BELOVED
STRANGER

JUDITH PELLA

BELOVED STRANGER

Their love-at-first-sight relationship was more than she
had dared to dream. Why did she now feel so lost?

BETHANY HOUSE PUBLISHERS
MINNEAPOLIS, MINNESOTA 55438

Beloved Stranger
Copyright © 1998
Judith Pella

Cover by D² Designworks

Scripture quotation on page 295 is from the *Holy Bible,* New Living Translation, copyright © 1996. Used by permission of Tyndale House Publishers, Inc., Wheaton, Illinois 60189. All rights reserved.

Scripture quotation on page 316 is from the New King James Version of the Bible. Copyright © 1979, 1980, 1982, by Thomas Nelson, Inc., Publishers. Used by permission. All rights reserved.

Published by Bethany House Publishers
A Ministry of Bethany Fellowship International
11300 Hampshire Avenue South
Minneapolis, Minnesota 55438
www.bethanyhouse.com

Printed in the United States of America by
Bethany Press International, Minneapolis, Minnesota 55438

Library of Congress Cataloging-in-Publication Data

Pella, Judith.
    Beloved stranger / by Judith Pella.
        p. cm.
    I. Title.
PS3566.E415B45   1998
813'.54—dc21   97–45453
ISBN 0–7642–2040–3   CIP

To the Greatful Threads,
Bev, Brenda, Christie, Lynn, and Susie,
my small quilt group whose
lively gab adds lots of spice to my writing.

JUDITH PELLA began her writing career in collaboration with Michael Phillips on several major fiction series. THE RUSSIANS was begun as a team effort, but eventually they mutually agreed that Judith would continue the series on her own. These extraordinary novels showcase her creativity and skill as a historian as well as a fiction writer. An avid reader and researcher in historical, adventure, and geographical venues, her storytelling abilities provide readers with memorable novels in a variety of genres. She and her family make their home in northern California.

1

THE SOMBER NOVEMBER DAY seemed a perfect setting for Shelby Martin to say farewell to her father. The gray chill encircled her heart, making her shiver. She found no comfort from the large crowd of mourners gathered at the graveside, nor in the knowledge that her father was a hero. An old man whose life was nearly over anyway lived today because Mike Martin had saved him from a burning building. Mike Martin was dead, but an eighty-seven-year-old man was alive.

What a cruel irony.

Shelby reminded herself for the hundredth time that her father wouldn't have been bitter. He had been doing his job, a job he loved and took pride in. Mike Martin was a Los Angeles fire fighter. He might well have died to save a kitten. He always told Shelby he was taking a certain risk every time he put on his uniform. She supposed she never really listened to him. She never believed he could die. Her dad just couldn't die . . . couldn't leave her alone.

A gust of wind swept over the cemetery, but Shelby took little notice of it. The words of the minister echoed around her as he droned on about eternal life and resurrection and other things of which Shelby knew little, and perhaps cared about even less. Aunt Lynn had stepped in and planned the service when Shelby had responded to her inquiries with blank stares and shrugs. It didn't matter to her how a dead body was disposed. The vibrant life that used to be Mike Martin, that used to care for Shelby—to protect her, to love her—was over.

A blur of tears rose once more to Shelby's eyes as she faced yet again the finality of her father's death. Through that haze a man in the crisply pressed dress uniform of the Los Angeles Fire Department handed Shelby a folded American flag, and she realized the service had ended. She hadn't even noticed the ceremonial folding of the flag and the solemn salute of Mike's co-workers. A hand reached out and touched her arm, startling Shelby, but it was only her aunt nudging her into motion. The time had come to file past the open grave, then move on to a catered meal at the house she had shared with her father. It was only right that friends and family came to express their love. Everyone had loved Mike. She was not the only one to grieve.

Shelby turned, gave a weak smile to her aunt, and began the long trek that would eventually lead her home. But the thought of home—empty of her father's presence—brought an unbidden sob to her lips. She wanted to curse the show of emotion. Dad would want her to be strong. She sniffed, but another sob managed to escape.

"It's okay, Shelby," said Aunt Lynn. "God will comfort you."

Shelby shook her head. "No . . . it's not okay." And she wasn't going to ask God for comfort now, when she had done without Him thus far in her life. Not even if she desperately needed comfort.

Vaguely Shelby wondered why Lynn was here anyway. She lived in Ventura, two hours away from Shelby's home in Whittier, California, but more than that, she wasn't even Mike's sister. She was a sister to Shelby's mother. True, she had been faithful about maintaining a relationship with Mike, and especially Shelby, over the years, but they hadn't seen each other since last Christmas. Maybe the woman just couldn't pass up a prime opportunity to preach about God. Lynn meant well, and actually she hadn't preached hardly at all that day. Shelby pushed aside her critical thoughts. It was just good to have someone close to tell her what to do next. Her best friend, Christie Duncan, had come to the funeral service in the church but left after that for an unavoidable meeting. She had promised to try to make it back for the reception.

Lynn helped Shelby into her minivan. Shelby had refused to ride in the black limousine provided by the funeral home, and since Lynn deemed Shelby unable to safely drive herself, she offered her vehicle instead. That was just as well because the twenty minutes on the freeway to Shelby's house passed in a complete fog. In fact, during the next hour the fog did not depart. Over a hundred people passed through the house, for the most part Mike's friends from his years with the fire department. A few of Shelby's co-workers had come, as well, but she hadn't expected many, since she tended to keep to herself. She wasn't exactly shy or reclusive, but neither was she a social butterfly. Only now did she realize how much of her life revolved around her dad.

Shelby stood in the living room surrounded by the buzz of conversations . . . not a part of them, not even able to discern the specifics of them. She was merely a machine, smiling bravely, shaking hands, embracing many and weeping with many. Later, she was certain, people would remark on her poise and grace. How courageous in the face of her grief. They would never know that it was neither courage nor grit that kept her in place, but rather a cowardly sense that without the presence of these people she would break into a thousand pieces.

She hardly noticed when another hand was thrust out to her. Shelby took it absently with the now frozen smile on her face.

"Thank you so much for coming," she said automatically.

"Shelby?"

The oddly familiar timbre of the voice forced her from her daze, and she gave the figure in front of her a closer look.

"Dawn?"

The person standing before her was an attractive woman in her early forties. She had long reddish hair that had to have been dyed to obtain such perfect "natural" color. The hairstyle, full and wispy, was one that might be expected on a much younger woman—perhaps someone in her mid-twenties, like Shelby. In fact, the woman was dressed in a youthful fashion, also—a black skirt that was quite short but not entirely unattractive because her legs were tan and shapely, and a white sweater that was just a bit too tight for a funeral.

But that was Dawn, wasn't it?

"I . . . I had to come," Shelby's mother said tentatively.

"I suppose you did." Shelby had used a warmer tone a moment ago when speaking to a complete stranger.

"I just can't believe it. You think someone is gonna live forever. Your daddy was a rock. It's just inconceivable—" Dawn's voice broke, and tears spilled from her eyes, smearing her immaculate mascara.

Suddenly, in the face of Dawn's emotion, Shelby felt very cool, calm, and controlled. She knew it was simply a determination not to share her grief with this woman.

"Why don't you get yourself a drink, Dawn?"

"Shelby, I had hoped we could talk a little." Dawn sniffed and dabbed her eyes with a tissue.

"This really isn't a good time."

"I know, but—"

"There are so many other people I have to see."

"Shelby, I'm your mother."

Shelby gave a slight start, then looked quickly around to make sure no one had heard the woman.

"Maybe later." Shelby turned and walked away, hoping later would never come.

Shelby's mother had left—or more correctly, deserted—her not long after her first birthday. Her dad always told Shelby that the woman had probably done Shelby a favor by leaving. She simply had not been cut out for motherhood, a fact that Mike had not realized until too late. Dawn was a child herself in many respects, and even at forty-two still wore the aura of teenage immaturity. Mike did what he could to keep Shelby from resenting Dawn, but he had been mostly unsuccessful. However, for Mike's sake, Shelby tried not to admit even to herself that she hated her mother. But she certainly had no qualms about using softer words like "I have no use for her" or "She means nothing to me."

It was to Mike, her daddy, that Shelby poured out all her love. Maybe she had loved him too much, maybe they had been too close. But Mike had been the rare type of parent who had been able to wield true authority while also nurturing a genuine friendship with his child. Shelby and her dad had talked about everything. Mike had helped her pick out prom dresses and had taught her how to rebuild the engine of her '65 Mustang. He had been involved in every aspect of her life—her education, her social life, her dreams.

He had known how much it had hurt Shelby to be abandoned by her mother, and so he had made a point to do everything he could to give her even more of a "mother" than many of her friends' real mothers. And the sad fact of it was that Dawn had left Mike solely *because* of motherhood. She had left Shelby more than Mike, though Mike was not the one to reveal this to Shelby. She had learned the truth on her tenth birthday. During one of Dawn's rare visits, Dawn had displayed the poor taste to actually say as much to her young daughter. She had given Shelby a silly present, something suitable for a four-year-old, and Shelby had responded to it less than enthusiastically.

"Guess I blew it again," Dawn had said. "I'm still not the motherly type. Be glad I left you, kid. We're both better off."

Shelby saved her tears until after Dawn was gone, then threw the ridiculous stuffed rabbit into the trash. That had been the turning point in her relationship with her mother. The tables of rejection had turned. Instead of being a child longing for a mother and wondering how she could be good enough to get her mother back, she began to accept the fact that she had no mother—and wanted no mother. Her daddy was good enough for her.

So Shelby had no sense of guilt about her cool reception toward Dawn at the funeral. She believed Dawn didn't belong there in the first place, and had she known the woman would have the nerve to attend, Shelby would have had her thrown out. Well, she might not have gone that far, but only out of respect for her father. She wouldn't have wanted to cause a scene in front of his friends and colleagues.

Dawn approached Shelby an hour later, when only fifteen or twenty friends remained in the house. Strangely, Shelby found she could not conjure her deep ire. Perhaps her grief had temporarily numbed it.

"Honey, I noticed you haven't eaten a thing," said Dawn, "so I brought you a plate of cold cuts and a roll."

"I'm not hungry," Shelby replied.

Aunt Lynn came up to them, and Shelby immediately recognized how different she was from Dawn. Conservatively garbed in a black knit dress that reached mid-calf, she was adorned with only a string of pearls. Lynn was a few years older than Dawn, slightly overweight, and attractive, but not strikingly so like Dawn. She was a housewife, married to the same man for twenty-five years. "You ought to eat something, Shelby, it's been hours."

Shelby rolled her eyes and took the plate, comforted only in that she was technically listening to her aunt and not really to her mother.

"I'm surprised you're still here, Dawn," Shelby said after taking a few halfhearted bites of food.

"I had hoped to talk to you more."

"I'm really not up for it."

"I'll leave you two alone," said Lynn.

"No, Aunt Lynn!" Shelby barely masked the desperation in her voice. "Anyway, you and Dawn probably have far more to talk about—you are sisters."

"It's you I want to talk to, honey," Dawn said to Shelby.

"Look," said Lynn, "let me leave you two." She hurried away too fast for Shelby to react.

"You're stuck with me now," said Dawn, giggling like a teenager.

With a resigned sigh, Shelby said, "What do you want?"

"I'm worried about you, honey—"

"Would you please stop calling me that," Shelby cut in sharply. "I'm not your *honey*—it's simply not going to happen. You're here and I'm trying to be cordial. Dad taught me very well—but he also taught me not to stand for phoniness. So you want to talk—fine. But my name is Shelby."

"I know. I picked out that name for you," Dawn said softly, no rebuke in her tone.

"Oh great."

"Your dad liked it a lot, though."

"Okay, thanks, you picked a lovely name. I like it. Now, what do you want?"

"Like I said, h—Shelby, I'm worried. You don't have to tell me it's no use for me to start now. Believe it or not, I have always worried about you . . . well, mostly I've thought about you and wondered. But still, it wasn't like you didn't exist, even if I acted that way. This isn't the time to get into all that. I just want you to know that I'd like to be there for you. You don't have to be all alone, okay? Maybe we could start over or something. Who knows what could happen?"

Shelby wanted to laugh in the woman's face. For one thing, she didn't know if she'd ever heard so many clichés strung together. *I want to be there for you . . . you don't have to be alone . . . start over.* The woman really was living in a dream world.

"I don't need anyone, Dawn," Shelby replied. "I'll get along fine."

"It's not going to be easy with the holidays coming up."

"I'll manage."

"Why don't we spend them together?"

You have got to be kidding! Shelby thought silently. Did the deluded woman actually think Shelby would enjoy celebrating Christmas with a despised absentee mother? On the contrary, Shelby was certain she'd have a better time standing on a ledge than spending the holidays with Dawn.

"That's kind of you, Dawn, but . . ." Shelby wracked her brain for a viable excuse. "Well, I already have plans for the holidays." There, that should do it.

"This early?"

"Yes . . . I . . . actually, my girlfriend and I had planned a trip before Dad died—and well, I think it'll be good for me to go ahead with it."

"Where to?"

"Puerto Vallarta." Shelby was pleased at how quickly she'd come up with a response. Actually, she and Christie had once talked about going to Mexico during winter break—about three years ago when they had still been in college.

"Oh . . . well, that should be nice." Dawn made no attempt to hide her disappointment.

Shelby was starting to feel slightly rotten for her lie. She comforted herself with the fact that it was only a little lie—hardly on a par with deserting a daughter.

2

CHRISTIE THOUGHT IT WAS a great idea and was certain she could get the time off work.

"I haven't had a day off in over a year."

"Christie, I told you it was just a lame excuse I gave to Dawn."

"But it's still a good plan for the holidays."

"The last thing I feel like doing is tramping off to some resort for sun and fun."

Christie smiled sagely. She was tall and willowy, with voluminous, silky chestnut hair that made her look like a model. If that wasn't enough, she was very self-possessed, graceful, and ladylike. The high contrast between them was probably what had kept them friends through high school and college. Shelby was trim, but petite by comparison and far more athletic, with large brown eyes and shoulder-length blond hair with often unruly natural curls. She was the ingenuous one and Christie was the sophisticated one. Christie glided like oil through the world of high-stakes advertising. Shelby, a teacher, chased kindergartners all day. Shelby was far less "together,"—perhaps even flighty, though she would vehemently deny these qualities because she knew how much they reflected her mother.

"Not now, Shelby," Christie was saying, "but in a couple weeks when the initial shock wears off and you really start to miss your dad, you might think differently."

Exactly two weeks later when all the Christmas decorations were in place—everywhere but at Shelby's house, that is—Shelby began to see that her friend was right. It had been almost impossible for her to make it through the usual onslaught of school Christmas preparations. Shelby helped her students make gifts for their parents, remembering the little dough ornaments she'd made for her dad when she had been in kindergarten. Mike had kept everything she'd ever made him and always put all her funny, lopsided ornaments on the tree.

So far, Shelby hadn't had the heart to get the Christmas decorations out of the closet.

She went to the mall one day and without even thinking, bought a Christmas gift for her dad—something he had hinted about a couple of months ago when they had been in the bookstore.

"Look at this, Dad," she had told him upon finding the book *The 1956 Corvette*. That had been his dream car, and he was in the process of saving to buy one to restore.

"Yeah, and the book costs almost as much as the car." He tapped his finger against the fifty-dollar price sticker.

"You're worth it."

"Maybe Santa will bring me one."

Shelby had smiled coyly. "Maybe so."

When she walked into the store and saw the book at ten percent off, she bought it, not remembering until she was leaving the store that Dad was not there to receive her gift. She went home and cried for the rest of the evening.

And that was not an isolated incident. Throughout each day she'd think of things as if he were still alive—unfinished plans, meals he'd like, errands to run for him. Because of his sudden, so very unexpected death, there had not been a chance for closure, for getting used to being without him. Luckily, all their friends knew he was dead—his heroic deed had made the *Los Angeles Times*. But there was still the bank, the dry cleaners, or the guy who provided them with succulent, all-natural turkeys for the holidays who confronted her yesterday with inquiries about Mike. There were reminders of Mike Martin everywhere and every day.

People told Shelby that soon she'd be able to remember her father without the pain, but Shelby didn't think that time would ever come. Another week passed with no change. She was fine during school, but it was in the evenings, when she was home by herself, that it really hit her hard. In another couple of days school would be out for Christmas break and the lonely, empty hours would seem endless. So Shelby sat on the sofa one evening and thought a lot about her conversation with Christie. She had no appetite for the frozen chicken pot pie she had cooked, now sitting on the coffee table untouched. A couple of weeks in surroundings that weren't so painfully full of her father could be just what she needed.

Then Shelby noticed the old recliner adjacent to the sofa—her father's favorite chair. She had thus far been successful in avoiding the chair because it was positioned in the room in such a way so that she never had to walk past it, and if she was watching television she didn't have to look at the chair at all. It was twenty years old—and looked it. Dad had refused to have it reupholstered because, in his words, "It's broken in just right." It was shabby and out-of-date, and the indentation his body had made in the cushion was clearly evident.

Shelby rose from the sofa and ventured toward the chair. She stood before it a moment as if viewing a museum piece. Then she leaned down and placed her hands on the well-worn arms. She caught a whiff of aftershave. Old Spice. A knot rose in her throat, and without thinking, she slipped into the chair. It creaked, but nothing like when her dad would lower his muscular two-hundred-pound frame into it.

All at once a peculiar sense of security washed over Shelby. It was eerie in a way, but she didn't let herself think of that. She just wanted to enjoy the feeling that was almost as good as getting a hug from him. As a child she had snuggled up with him many times in this chair to hear stories, to watch television, or just to get a bit of affection.

"Dad, what do you think?" she found herself saying. "Would you mind if I went on a trip? I mean, if I up and left for Christmas? I guess I really want to know if you'd mind if I went off to some beach resort and had a few laughs, had some fun. If, for just a while, I could try to forget . . . not you, of course, but just forget how awful I feel. Sometimes I think I'll explode if I have to rattle around this house another minute. You were always in favor of having fun, and I know you wouldn't mind. Maybe my biggest fear is that I'll get there and find I just can't laugh or even smile anymore."

Shelby ran her hands over the rough arms of the chair, then lifted her hands to her nose. The scent of aftershave she had noticed earlier seemed to be gone.

"No, Dad . . . I think my biggest fear is that I will have fun and that I might forget." She closed her eyes, almost as if she hoped for a response to her words. But the recliner wasn't some magic place that could bring her an image or even the voice of her father. Yet she still had his voice in her mind and heart. She could still remember many of the wise things he'd told her over the years.

Was there something that applied now? She was sure there must be. . . .

"*Shelby, follow your heart and trust your gut,*" he had often said.

She smiled. So her dad was no intellectual. He was still the wisest man she knew. And right now her heart *and* gut said she had to get away . . . and maybe even have a few laughs.

She sat in the chair a few more minutes then rose and went to the phone.

"Hi, Christie," she said when her friend answered. "You still interested in taking a trip?"

"Sure, I'd love it."

"Puerto Vallarta?"

"Well, that'd be great, but this is the busiest season of the year. Do you really think you could get reservations?" It was just like Christie to be so practical.

"Well . . ."

"And plane tickets will cost a fortune on such short notice."

"I hadn't thought of that. Maybe we could go somewhere else."

"Wow, you sure give up easily!"

"It was the first place I'd thought of . . . but really any place will do." Shelby didn't know whether to be relieved or terribly disappointed.

"What if it could be arranged?"

"It'd be great."

"What if a very wise and good friend had reservations at a five-star hotel and plane tickets already?"

"You?"

"Yeah . . . I made all the arrangements right after we talked about it."

"When were you going to tell me?"

"I was starting to get a bit nervous, but I knew it would be best if it came from you rather than me strong-arming you into to it. If nothing happened by this weekend, I was going to start to put on the pressure."

"So we're really going?"

"I have two weeks reserved at a great place. It's a bit outside of town on this idyllic beach. One of the executives at work got us in—and even three weeks ago it wasn't easy."

"I love you, Christie!" Shelby paused. "This is going to be good . . . I know it."

She glanced over at the recliner as if for further affirmation. And in her mind she saw her dad sitting there, smiling encouragement.

3

THE PUERTO VALLARTA AIRPORT was mobbed with locals vying for the attention—and the money—of arriving tourists. Shelby spotted the man holding a sign that read *Mismaloya Bougainvillea*. She nudged Christie and they waved at the man, then grabbed the cart holding their luggage. But before they could reach him, the crowd moved in between them and they were stalled. Several shouted "Taxi" at them and others offered more services, though Shelby's rusty Spanish could decipher little of it. The man holding their hotel sign finally wormed his way through the crowd toward them.

"You are going to the Bougainvillea?" he said when he reached them.

"*Sí*," said Christie.

"Follow me."

Shelby marveled at how the crowd melted before the man, and in a minute they were distanced from the mayhem. Soon they were loaded into a waiting shuttle along with three other passengers. Shelby was still in a bit of a daze and hardly heard the driver expounding on points of interest as they drove through town. She had never been to a foreign country, and despite the fact that as a Southern Californian she was very familiar with the Mexican culture, *Mexico* was foreign.

The late-afternoon air was warm, but in December it held only a hint of the humid, tropical climate that would descend later in the year. There was little chance to take in much of the scenery along the way until they left the narrow and busy streets of town behind and drove on a two-lane mountain road. Tall cliffs adorned one side, and on the other side a steep drop to the beach displayed a beautiful view of the bay. Just as Shelby was about to relax and enjoy this, the vehicle suddenly lurched to the right to avoid an oncoming bus. It seemed to her that they had barely escaped with their lives, but the driver appeared completely unruffled and was even humming a little tune as he jerked the van back into the right lane.

The hotel itself made up for the harrowing drive and helped to soothe frayed nerves. It was absolutely lovely, like a picture postcard or a movie set. Open breezeways with tiled floors and arched porticos were abundantly flanked with rich tropical plants and, of course, brilliant red and fuchsia bougainvilleas hanging from planters overhead. Three pools in rock garden settings had clusters of palms alongside other exotic plants, effectively eliminating the sterile "resort" feel. Shelby and Christie's suite was open and cool and very comfortable. Five floors up, they had a marvelous view of the ocean, and Shelby thought she could spend every day just sitting on the balcony enjoying it. Christie, however, was ready to go exploring the minute she deposited her luggage in her room.

"I'll let you kick back this evening, but tomorrow . . . 'no rest for the wicked,' " Christie warned her.

Shelby smiled. "Okay—" she began, then suddenly changed her mind. "Oh, I'll go with you now."

The late Saturday afternoon breeze was still warm as they explored the resort and walked quite a ways down the beach, where they discovered a small shopping area closed for the day. The place was quaint, with thatched roofs and bamboo walls, and would be worth visiting another day. The sun was setting when they got back to the hotel, and Christie suggested going to the hotel club for drinks and some socializing.

Despite the fact that it was a busy Saturday night, Shelby and Christie found a table in a good location for listening to the mariachi band. Shelby knew Christie would soon meet a guy, and for the sake of not being left out, Shelby hoped the guy might have a friend. That was one of several areas where the two young women differed. Christie always had a guy, whether he was a steady boyfriend—someone she had dated more than twice—or a one-night stand. And the guys were always good-looking and usually successful—or at least on the road to success. Christie made no excuses for approving a man's car before accepting a date.

Sometimes Shelby would go along with the singles-on-the-prowl scene, but she usually let her friend go alone. Shelby preferred quiet evenings spent at the movies, walking on the beach, or hiking through the woods. If she happened to meet a guy she liked she would go out with him—if he asked. But she hated looking for men. Consequently, her dates were about one to Christie's five, but she liked to think that her one was far more meaningful. There was no one special in her life now—in fact, she'd not had a steady boyfriend for several years. Getting established in her teaching job was far too demanding to permit time to properly devote to a relationship. Now, after two years, she was fairly confident in her job. Maybe she'd start to think about dating seriously again.

From the beginning, Shelby had realized that her idea of a vacation in Mexico would be far different than Christie's, but their relationship was such that they were quite comfortable in letting each other follow her own path. They would have fun together, but they also would have the freedom to be independent. The only flaw in this plan was the present situation. Christie was feeling especially protective toward Shelby and by the end of the next day had been rather overbearing about leaving Shelby alone. Shelby attributed this to the fact that it was Christmas Eve, although they had both agreed to downplay the holiday.

On Christmas Day the only recognition of the holiday they gave was exchanging gifts in the morning. Then, after a visit to town together, Christie was ready to go to a fiesta on the beach.

"I think I'll stay in this evening," Shelby said, knowing Christie wouldn't be alone for long.

"Come on, Shelby. I've heard these things are a lot of fun."

"I'd like to watch a movie."

"You can do that any time. Come on."

"How come you are suddenly so insecure, Chris? I'm sure you'll have a blast without me."

"It's not that, it's—"

"What?"

"We're here to have fun, that's all."

"And tonight I'm going to have fun watching a movie."

"I just don't think . . . that is . . . well, this fiesta thing will be great. Maybe Mr. Right will be there."

"I'm not looking for Mr. Right." Shelby eyed her friend warily. "You're afraid to leave me alone, aren't you?"

Christie shrugged noncommittally. "Well, it is Christmas. You can't stay alone."

"I'd rather be alone than with a bunch of celebrating strangers."

"Than with me?" Christie was actually pouting.

"You know that's not true. In my mind, the holiday is over."

"I'm not going to leave you alone on Christmas night."

"Maybe we ought to set some ground rules," said Shelby. "We always have a good time together because we don't place expectations upon each other. That should be no different now. I'll be okay alone once in a while—I promise. Now, go to your fiesta and let me watch a movie. And when you get home tonight we'll find some ice cream and stay up late sharing our experiences."

"You'll tell me all about your movie?" Christie asked with obvious sarcasm.

"If you're really lucky."

"I don't know. . . ."

Shelby knew Christie well enough to know she wanted to be where the action was, not sitting home with a girlfriend.

"Get out of here. Shoo! I want to be alone!" Shelby intoned the final phrase with her best Greta Garbo impression.

Christie was soon gone. And Shelby was alone.

She flipped on the television, quickly surfing past the Spanish shows and pausing at a familiar scene from *It's a Wonderful Life*. Jimmy Stewart was standing on a bridge, contemplating jumping. That hardly seemed like a good viewing choice. There was static on the next two channels, then another channel and a different scene from another showing of *It's a Wonderful Life*.

Sighing, she sat back. The movie was almost over, and maybe something more appropriate would come on after it. Anyway, it was pretty harmless spending the holiday with Jimmy Stewart. Contemplating the problems of poor George Bailey was a perfect way of burying her own.

Shelby forgot how the end of the movie had always gotten to her—even in the best and happiest of circumstances. This time, however, it wasn't the touching response of friends and family coming together to rescue Bailey. Nor was it the "richest man in the world" rhetoric. This time it was a small, almost insignificant thing: George Bailey holding his little daughter. Shelby thought about how close the child had come to losing her daddy.

And that was it. Shelby spent the next half hour bawling.

What a fool she had been to believe she could spend this, of all evenings, alone! For that matter, did she really think this trip could heal her heart, ease her grief? The whole thing was a sham, a huge pretense. Being around happy, carefree people was the worst idea she'd ever had in her life. But that was the awful dilemma she now had to face—to be miserable alone or in a crowd.

Shelby sniffed noisily and tried to blot away her tears with a tissue, then suddenly jumped up. If she didn't get away now, she would spend the rest of the evening crying. At least the presence of a crowd would force her to rein in her emotions. She went to her room and changed into something suitable for the evening—loose-fitting pants and a sleeveless white cotton sweater to highlight her new tan. She didn't take the time to put on eye makeup—her eyes were too red and puffy and it would have only drawn attention to her state. She did put on lipstick and a bit of blush in hopes of eliminating her pallor. Then she headed out the door.

Shelby was relieved when she spotted Christie at a table in the bar. True to form, Christie was accompanied by not one, but two men.

"Oh, Shelby, we were just talking about you." Christie grinned. There was a bit of triumph in her eyes. "This is Dan and Larry. I didn't know what I was going to do with two handsome men, and I was about to drag you away from that movie."

"Guess I saved you the trouble."

"You'll join us, then?" Larry asked. Shelby discerned immediately that Christie had already staked a claim on Dan. Not that it mattered to her. Both men were tall, good-looking specimens.

"Why not?" Shelby could think of a million reasons why not, but she saw no reason to ruin everyone's evening with her negative attitude.

She tried her best to match Christie's bubbly persona. She laughed at all the appropriate times, she danced when asked, she drank every margarita that came her way. And no one really seemed to notice or care about her forced behavior. Maybe it was only evident to her.

They went out to the beach where a band was playing and people were dancing, eating, and socializing. It dawned on Shelby that it really didn't matter to any of them who they were with, as long as there was someone filling the empty space next to them. But she also realized that she would not have enjoyed this situation even under the best of circumstances. It wasn't her depression or grief that made Larry and Dan two very dull men. They were handsome, tan, muscular—Christie would attract no less. But . . .

"So, Shelby," Larry said as they relaxed between dances, "how much do school teachers make these days?"

"I guess we're not in it for the money," Shelby hedged. She was not about to reveal anything so personal to a total stranger.

"Thirty, forty thousand dollars, I'd say."

"As I said—"

"Why go into teaching when there are so many fields open to women these days?" He signaled the waiter for another drink. "The stock market is where the money is." He paused and laughed loudly. "No pun intended. But I pulled in six figures this year, and I'm only twenty-five. I'll be able to retire in another five years if I want."

"I'm very happy for you." Could he see how disinterested she was?

He continued. "What kind of portfolio do you have? After the loss of your father, you really have to think about what to do with your money. I imagine you got some good bennies out of the fire department. Well, don't let your grief make you act foolishly. Sure, it's hard now, but in a year it'll be a lot worse if you wake up one morning and realize you've lost a pile of interest by letting your money lay around."

Shelby just stared at him, unable to conjure even a glib response.

"I could direct you to some good investments. Nothing volatile like commodities. Aggressive but secure—that's what a gal like you would want."

"I . . . I really . . . uh . . . I'll think about it, Larry." She gulped down her drink. "Do you want to dance?" Maybe that would shut him up for a while.

Shelby stuck it out for two hours, then pleaded jet lag and made an escape. Larry was obviously perturbed. And Christie was so unhappy with her that she didn't even attempt to talk Shelby into staying.

At eight the next morning, Shelby was already dressed and thinking about going to the restaurant for breakfast. She was pleased to note that Christie, who had come in sometime during the night, seemed to hold no grudge against her—in fact, by the time Christie came out of her room, she had cooked up yet another diversion for them.

"Dan wants to go for a sail. Are you game?"

"Chris, I was kind of a wet blanket last night."

"I don't hold that against you. It was Christmas and I could tell you'd had a rough time. Come with us. It'll be fun."

"You mean Larry wants me to go?"

"No . . . actually, he met someone else. Anyway, they made other plans."

"So it's just you and Dan?"

"He said there would be other people."

"I don't know. . . ."

When Christie exhaled an exasperated sigh, Shelby knew she couldn't disappoint her friend again.

After meeting Dan in the lobby an hour later, they took a taxi to the marina half an hour away from the resort, on the north side of town. On the way, Dan mentioned casually that the sailing trip was actually a bit of a business venture. He was taking the boat out for a "test sail." The boat was on the market, and it was a good way to go sailing in a private vessel for free.

"So you're not really planning to buy a boat?" Shelby asked warily.

"Oh, sure, my plan is to buy a boat someday," Dan said quickly. "But you gotta look at a lot of boats before you make such a big decision."

"Someday. . . ?"

"You're not gonna spoil this by asking too many questions, are you, honey?"

Shelby rankled at the glib familiarity of his tone. "I don't think I feel comfortable in this situation."

"Shelby, we're not doing anything wrong," said Christie.

"Hey, if she doesn't want to go . . ." Dan obviously had not forgotten how Shelby had deserted his friend the night before.

"Well, I'm not going if she doesn't," said Christie.

Shelby wanted to scream.

The taxi pulled into the marina. There was a huge section for commercial vessels, from which most of the tour boats launched. Off to the side was a private boat marina, surrounded by restaurants and shops.

"Maybe I'll just hang out here," Shelby suggested.

"Shelby, please come with us. It won't be fun knowing you are here all alone," Christie said.

Shelby suddenly thought better of further protests. It was ruining the trip for everyone. Instead, she shrugged, deciding it might well be an interesting experience, if she could just stay away from Dan.

They found the dock where the boat was tied up. It was called the *Seabird*. A man coiling some line on deck glanced up when Dan called to him.

"Are you Frank Stefano?" Dan asked.

"You must be Dan Thomas."

At Dan's nod the man named Stefano added, "Come aboard."

"Hope you don't mind that I brought a couple of friends."

"No problem."

Introductions were made as Stefano helped everyone aboard.

The man was in his mid- to late twenties and looked Mexican, with tawny skin and short, black wavy hair, but his English was completely unaccented. Shelby glanced around to see if anyone else was aboard, but he seemed to be alone.

"Nice vessel," said Dan. "How old?"

"Twenty years," Stefano replied. He gently rubbed his hand along one of the wood rails, and Shelby noticed that the wood was rough in places. "Needs some TLC. I just don't get down here enough to keep up the brightwork. The marina does what they can but . . ." He shrugged to complete his thought.

"Down here?" asked Dan. "So you're not from Puerto Vallarta."

"Southern California. My family used to spend most of our vacations here, but not much lately. That's why we're selling the boat. It's a shame for it to sit here never used. Not to mention that the marina fees aren't cheap. It's a great-looking boat when it's polished up. Forty-one feet and fairly easy to single hand. But you can be the judge of that. Why don't we cast off."

Several minutes were spent in starting up the engine, bringing in dock lines and fenders, and turning on instruments before Stefano maneuvered the boat out of the dock. When they were still negotiating the marina waters he offered the wheel to Dan.

"Well . . . I'm not much of a sailor myself," Dan hedged. "I've got a partner in this deal but he couldn't make it. He's teaching me. For now, why don't you just handle the boat. I'll be able to tell a lot from that."

"Sure. Feel free to ask any questions." Stefano paused, then added, "Oh, and by the way, there is a fully stocked bar in the salon below. Help yourselves whenever you want. I'm sure you'll want to check out things below anyway."

"Great idea." Dan headed for the companionway, and Christie started to follow.

"Are you interested?" Christie asked Shelby.

"Not now." Shelby felt uncomfortable enough just riding in the boat, much less consuming the man's food and drink.

Besides, she was finding she liked being on the water and was enjoying the view from the deck—the cluster of boats at the marina, the cliffs dotted with bungalows and fine houses, even the lines of laundry in the poorer areas. And the translucent water shimmered and danced as the morning sun reflected off its surface. At ten in the morning it was already warming up. However, dressed only in white shorts and a sleeveless navy blue shirt, Shelby was still a bit chilled. She got a sweat shirt from her tote bag, glad she'd had the insight to pack it.

"It's a little windy today," Stefano said.

"Yes. Actually, it's cooler in Puerto Vallarta than I thought it would be."

"You came prepared, anyway." He nodded toward the sweat shirt. He himself was dressed in a white T-shirt, tan shorts, and sandals, and appeared comfortable with the temperature.

She smiled and nodded, and though the conversation died away, his gaze lingered on her for a moment longer. His lips bent into a slight smile, obviously embarrassed that he was caught staring. Then his attention was drawn to steering around two approaching vessels.

Shelby watched in silence. She had never been good at small talk and didn't feel like getting too friendly with Stefano because she still felt bad about what Dan was doing. Yet she could hear Dan and Christie below laughing and talking and felt if she kept to herself, this trip might get really awkward. She wished she would have listened to her first instinct and stayed at the marina to shop. But as she glanced over at Stefano, she found a little comfort in noting that he seemed to be enjoying himself and not at all concerned that his prospective buyer was more interested in the salon than in the handling of the boat. She studied him with a covert glance, intrigued at the way he seemed so absorbed in what he was doing. When he suddenly looked in her direction she jerked her eyes away, too quickly to be subtle.

"Would you like to help . . . Shelby, isn't it?" he asked.

"Well, I've never sailed," Shelby said.

"I'm ready to hoist the sails. All you have to do is take the wheel and keep the boat pointed into the wind."

"Into the wind . . . and that would be. . . ?"

He motioned for her to come to the wheel, and when she was next to him he turned the boat so that she distinctly felt the wind in her face.

"Like that," he said. "If you want a further indicator, just look up at the top of the main mast"—he pointed in the proper direction—"to make sure the arrow on the wind indicator is pointed away from you, toward the bow."

"Okay."

Before he began the procedure, however, he called down to Dan and Christie to let them know what was happening. Dan said they'd be up in a minute. Stefano removed the sail covers, and when his other passengers still had not appeared, he pulled at a line in the cockpit that controlled the mainsail. When the sail was halfway up, it stuck and he had to jog to the forward deck and jiggle at the line, which he called a halyard, to loosen it before returning to the cockpit and giving the line another tug. This time it went up smoothly. He fastened that off, then unfurled the jib—Shelby picked up the proper lingo as he explained what he was doing. All the while he wore the animated expression of a boy on a lark.

When he finished, Shelby was a little disappointed she had to relinquish her job. It had been quite exhilarating to hold the wheel of the boat, though in fact she had done little besides stand there with a steadying hand on the shiny wood surface.

"We should have a nice sail if the wind keeps up," he said, taking the wheel and steering them into the bay.

"That was kind of fun," Shelby said.

"In that case, you can keep it up if you'd like."

But seeing several other boats in the bay, Shelby lost her nerve. "Maybe when there's not so much traffic."

He smiled and chuckled—a nice, warm smile and a sincere chuckle, even though both were more reserved than boisterous. Shelby was feeling more and more strange about this whole outing. She considered telling Stefano about Dan's little deception rather than let him go to so much trouble for nothing. But he spoke before she could.

"Your friend Dan doesn't seem very interested in the boat."

"He's not my friend," Shelby answered quickly, defensively. "That is, I just met him. Christie—now, she *is* my friend—met him last night and he invited us."

"I see."

"Do you really?"

"Well, I have to wonder if Dan is seriously interested in buying my boat—or *any* boat. If I were going to lay out sixty thousand dollars, I'd have just a few more questions about the prospective purchase. And if I were really interested in sailing, I probably would have made sure to be present for the hoisting of the sails. That tells a lot about a boat. The salon is very nice, but—"

At that moment Dan and Christie climbed up on the deck, each carrying some kind of red fruit juice drink.

"Some digs down below," said Dan.

"Hey, look, the sails are up," Christie commented.

"It's okay for us to walk up forward, isn't it?" asked Dan.

"Make yourself at home," Stefano said.

Shelby gave him a puzzled look after the others had departed. "It doesn't bother you?"

"It's a chance to get out on the water."

"Yes, but with a bunch of strangers?"

"It doesn't bother me, really. So you can relax. Enjoy yourself. You'd pay fifty bucks apiece for a trip like this from the commercial boats."

"I still feel funny. . . ."

He shrugged, then with an ironic smile said, "Here, take the wheel and earn your keep, then."

"Aye, aye, Captain!" she said, then laughed, feeling her previous tension melt away.

As she steered, he offered frequent verbal guidance while tending to the trim of the sails, and an easy conversation flowed between them.

"So where are you from, Shelby?"

"California. Whittier."

"Steer a little starboard—that is, to the right. Been in P.V. long?"

"Just three days. How about you?"

"A week or so. It's easy to lose track of time."

"I guess I haven't experienced that, yet."

"Not having a great time?"

She shrugged. "I doubt it has anything to do with where I am." She sighed, feeling a familiar melancholy begin to take over. "I don't know . . ." Then determinedly, she changed the subject. "You must know this place well if you used to come here a lot. Are you Mexican?"

"Yes, to both questions. But I was born in the States. My parents were born here but were babies when they came to the States. My grandparents on both sides immigrated forty-some years ago."

"But they came from here, Puerto Vallarta?"

"Back then Puerto Vallarta hardly existed. They were from Guadalajara, but my mother's parents owned land here and came often for the sea air. They were considered well-off by Mexican standards and lived a fairly decent life. But there was so much political instability that they never knew how long it might last. Finally my grandfather on my mother's side fell afoul with the government and left for America. They lost their holdings in Guadalajara, though they somehow managed to maintain the land here. My father's parents were migrant workers in California."

"Sounds like you could write a book about your family."

He shrugged, scowling slightly. Whatever she'd said had caused some tension. She quickly changed the subject.

"Land values must have skyrocketed after Richard Burton made *Night of the Iguana* and he and Liz Taylor had their famous love affair," she said.

"My family could have made a fortune on the property, but one of the best things we always did was come here every year on vacation. Grandma wouldn't dream of selling it. Not even now when it gets so little use. Still, I resent Richard and Liz. It was a great place before they made it famous. Of course, I wasn't even born then, but my grandma's stories make it sound like the most idyllic place on earth."

"It's still lovely . . . I suppose I just need to look at it with better eyes."

Stefano studied her for a brief moment, then smiled, embarrassed once again. "There's nothing wrong with your eyes."

Such an endearing earnestness mingled with his embarrassment that

Shelby forgot to be flustered herself at his compliment. Instead, she met his gaze and found a depth in his eyes that made a striking contrast with their trivial conversation. She wondered at this man whose expression could be so filled with boyish wonder when involved in sailing, then shadow mysteriously or brighten when a slight ironic smile bent his lips. She knew it would be an adventure finding out all the nuances. She was tempted to compare him to Larry, but even from this brief encounter she could tell there was a world of difference between the shallow stockbroker and this man before her now.

Their brief, silent exchange—a quick look in which strangers are transformed into something far more—seemed to last a very long time. Shelby felt her heart pounding and forced her eyes toward the bow of the boat. Christie and Dan were still there drinking and laughing.

"I should be paying more attention to the water," she said nervously.

"You're doing great. It seems to come naturally to you."

"It's fun, but I'd still feel pretty crummy if we crashed into something."

"I wouldn't want you to feel crummy." He smiled and put a hand on the wheel, disconcertingly close to hers. She started to let go, but he moved his hand quickly on top of hers.

"You don't have to stop. We can both share the burden, eh?"

"I've never been on a sailboat before. It is wonderful."

"There is nothing that compares."

Again, that earnestness. He deeply meant what he said, and, Shelby thought, he meant so much more besides.

"Do you sail in California?"

"I have my own boat. The *Seabird*, by the way, belongs to my grandmother. Anyway, I have a smaller boat in King's Harbor. I don't know what I'd do without it. I feel like it transports me to another world. Maybe I'm even a different person when I'm on the sea. For a short time, at least. . . ."

"I think everyone needs something like that."

"And what is your escape, Shelby?"

"I guess I escape through books and movies. But mostly—" She stopped, realizing she was about to say something she had seldom told anyone. She breathed a nervous laugh. It was her turn to be embarrassed, for she was not accustomed to talking about personal things, not even to people she knew well, much less a stranger. But she plunged ahead, somehow sensing her thoughts were safe with this man. "I haven't told this to many people. Maybe I haven't even given it much thought. I love to repair cars—learned it from my dad. When I put my head under the hood of my Mustang, all my problems seem to fade away. But like you said, only for a while."

"The problems never really go away, do they? We can only pretend."

There was a sad, mournful quality to his tone, and Shelby didn't know how to respond. Before she could say anything at all, Christie and Dan made their way back into the cockpit.

All the awkwardness returned, along with the small talk. Which was how the next hour passed until they returned to the marina. As Stefano maneuvered the boat into its slip, Dan gave a very unconvincing speech about having to think about the boat and see where his financing stood. Stefano, with a covert wink toward Shelby, shook Dan's hand and told him to reach him through the broker if he wanted to know more. Dan jumped off the boat and Stefano handed Christie down. But as Shelby turned to leave, he gently laid a restraining hand on her arm.

"Would you like to have dinner with me tonight?"

"Yes," she said simply. The invitation did not really surprise her.

"Where are you staying?"

"The Mismaloya Bougainvillea."

"I'll come at six."

4

IT WAS ONLY DINNER, but something incredible happened that evening. Was it just a matter of the right place and the right time? Or could it have been something destiny had arranged?

Shelby didn't know the answers to those questions but decided they hardly mattered. From the moment Frank—for that is what she knew him as now—arrived at the hotel, she knew she didn't want to clutter what was happening with philosophizing. She hadn't been looking for a man or a relationship. Yet both had found her in a way so beautiful, so sweet, that she instinctively knew that to probe too deeply would ruin the quiet power of it all. Her heart had been so broken by her father's death, and she found herself pouring it all out to Frank. Somehow, Frank had taken each shattered piece of her heart and held it with gentleness and respect—no glib responses, no talk about investments and profits and interest.

"I am sometimes so weary with grief," she confided over salsa and chips in a little restaurant on Badillo Street in downtown Puerto Vallarta. "Yet I don't want to let it go completely. I don't want to forget how much he meant to me."

"Maybe grief isn't always a bad thing. In some cultures the extremity of their grief is how they honor their lost loved ones. You honor Mike Martin this way."

"Have you ever lost someone close, Frank?"

He shook his head and a deep furrow formed between his brows. Silence hovered over the table for a moment. "I grieve more over the living," he stated softly.

"Do you want to talk about it? I feel bad monopolizing the conversation."

"You shouldn't feel that way on my account. I'm incredibly honored that you divulged such things to me."

Shelby gave a little grimace. "I laid too much on you, didn't I?"

He smiled. "No . . . at least it didn't seem that way."

"No, it didn't. . . ."

Their meal arrived and they fell into small talk, an exchange of basic information about each other. Shelby loved spicy Mexican food; Frank had grown up with it and preferred a good steak. Shelby talked about teaching; Frank described his job managing one of the Mexican restaurants his family owned in Southern California. Shelby told of her hobby of auto mechanics; Frank talked about sailing. It was the kind of conversation you engaged in over food, but all the while Shelby had a feeling of discontent, like they were merely marking time and there were far more important things to discuss. She wanted to tell him about her mother—and she never talked about Dawn to anyone if she could help it.

She wondered if he was feeling the same way. Though he talked far less about himself than she did, she sensed that had more to do with the kind of person he was than with reticence toward her. Still, Shelby wanted to know everything about him, and she didn't mind having to work at getting him to talk.

Was it possible they had only known each other a few hours?

When their leisurely meal was over, Frank asked Shelby, "Would you like to walk around town for a while before we return to your hotel?"

"I'd like that."

But in typical Mexican fashion, it took a long while for the check to arrive. When they finally left the restaurant, darkness had descended but the streets were still busy with both vehicles and pedestrians. Many of the streets were ancient cobblestone, and though some were asphalt, none were in the best repair, even if they were fairly clean. But Frank maneuvered confidently and skillfully through the wild traffic, making Shelby wonder if it was from experience or if it was just his nature. Probably a bit of both.

She knew so little about him.

"Frank," she began as they strolled over the old brick and cobblestone bridge spanning the Cuale River that bisected the town, "I have to tell you something." She glanced up at him, and he nodded encouragement for her to continue. "I don't usually open up this freely with people I don't know. Honestly, I'm not one to wear my heart on my sleeve. And I don't want you to get the wrong impression. It's just that—" Shelby paused because she found it difficult to put into words what she felt was happening between them. Perhaps she was also a little afraid that it wasn't mutual.

He pulled her aside as they reached the middle of the bridge. They stood looking out upon the dark river below them, flowing as sluggishly as a Mexican siesta. "There was a moment on the boat today," he said, studying the water as he spoke, "when I knew I would be standing in a place like this with you—and I would see into you and you would see into me. I couldn't have predicted it would happen this soon, but I knew it would happen."

"How . . . what was it?"

"You are a real person, Shelby. I saw that almost as soon as you came aboard the *Seabird*. The contrast between you and the likes of Dan and even Christie was like night and day. And you were day—bright and shining day! I am so tired of people with agendas, men and women with perfectly honed skills attracting the opposite sex. You didn't try to attract me, yet that's exactly what you did—just as simple as that."

"On the boat?"

"You felt nothing on the boat?"

"You know I did. I can probably even tell you the exact moment you are talking about."

"Is this love at first sight?"

"Oh . . ." An electric charge coursed through her. Did that really exist? Love at first sight. Love. . . ? Was it possible?

"Now *I* am wearing my heart on my sleeve." Frank looked at her now, his dark eyes penetrating her with an intensity that made her hold her breath. "I have never been in love, Shelby . . . and I was married once before. But her soul never touched mine, not like now."

"Have you opened your soul to me, Frank?"

"No, but I could . . . I truly could."

"I think I want you to, but not now. It's too soon and too hard to take everything in." Shelby started walking.

He strode beside her. They didn't touch, yet she knew his nearness and it felt so very *right*. She stole a glance at him and wondered again at this connection between them. He was handsome but not strikingly so, with an average build not more than one hundred and sixty pounds. He was no broad-shouldered hunk, and muscles did not ripple under his white polo shirt. But there was a solidness about him in his physique and in his features. His jawline was well-defined, and his eyes, narrowly set, were dark and incisive with a strong ridge of thick, dark brows over them. His distinctive nose added to the overall dramatic sense of his face. Shelby wanted to take more time to study him; she wanted a closer look at the scar that ran from the corner of his right eye to the corner of his jaw, a scar he tended to finger unconsciously. She wondered what had caused it and instinctively knew he bore other scars she could not see—scars on his heart rather than his body.

"What did you mean before," she asked suddenly, "about grieving the living?"

"There are people I wish I had a better relationship with, that's all. My parents . . . my brother."

"I'll never know why families can be so tedious at times."

"But you had an idyllic relationship with your father."

"And now he's gone and I just have my mother left."

"You never mentioned her."

"That's because I wish she didn't exist. But she does, and I suppose I'll have to face it eventually. She ran out on me when I was a year old. Couldn't hack the responsibility. She's a really flaky person—even now she still has no idea who she is and what her life is all about."

"Do you? Does anyone?"

"I guess it just seems a person's mother ought to know where she's going so she can direct her children. Maybe it's asking too much."

"And perhaps one can get too much direction from a mother."

"Is that a description of your mother?"

His lips quirked in a slight smile. "My mother is a rock—no, she is a rudder. The whole ship goes her way or no way."

"At least she's not an anchor."

He laughed a dry, humorless laugh. "Sometimes she can be that, too."

Soon they were back to his old black Dodge pickup. It was only nine o'clock, and they both agreed they weren't ready for the evening to end. He drove south through town, then along the winding two-lane road that led to Shelby's hotel. Three miles before reaching the resort, he turned up a side road that was gravelly and steep. He had to engage the four-wheel drive to negotiate the road, and even with that, the rusted old pickup had to labor over the pitted terrain. A five-minute drive dotted with lush tropical vegetation brought them to a level, more cultivated area leading up to a white stucco house with a red-tile roof. The house and landscape provided the atmosphere for a typical tropical Mexican scene.

"My grandmother's house," Frank said simply.

The house itself was modest, no bigger than an average family home. It was old, though kept up well despite the fact that the plants and bushes around the house were a bit overgrown. The setting was what made it truly spectacular. Perched on a cliff, the back of the house held a sweeping view of the lush valley below while the front faced a panorama of the ocean. Frank and Shelby got out of the truck and walked to the ocean side, where the moon sparkled enchantingly on the water and phosphorescent waves crashed against the sandy beach. Since her arrival in Puerto Vallarta, Shelby had often gazed up at the homes nestled into the cliffs, wondering what they were like—or rather, wondering what it would be like seeing everything from such a vantage point.

"We will come here one day and watch the sunset," he said quietly, reverently.

"Oh yes . . ."

"You can see Los Arcos." He pointed toward a distinctive formation of rocks about a half mile off shore. "There is good snorkeling there. We will sail out there one day."

She nodded.

"And of course, Playa Mismaloya. Your hotel is slightly south of Los Arcos. And a little more south of that are the remains of the set where *Night of the Iguana* was made. We'll go there, too."

She looked at him and smiled.

"Too much?" he asked with a slightly embarrassed smile. "I want to show you everything, to be with you."

"I want to be with you, too."

"But. . . ?"

"It's not too much, and yet it is scary. I keep trying to analyze it—"

"Why?" Frank cut in. "Can't we just accept it as a rare, magical event to grab and enjoy? Most people never experience what we have found today."

"Are you saying we should live for the moment?"

"No, I'm saying live for today and tomorrow—and even forever. If there is a forever, if there can possibly be such security in life, I want you to be part of it with me."

"How can you know that?"

Instead of answering immediately, he reached in his back pocket for his wallet, which he opened, removing a photograph. It was a family portrait, a man and woman in their early thirties with two children, a boy about six and a curly-headed girl about four. Cleaned and scrubbed and dressed in their best clothes, they looked like all-American folks.

"Who are they?" Shelby asked.

"The photo was sent to my grandmother by a friend whose son is pictured here with his family. I don't know their names, I've never met them. I asked my grandmother if I could have the photo simply because I liked the way they looked, I guess." Frank paused and bit his lip, focusing his gaze on the ocean. "I carry it as a reminder of what I want from life. It's a pretty ridiculous gesture because my whole life has been a total contradiction of such a normal life. In fact, there was a time when I would have laughed at such ordinary, even boring people. But no more. I now covet it instead."

"So I am a convenient way for you to fulfill your dream?"

"You don't understand." He placed his hands on Shelby's shoulders and turned her toward him. "I have been looking for a long time, judging women by the wife in the photo. I have given it much thought. I know what I want."

"Me?" Shelby whispered.

"I knew when we met on the boat." He sighed. "I suppose I am overwhelming you. But imagine after all this time of looking, to find you and realize that you felt something for me also. I guess I've let it go to my head."

Shelby reached up and brushed an errant strand of wavy hair from his forehead. And in the next moment she leaned very close, her eyes shut, her lips seeking his. When they embraced, the passion shuddered through her as if her soul had been awakened from a deep sleep. He responded, holding her with such strength and yet such tenderness she did not know what to think or what to do. So she simply surrendered to his embrace, trying not to question how such a thing could happen.

Then he stepped away from her.

"You must understand, Shelby, that this is not what the evening is about. I did not bring you up here to seduce you. I only wanted for you to see this part of me so that you could know a little more of who I am. More than anything, I fear ruining what has happened here by doing something we might later regret." Frank studied her closely with dark, penetrating eyes. "You fear this, also?"

"I don't know what I fear most," Shelby replied breathlessly. "Falling in love . . . or losing the most incredible love I could ever attain."

He nodded and took her hand. "Let's drive down to the beach, walk for a while, and get to know each other better. Only then can we put aside our fears."

5

"I COULDN'T STAND IT," Christie said when Shelby walked into the living room of their hotel suite at midnight. "I had to wait up for you." She set aside her magazine and perched on the edge of the sofa.

"You probably just got in yourself." Shelby pulled up a chair opposite her friend.

"A little bit ago," Christie confessed.

"Dan?" For some reason she couldn't explain, Shelby didn't want to talk about her evening. Christie, who kept her relationships with men light and uncommitted, probably would not understand what Shelby had experienced.

"No, he turned out to be a real bore. I dumped him after lunch. I met another guy. He's much nicer—rich, too. He's a computer systems analyst—don't ask me what that is—but he also has family money. We had dinner and then went to a beach fiesta. It was fun. What about you?"

"Frank's nice, too. We had a good time."

"Will you see him again?"

"Tomorrow for breakfast and then some sight-seeing. Do you mind?"

"Now, don't you start being protective of *me*. Anyway, I'll probably see Ted—that's the new guy I met—again. You and I can see each other anytime."

"Are you sure?"

Christie rolled her eyes. "No more discussion. Who knows? One of these guys may be Mr. Right."

Shelby shrugged casually, then got up and stretched. "Well . . . I think I'll go to bed. Frank is picking me up at eight-thirty." She went to her room, relieved nothing more had come of the conversation.

They ate breakfast in an outdoor café facing a busy street and a large market area that was just beginning to open for business. Shelby felt relaxed with Frank, able to take in the activity around them without the burden of small talk. She ordered a sausage-tortilla dish with scrambled eggs, melted cheese, and lots of salsa. He ordered eggs and plain tortillas. They sipped strong Mexican-style coffee while they waited for their meal.

Out in the street a man with a deformed leg and a severe limp was directing traffic around the busy corner. He was wearing an official-looking orange vest, though in every other respect he hardly looked right for the position. However, for a man who at times appeared as if he might topple over, he did his job with amazing authority, blowing his whistle or waving his arms with distinctive hand motions. The drivers obeyed him instantly, and those who didn't received a scathing tongue-lashing from the man. It was quite a sight, and Shelby watched it, mesmerized, for some time.

"Only in Mexico," Frank commented dryly.

"He's great," said Shelby. "I wish I had a video camera. It would be a great lesson for my students in accepting people with physical challenges and seeing their amazing abilities."

"You enjoy teaching?" he asked as their meal arrived.

"I love it. There is simply nothing else I'd rather be doing."

"It is a rare thing for a person to be so content with their work."

"You haven't talked much about your job. I gather you don't feel the same."

"It's just a job. I suppose I should be thankful my family had such a convenient position for me when I needed it, though I'm sure my grandmother made them give it to me. My parents wouldn't have done it on their own."

"What do they have against you?"

His gaze shifted from her to the street. She wondered if he was going to attempt to avoid her question. It was obvious from the shadowed look in his eyes that he didn't like talking about himself, especially his family.

"You know, Shelby, I wasn't always the saintly specimen before you now." His voice was light, but his eyes remained the same. "I used to look for trouble—and had no trouble finding it. I only have one brother and he is younger than me, and the idiot looked up to me, wanted to follow in my footsteps. When I decided to clean up my act, for some reason he wouldn't follow me there. Maybe he was in too deep, maybe he had matured out of his hero worship. Well, my parents have blamed me for leading him astray."

"You didn't force him into it, did you?"

"No, of course not." Frank's tone was abrupt, defensive. He glanced away, his eyes clouded. "It's impossible to convince a kid to stay in school, to listen to his parents. But I didn't practice those things myself, so I shouldn't have been surprised that he didn't. It was my fault."

"It sounds like an awful burden to carry."

"I'd do anything to help him now, but he wouldn't accept my help."

"Were you . . . in trouble with the law?"

"It's all behind me now, I promise you. But it is a past I don't want to remember."

"Sounds like your parents won't let you forget."

"That is an understatement." He spread a tortilla with butter, rolled it up, and concentrated on eating it. Shelby took the hint and said no more about his parents.

"Do you want to do some shopping when we finish?" she asked instead.

"Good idea. It is an adventure I'd very much enjoy experiencing with you."

"I went with Christie when we first arrived. We were a bit overwhelmed. My Spanish is very rusty."

"It will be fun to show you the ropes."

When they finished their meal and walked to the main market under and around the two bridges that spanned the Cuale River, Frank displayed his fluent Spanish and true talent for bartering.

"They expect you to bargain," he told her. "In fact, they would be disappointed if you accepted the asking price."

Shelby found a beautifully embroidered tote bag in a shop, and Frank gave her a lesson in Mexican shopping.

"*¿Cuánto vale?*" he asked the man tending the shop.

"Ah, you have very good eye," the man said in heavily accented English. "This handwork, very much difficult. I can sell for *ciento cincuenta pesos*. Good deal."

"I'll give you *ochenta* pesos."

"Oh no . . ." groaned the man, and Shelby wasn't surprised at the clerk's pained expression. She thought Frank had made a pretty low offer herself, less than half the asking price. "This all handwork, very intricate. I watched the women in the village make it. It takes them a long time," the clerk insisted. "I already take a great loss. One hundred thirty pesos is as low as I can go."

They bartered back and forth for a few moments. Frank came up to ninety pesos, but the clerk would only go down to one hundred and twenty pesos. Finally Frank turned to leave.

"No, *gracias.*" He took Shelby's hand and exited.

The bag was beautiful, but she hadn't had her heart set on it. They were out in the breezeway between shops when the clerk called after them.

Frank winked covertly at Shelby, and she realized this was all part of the game.

"Okay," the clerk said with a long-suffering sigh, "for you I give for one hundred ten pesos. I make no profit if I give it for less."

Frank shrugged. "We're not that interested. A hundred pesos."

"Oh, but there's no profit in it for me," whined the clerk.

Frank ambled about the shop looking casually at other items. A few more customers came in and soon Frank and Shelby started to leave again. But the clerk caught them before they reached the door.

"Okay, for you I let it go for a hundred pesos," he said in a soft voice. "Tell no one. I make no profit, but the pretty lady would look good with the bag, eh?"

The deal was sealed, Frank paid the money, and Shelby took the bag from the rack. When they were outside she tried to give Frank the money, but he wouldn't take it.

"This is too much fun," he said. "It's worth it."

"Well, I'll pay next time."

They strolled around the market, which consisted of many three-sided stalls each filled to the brim with south-of-the-border merchandise. The shopping district wasn't crowded at that hour in the morning, so they received much attention from the clerks. Often, if Shelby just casually touched an item, she found herself suddenly caught up in bartering for it. She ended up buying a silver bracelet that hadn't especially interested her simply because the clerk made the deal so enticing. After a while she was drawn into the routine, bartering with the best, and making some very good deals. She tried not to think about the fact that half the stuff she purchased she neither needed nor wanted. Frank joked that she was doing her part in keeping the economy of Mexico fluid.

When they tired of shopping, they had lunch in another café. Then they walked to the south side of the river and to the Playa de los Muertos, one of the more popular beaches in town. By now it was crowded with tourists, and vendors weaved in and out of the crowd, hawking their goods carried in suitcases or draped over their arms—lace tablecloths, silver jewelry, carved masks, or grilled fish on a stick. It hardly made for a peaceful, romantic stroll when they were fending off vendors at every turn, but it was an adventure, and it was with Frank. Shelby found herself enjoying his company more and more. He was like a multi-facetted gem. He had his solemn moods that Shelby felt she could not penetrate, but he also had a wonderful sense of humor, often making her laugh. Her father's death soon became a dim, faraway memory.

And so the days passed. They spent every waking moment together, exploring the town, seeking out the many quaint places tourists seldom saw. They took the boat out to snorkel or swim in places off the tourist-beaten track. Sometimes they held hands, sometimes they kissed, but never more than that. There were times when the passion ignited within Shelby was almost unbearable. But Frank consistently made it clear he would not sully what they had by succumbing to physical passions. Shelby agreed—she truly did—but it did not come easily when he was near, when she could still taste the sweetness of his kisses long after they had parted.

One day, when Shelby had been in Puerto Vallarta a week and had known Frank less than five days, they walked to the set of the movie, *Night of the Iguana*, which was just down the beach from Shelby's hotel. They had to hike up a steep path, and only because of a few old signs did they know they had reached the famous spot. There was nothing left that resembled the movie, and what little did remain was in ruins. But the landing at the top of the hill offered a wonderful view of the sea.

"I love the sea," Frank said, studying the endless expanse. "It makes me feel alive. Sometimes I think I'd like to walk out into the middle of it all and be forever surrounded by it."

"But that would defeat what you love about it."

"Ah yes . . . isn't that the great dilemma of life?" He absently rubbed his scar. "It is but the other side—so close you can hardly tell when joy is swallowed by death."

"That's pretty deep stuff, Frank," she quipped. "Not to mention depressing."

He turned to her, and his gaze held such sadness it made her shudder. "I don't ever want to depress you, my love. I want to be your joy, your life, even if it means—" he stopped, jerking his gaze back to the sea. "Do you know there is a little village over there"—he pointed along the coast to the south—"that you can only reach by sea? It's called Yalapa. Many of the local women still wash their clothes in the river, and if it wasn't for the daily invasion of tourists, the residents would carry on their lives the same as they have for hundreds of years."

"I'd like to see it." Shelby was both relieved and disturbed that he had so abruptly changed the subject.

How she wished she could unlock the deeper mysteries of this man before her—discover the endings of the statements he so often left unfinished or the meaning in those shadowed looks of his. Yet she was reluctant to probe too deeply, desiring such revelations to come naturally and from him. She knew it wouldn't change anything. No, it would simply make her love him more.

6

THEY SAILED TO YALAPA the next day, and the village proved to be as quaint as Frank had promised. A hike inland revealed a true step back in time. The path Frank followed was narrow in places, rocky, and often blocked by overgrown shrubbery. Occassionally they would pass an adobe hut or a shack, but for the most part they were traversing a rather wild and unfrequented area. Once, two men with a mule approached from the opposite direction. They ignored Shelby's friendly greeting but gave a quick *Hola* to Frank. Later, the same thing happened as another male local passed them.

"Are they hostile against tourists or something?" Shelby asked Frank. "I'm trying to be friendly."

"Tourists are their bread and butter," Frank replied. "It has nothing to do with that. Nor should you take it personally. They simply don't want me to take offense."

"You? Why?"

"The Mexican male tends to be a rather jealous creature. So these men ignore your greetings because they don't want to appear to be flirting with you while you are with another man."

"You're kidding?"

"Not at all. It all has to do with machismo. You've heard of that, haven't you?"

"Of course. But I don't see what it has to do with jealousy."

Frank reached up to push aside a protruding branch from their path. "In order for me to be a real man, I would have to react to their perceived flirting. They expect my—uh . . . reaction, and so to avoid trouble, they ignore you."

"You mean they're afraid you'd pulverize them if they flirted with me?" Her tone held a hint of amusement.

"Yes, because that's what they would do. It could become a very serious matter."

"You wouldn't really beat up a man for saying hello to me?"

"I'm far too evolved for that. . . ." His comical tone almost matched hers, but there was little humor in his eyes. "I suppose I know of no one more docile than my father, but when I was a boy, a friend of my father got fresh with my mother—I don't think he did more than wink at her. My father nearly beat the man to a pulp. I watched it. And rather than being apalled, I remember thinking what a man my father was. It is something we learn at a very young age, and no matter how 'Americanized' we get, it's still hard to shake entirely."

"What do the women think of this?"

He turned suddenly somber eyes upon her. "They learn early how to work it to their advantage."

Just then they came to an opening in the brush with a view of the river. "Look over there," Shelby said, hardly even realizing what a relief it was to change the subject. They caught their first glimpse of a group of women crouched on the far bank of the river, scrubbing their laundry. The previous conversation was forgotten as they once more became caught up in experiencing the charming countryside.

Later, back at the Bougainvillea, Frank suggested a little restaurant called Tony's that was just east of the hotel in the little village of Mismaloya. Shelby hadn't even realized the village existed, though it was hardly a mile from her hotel, and felt it was a true discovery. As was common in Mexico, the village was rather shabby and could hardly be called picturesque, except in its uniqueness from towns in the States. Despite its close proximity to the hotel, it was obviously not intended to be a tourist trap. There was one main dirt street with a few less-than-thriving businesses on either side. Only one small shop offered the kind of wares to interest a tourist. The village did offer a church and even a children's play area with a trampoline and table games. This particular evening the village reflected a festive atmosphere with flags and paper decorations strung overhead in the main square of the village. Frank guessed there would be a fiesta that evening. He greeted several locals whom he knew and explained to Shelby that with his grandmother's house so near, he knew Mismaloya well and always made it a point when there to dine at Tony's.

As they strolled up the hill to the restaurant, two young boys caught up with them.

"Hola!" said the taller of the two boys. "You go to Tony's?"

"Sí," answered Frank.

"We show you the way?"

"*Está bien*," said Frank, not mentioning his familiarity with the place since the boys obviously appeared eager to be helpful.

Shelby realized this was what the village children did for fun, interacting with the few tourists who ventured into their small town.

"What's your name—" Shelby began, then suddenly stopped. "I mean . . . *¿Cómo se llama usted?*"

"You speak good Spanish," said the boy who had apparently elected himself spokesman. "*Me llamo* Miguel."

"Me llamo Raul," piped up the other boy.

"Glad to meet you. Me llama Shelby and—" But Shelby's Spanish failed her and she finished in English. "This is Frank."

"*¿Su esposo?*"

Shelby glanced quickly at Frank, and her cheeks grew warm. Frank responded to her look with only a smile. She knew he was curious what her response would be to the innocent question.

"No, not my husband. Just a friend . . . a very good friend." She gave Frank a little smirk and he took her hand, squeezing it gently.

"Where you from?" asked Miguel, unaware of the interchange between the adults.

"California," said Shelby.

"I got a brother in Los Angeles."

"Have you been to visit him?"

"Sí. Maybe I go live there someday, too."

"Did you learn English here in school?"

"No, in L.A."

"Well, your English is much better than my Spanish. You should get along well in the States."

As they neared their destination, they passed a large hibiscus bush. Miguel reached up and plucked off a red blossom and handed it to Shelby. Touched, she took it with a smile.

"Gracias," she said.

Not to be outdone, quiet Raul also plucked off a blossom and gave it to her. She accepted it with further thanks.

"Well, here we are," said Miguel, stopping in front of an ancient but charming adobe structure. A sign swaying above the doorway said simply, Tony's.

"It was very nice meeting you, Miguel and Raul. Thank you for escorting us," Shelby said.

Frank reached in his pocket and gave each boy two American quarters, which they accepted with wide eyes and effusive thanks.

"That made their day," Shelby said as they climbed the narrow flight of stairs that led up to the open-air, thatched-roof dining room.

"*You* made their day," Frank countered. "As you have made every one of my days since I met you."

The meal was the best Shelby had tasted since coming to Mexico, and the waiter served it with such flair that the enjoyment went beyond the delicious food. They lingered over dinner, watching the sun set over the ocean as they were served a pastry-and-whipped-cream dessert with flaming kahlua coffee, which was a specialty of the house. It was dark when they left, and the full moon had risen high in the sky. Back in the main part of the village, the festivities had picked up their pace. Many locals and a handful of tourists were strolling up and down the street while a dozen children enjoyed the play area, laughing and jumping on the trampoline with great enthusiasm.

Near the end of the main street, Shelby took a closer look at the church. It was really rather nondescript, built of gray cinder blocks with a flat roof—hardly what she expected of a Mexican Catholic church. Now, because of the lights and decorations strung around the courtyard, the church was very apparent. About thirty people were milling about in the yard, adding to the festive atmosphere.

"I wonder what's happening up there?" Shelby asked.

"Let's take a look."

Frank took her hand and led her up the steps and into the church's courtyard. The paper-flower garlands decorating the yard were fastened from the roof of the church to a small bell tower at the opposite end of the yard. It gave the building an inviting look. And a closer inspection showed that the people were standing outside because inside, the church was filled to capacity, with many standing at the back and in the aisles. However, because everyone inside was standing, even those in the pews, Shelby could not tell what was happening at the altar.

Frank approached an old woman who was standing near the door. "*¿Señora, es ésta la boda?*"

She gave him a broad, toothless grin. "*Sí! Es la boda de Juan Ramirez y Agueda Gómez.*"

"*No los conozco. Pero gracias, señora.*" He turned to Shelby. "It's a wedding," he explained. "They must have begun while we were in the restaurant. Typically there is a procession through town before the ceremony. Unfortunately, we wouldn't have seen or heard it from the restaurant."

"Oh, too bad we missed it." Now Shelby understood why there were several children playing in the courtyard, dressed in bright costumes complete with feathered head gear resembling Aztec warriors. They must have been part of the procession. "Can we wait a bit to get a glimpse of the bride and groom?"

"What is it about women and weddings?" Frank grinned.

"And weddings do nothing for you?"

"My own wedding will be the only one that matters."

"I'm sure your bride wouldn't argue with that."

"I hope not."

Suddenly Shelby sensed they were no longer talking about some undefined event. She felt herself grow warm all over at the way he looked at her, giving no doubt about what he was thinking.

"Frank, I . . ."

He put his arm around her and nudged her close. "You know it is inevitable that I will propose to you?"

"I—I hadn't thought about it." But she knew she was lying. She had thought about it several times, futilely trying not to dwell on those thoughts.

"I want to marry you, Shelby, and share my life with you. I have known that from the beginning."

"Maybe I knew it, too."

"Yet I know it is sudden, too sudden."

She gazed up at him. His dark eyes reflected the lights on the garland, giving them an ethereal quality. And, indeed, she felt almost as if she were floating in some dream. It was stunning to think she was standing there discussing marriage with a man she had known only a week. Yet it all seemed so very right. In fact, now that she allowed herself to consider the possibility, Shelby realized she could not imagine life without Frank.

"Who are we to place some arbitrary time frame on such a thing as love?" she found herself saying. "Will it be any better in a week? A month? A year? I hope it will always be deepening, I suppose, but will it be any more *right*?"

"What are you saying?"

"I don't know . . . except I feel certain I need not look any further for my soul mate."

"You are certain of this?"

"Yes. I want to doubt, to question . . . but all I feel is certainty."

"Are you saying that when we return to the States you will want to discuss a wedding date? We could even plan a honeymoon back here in Puerto Vallarta where it all began."

"Or we could take care of both at one time."

"What do you mean?" Frank looked at her warily, as if he well knew what she meant but couldn't believe it.

"We're here now, and I have a week before I have to return to work. Is that a long enough honeymoon?"

"Wait a minute! Am I hearing you right? Do you want to get married here and now?" It was the first time she had seen sheer incredulity on his face.

"I've gone completely crazy, haven't I?" Shelby giggled, ignoring the fact that she sounded so very like her mother.

"Insane."

"But I don't feel insane. Frank, if we know this is going to happen, why wait?"

"And I thought I was being overwhelming—"

"We could wait. I know I *would* wait if I had to. But I don't want anything else."

"Neither do I."

"Then why wait?"

"It's not as simple as you make it sound," he said. "There are forms to fill out and blood tests, and we'll need the proper identification."

"Are these insurmountable obstacles?"

He smiled slyly. "This is Mexico, where a greased palm here and there can dissolve any obstacle."

They looked at one another in the shadowy glow of the churchyard lights, and their eyes made the commitment their hearts had felt all along.

7

"YOU'RE GOING TO WHAT!"

"I'm getting married, Christie, and I want you to be my maid of honor."

It was the response Shelby had expected. Of course, she had an impulsive nature, but because she tried so hard to curb that tendency, it was not always evident. Even though Christie knew about her often-squelched impulsive side, her sudden announcement still caused some shock. Yet Shelby desperately yearned for Christie's support. She was determined to make this marriage happen, and she would do it alone if necessary. But having her best friend present would make a wedding in a foreign country a little less intimidating.

"Whoa, Shelby, slow down. I mean *really* slow down. Do you know what you're doing? Have you had one too many margaritas?"

"I know exactly what I'm doing," Shelby replied with such firm confidence it even surprised her a bit. "I love this man, we are going to marry, and so I see no reason to wait. I don't want a big, silly wedding in the States. There's no one left I really care about to attend except you."

"Shelby, are you doing this because you are afraid to go back home and be alone?"

"Don't try to psychoanalyze this, Chris. We love each other. It has nothing to do with my grief. It is love, pure love."

"Is he pushing you?"

"Christie! I thought I could count on you, but . . . forget it." Shelby stood and turned to leave the patio balcony where they were seated in the morning sunshine.

"Hold on," Christie said with more understanding. "Can't you just give me a chance to let it sink in?"

Shelby returned to the lawn chair. "It's hard to put into words the certainty I feel in my heart." She moderated her tone. "We could get engaged and wait six months or a year. Maybe we should, maybe that is the logical thing to do. But there are times when a person must follow an instinct that is much more visceral than logic."

"But how well can you know him in such a short time?"

"I know he loves and respects me with a depth that is almost staggering. I know he is tender and gentle and strong. He is all the things I desire."

"How can you be so certain, Shelby?" said Christie, whose usual aplomb was seriously ruffled. "How do you know he's not here just preying on helpless women—"

"Give me some credit, would you?" Shelby snapped.

"But you weren't even looking for a husband."

"And that's what convinces me more than ever. I wasn't looking, but now I can't picture my life apart from him. Without Frank, the emptiness would be akin only to what I felt when Dad died. Chris, you have heard of soul mates, the one true love. . . . Well, I know Frank is mine. That's all I can say."

Christie reached out and touched her hand. "Well, who am I to argue with that. When's the wedding?" She smiled and Shelby sighed with relief.

"Day after tomorrow. A civil ceremony at the courthouse."

"We better get to shopping, then."

An hour later they were in town scouring all the better boutiques for a wedding trousseau. Shelby had arranged to meet Frank at two in the afternoon at the courthouse to get the legal gears in motion. When they saw him waiting, Christie gave Frank an enthusiastic hug and what appeared to be sincere congratulations. A day of shopping had injected her friend with excitement for the event. Christie even suggested that she arrange to change Frank's plane ticket so that he and Shelby could return home together. Acknowledging their grateful thanks, Christie assured them it was the least she could do. She then gathered all their shopping parcels and returned to the hotel while Frank and Shelby began the arduous task of lighting a fire under the sluggish Mexican bureaucracy.

The receptionist in the licensing bureau was not encouraging. In fact, she smiled a bit when Frank informed her they wanted to schedule the wedding in two days. Because the interchange took place in Spanish, Shelby was lost except for brief interpretations offered by Frank. The woman gave them the paper work and put them on the schedule, but she was extremely skeptical that they'd get everything together in time. The biggest obstacle was the blood test—but Frank knew a way around it.

They drove to the village of Mismaloya. It was by then four in the afternoon, and the village had a far different air about it than it had the previous night. There was hardly anyone on the streets, and though some of the decorations were still up, all looked far more dingy by the light of day. Frank parked at the curb near the now empty children's play area. When they got out of the truck, he took Shelby's hand and led her down a breezeway at the side of a building to a door that had a shingle overhead that read R. Sanchez, M.D. He knocked on the door, but there was no answer.

"It's siesta time," Frank said to Shelby. "No doubt the old sot is asleep."

" 'Old sot'?" she said warily. "He's going to do the blood test?" She wasn't certain if she wanted a "sot" to be poking her with a needle.

"You'll be perfectly safe, my love. I won't let you within ten feet of his needles." He knocked again on the door, this time harder. When there was still no response, he turned the knob and the door opened. "Hey,

Doc," he called, stepping inside. Shelby followed.

The room looked like something out of the old West, only not even as clean or well-equipped. The examination table had rusty legs, and the leather cover was torn in several places. The glass on the medicine cabinets was so dirty it was hard to see the contents. A black cat lay on a counter in the midst of instruments and linens.

"Frank," said Shelby, looking about with horror, "if I ever get sick, shoot me before you take me here."

He smiled. "Few people ever come here for medical treatment. But Doc Sanchez has his uses, even if most of what he does these days is back-alley medicine, procuring illegal drugs, or filling out bogus forms."

"And giving phony blood tests?"

"Exactly."

"How did you know about him?"

"Oh, he's an old friend of the family. Once, he was a pretty good doctor—"

A voice, dull and groggy, intruded into their conversation. "*¿Quién está allí? ¿No sabe que la oficina está cerrada?*"

"*Doctor, soy yo, Francisco Stefano.*"

In a moment, an old man—probably in his late sixties or early seventies—appeared in a doorway that led off the infirmary. His white hair and stubble of beard made a stark contrast to his swarthy and leathery complexion. He was short and bent and dressed in a dirty undershirt and baggy trousers with suspenders hanging down at his sides. Even from a distance, Shelby could smell the cheap alcohol lingering about him.

When the doctor's bleary eyes focused on Frank, his lips parted in a wide grin revealing yellowed and rotten teeth.

"*Francisco! Mi amigo! Cuánto tiempo que no te veía.*" He grasped Frank's hand with a grimy, arthritic paw while slapping Frank on the shoulder with his other hand.

They conversed in Spanish as Shelby listened, grasping very little.

"So what brings you to my humble casa, amigo?" Dr. Sanchez asked in Spanish.

"I have a favor to ask of you, Doc."

"You know I am at your service. I still fondly remember your grand-father, may he rest in peace. He was a good man and helped me many times when my pocketbook was bare. Is your grandmother well? She has not come here for a long time."

"She is well, as spry as a seventy-year-old woman could be."

"Good. Now, what can I do for you? You know, I still maintain some of the connections you have used in the past. I think they would still be willing to do business with you even though it has been—how long? Over a year since I have acted for you—"

"No, no, Doc. That's not what this is about. A completely different matter. I want to get married here in Mexico the day after tomorrow. I need a few things expedited."

"And would this be the lovely bride-to-be?"

"Sí." Frank glanced at Shelby and smiled.

"A beautiful gringo girl. But, Francisco, why not marry in the States? Wouldn't it be simpler?"

"Things are never simple in the States, not for me. But regardless, we want to marry here where we met and fell in love."

"And you are in love, aren't you, amigo? I can see it in your eyes."

"I am, very much. So can you help us, Doc?"

"With pleasure! I know someone in the health department who can put the proper stamp on your paper work. I'll need to get some basic information about you first. And of course, it will take a few pesos."

They gave the doctor the information he needed, and he agreed to meet them the day after tomorrow—Wednesday—at one o'clock in front of the courthouse with all the documents they would need. Then Shelby and Frank returned to the Bougainvillea and, sitting by the pool, tackled another form the woman at the courthouse had given them. Shelby filled out the bride's section, then handed it to Frank. She peeked over his shoulder as he did the same to the groom's section. One inquiry caught her eye: "Highest school grade attended." He put twelfth.

"No college?" she asked.

Frank shook his head. "Does that bother you? To be better educated than me?"

"Not at all. It's just something I didn't know about you."

"Do you wonder how much more you don't know?"

"Yes, but I'll have a lifetime to learn everything."

"Maybe I should tell you some things. . . ." His tone was suddenly serious.

"Nothing you could say would change how I feel. I know your heart, Frank, and that's all I need to know."

"But—"

"Say no more, not now."

He returned his attention to the form, filling in his parents' address, the last item. He sighed as he laid down the pen, then focused a tender gaze upon her. "Just know I love you, Shelby. . . ."

She nodded and took his hand, bringing it to her lips. "I know."

8

SHELBY'S WEDDING DAY began at dawn when, after a sleepless night, she crept from her bed, dressed in jeans and long-sleeved shirt, and headed down to the beach that fronted the hotel. The dusky gray sky bore wisps of pink, hinting of the new day. The water was calm, almost glassy, with only gentle waves breaking against the sandy beach. Shelby was the only person out at that hour. Gone were the wall-to-wall sunbathers; gone, too, were the persistent vendors hawking their wares.

In a way, Shelby wished she had forced herself to go back to sleep. The day would have begun so much more simply had she awakened later with Christie and been plunged immediately into the flurry of wedding preparations. She had not been seeking an introspective walk on the beach. She didn't want to question what was coming and possibly ruin the beauty and spontaneity of it.

She was going to marry Frank. She didn't know why she was so determined to do it now. Maybe she was afraid that to wait would spoil the magic they had experienced here in Puerto Vallarta.

"I don't want to think about it!" she said out loud, kicking hard at the sand.

She started running, hard and fast, her feet pounding on the wet sand near to where the waves were lapping lazily. She ran and ran until her heart was pumping and her chest ached. After ten minutes, exhausted, she crumbled onto the sand, gasping and panting. It felt good. Then she jogged back to her suite, making enough noise so as to be sure to wake Christie.

The rush of activity after that was more welcome than she wanted to admit.

If Shelby nursed any doubts, they were quelled the moment she first laid eyes on Frank. He was waiting for her in the square in front of the courthouse, and the love reflected in his eyes was more than any woman could desire. He was dressed in tan chinos and an off-white linen sport-coat with a matching dress shirt and a conservatively printed necktie in neutral tones. She had not seen him so dressed up before. He looked wonderful.

He must have felt the same way about her, at least by the pleased look with which he appraised her. She was wearing a white cotton batiste dress with a tiered skirt. The hem was richly and colorfully embroidered in Mexican fashion, as was the neckline of her blouse. Christie had done wonders with her hair, pulling it back loosely into a French twist and tucking in a pink Hibiscus, leaving soft tendrils to frame her face. Shelby knew she looked good, she knew she was glowing, she knew this was right.

She and Frank and Christie continued to stand in the cobbled square as they waited for Dr. Sanchez. The wrought-iron park benches nearby were too rusty and dirty to invite sitting, especially in their good clothes. They double-checked to be sure they had all the necessary identification. Frank had a passport and driver's license, but Shelby only had her birth certificate and driver's license. Frank told them he had cleared up a few other matters with the records clerk—that is, he had given the man a bribe to overlook the fact that they had no tourist cards and he had no verification of the validity of Frank's divorce. He also had all the necessary papers translated into Spanish.

"All we need is Doc," Frank said. He studied her a moment. "Are you nervous?"

Shelby shrugged noncommittally. It wasn't something she wanted to think about. "Will the ceremony be in Spanish?"

"Probably. Will you mind?"

"I don't care—as long as it's all legal."

"It will be."

Finally Doc arrived with two friends who would act as additional witnesses, since four were needed. He also had an officially signed health certificate. At last they headed into the courthouse, up a wide flight of stairs to the second floor, where the licensing bureau was located. Another couple was ahead of them, so the group milled about in the corridor until they were called.

"Are you sure you don't mind that this isn't a big church wedding?" Frank asked. They were standing apart from the others, holding hands.

"I suppose it would be a sham if it were. I haven't been to church in years. Does it bother you that I'm not Catholic?" Here they were, moments before their wedding, still discovering elemental things about each other. Shelby pushed such thoughts from her mind once more and focused even harder on Frank's response.

"My family is Catholic, but I quit the church years ago."

"Another thing we have in common—we're both spiritual reprobates."

"I don't attend church, but I'm not sure about everything else. Don't you believe at all, Shelby?"

"I'm not sure. Maybe I'm more of an agnostic. I just don't think about it much."

"I doubt I could be either an agnostic or an atheist . . . because of my grandmother."

"Out of respect?"

"Somewhat, but—"

The conversation was cut short as the clerk called their names. Still gripping each other's hands, Frank and Shelby stepped up to the counter. The clerk motioned for them to come around to where an older, distinguished-looking man stood.

After that, everything happened quickly, even with Frank interpreting the judge's words. In less than five minutes, Shelby was saying, "I do."

And the Judge said, *"Los declaro marido y esposa."*

It was Christie who declared the next traditional words. "Okay, it's time to kiss the bride!" And she started snapping pictures with her camera.

Shelby awoke in the night. Moonlight flooded through the window, illuminating a large swath of the bed. Still groggy, she didn't know what had caused her to wake. Then she heard a sound and sat up, startled. For a moment she had forgotten she was not alone in the bed. Frank was lying beside her, but he was stirring restlessly. Sweat beaded on his forehead, and he gave an anguished moan.

"Oh no . . . no!" he murmured, tossing even more violently.

Shelby reached out a hand, thinking it might be best to wake him. But all at once, with a shuddering cry, he sat upright in bed, panting heavily.

"Frank. . . ?" she called quietly.

He gasped in surprise. "Shelby. . . ? Oh, Shelby! Tell me you are real . . . and the other was a nightmare."

"I'm real, my love. It's okay," she soothed.

"Is it? Is it really okay?"

She moved close to him and put her arms tightly around him. "Do you want to tell me about your dream?"

He looked aghast at her and shook his head. "No! Just hold me. It'll go away. Oh, God, please make it go away!"

Shelby put her arms around his trembling shoulders and held him the rest of the night.

The light of dawn angled through the window when Shelby woke again. The disturbing interruption to their sleep last night by Frank's nightmare hardly seemed to have happened. Yet she knew she had not imagined it. Frank had been emotionally shattered by the dream, trembling and afraid. She had needed to soothe him like a frightened child— Frank, who was usually so cool and indomitable. What had brought on such fear after their incredibly wonderful wedding night?

Frank now slept soundly and quietly. Shelby thought perhaps the whole episode had been a fluke. People had nightmares—it could just as easily have been her. Why dwell on it? Instead, she snuggled close to her new husband. My new husband. She was now Mrs. Frank Stefano. She tried the name out several times silently in her mind. It sounded so very good. Frank and Shelby. Shelby Stefano. Her students would now call her Mrs. Stefano.

She was married! And the thought made her tremble with excitement and fear and wonder and anticipation. A new life stretched out before her. Two months ago she had felt so lost and hopeless, so empty and alone. With some guilt she thought of her father. He would approve, she knew he would. He would like Frank. And, had he been alive, he would have been included in her wedding. But one thought flickered through her mind that she tried unsuccessfully to ignore. Would this be one of those times he'd say, usually not in a complimentary fashion, that she was just as impulsive as her mother? No . . . he would understand. He always understood.

Frank did not stir, and though Shelby longed for his company, she didn't have the heart to wake him. She slipped out of bed, donned her silk robe, and padded, barefoot, from the bedroom. They were staying at the Stefano home nestled in the cliff overlooking Mismaloya beach. It had been a perfect setting for their first night as man and wife.

Shelby went to the kitchen and filled the coffee maker with grounds and water, ready to turn on when Frank awoke. She chopped vegetables and grated cheese for omelettes, then set it all aside and walked into the front room. The large bay window in this room looked out on the ocean with a breathtaking view. This was a charming house in every way. Shelby could live here forever, in this world not unlike the fairylands she had read about as a child. Standing before the seascape, she let her mind wander down picturesque paths of the future where there was only "happily ever after." She had no reason to believe it could be otherwise. Life for her now was simply too blissful.

So absorbed was she in her sweet thoughts that she started and gasped when a hand touched her shoulder.

"I didn't mean to frighten you," Frank said.

"I was just deep in thought."

"Pleasant thoughts, I hope."

She nodded and leaned ever so slightly back until she pressed against his chest. He put his arms around her. "I have never been happier in my life, Frank."

"That is good. It is how I always want you."

Smiling, she sighed contentedly. "Always . . ." she breathed.

They had finished breakfast and were lingering over a final cup of coffee when a rumbling sound broke into the peaceful morning. In a moment the sound took form and seemed to be that of a vehicle, possibly a truck with a loud motor and wheels that sounded like an army tank on the dirt road.

"Visitors?" Shelby wondered aloud. Had Christie found transportation in order to visit her newly married friend?

Frank rose and looked out a window.

"Who is it?" Shelby asked.

"Stay here. I'll take care of it," Frank replied and strode from the room.

Shelby went to the kitchen window herself just as Frank was crossing the yard. The window faced the back of the house, where the road came to an end. It was indeed a truck—an ancient half-ton pickup with a battered, rusted camper shell. Two Mexican men jumped out of the cab to meet Frank.

They spoke in Spanish, and Shelby decided that she was definitely going to brush up on the language once she got home. At first the conversation seemed congenial, then one of the strangers gestured toward the back of the pickup. Frank yelled at the men, but the only word Shelby could interpret was "*Stupido!*"

The three argued back and forth for a few more minutes. Frank's voice was sharp and angered, but Shelby couldn't decipher his words. Finally the two strangers none too happily got back into the truck and drove off, tires screeching and spinning as they sped away much too quickly for the poor condition of the road.

"What was that all about?" Shelby asked when Frank returned.

"Nothing," he snapped, and for a brief instant his features were as hard as when he had been dealing with the strangers. Then he seemed to think better of his response and added more civilly, "They were just lost."

"You acted like they might have been terrorists or something." She made an effort to lighten her tone, countering the tension emanating from Frank.

"They . . . wouldn't leave when I told them to. I was afraid they really might try something."

"They did look pretty seedy."

"You can't be too careful around here."

She went to Frank and put her arms around him. "Well, I feel very safe with you, my dear husband." When he didn't respond immediately, Shelby stepped back and found herself gazing into dark, pained eyes. "What is it, Frank?"

"Nothing."

"I . . . I don't know what to think when I see such an expression on your face." The thought that she knew so little about him edged into her mind. When Frank was out there in the yard he had seemed as much a stranger as the two intruders.

"Are you worried you made a mistake?" His voice matched the vulnerable, haunted look on his face.

"Let's not even talk like that, okay?"

He placed his hands on her shoulders, and their sweaty heat pressed through the thin cotton of her blouse. "What have I done, Shelby?"

"It sounds like you are the one who thinks we made a mistake." The words, spoken through a dry mouth, were difficult.

"No . . . I love you. But what if I can't protect you?"

"Is that all that's bothering you?" She again forced herself to speak lightly, letting a smile grace her lips. "I'm a modern girl, you know. Hardly helpless."

"But you have married a Mexican." He, too, made an effort at levity. "And no matter how hard I try to be modern, the old ways are hard to shake. So to me you are a precious jewel, to be placed on a pedestal—"

"Oh goodness! Now I really am afraid."

"I will try to curb my instincts. But I will still cherish you." This time Frank wrapped her in his arms, and his strained mirth turned to tenderness. "You are a gem, a gift—even if an independent, modern one. I will never stop being amazed that I have found you, Shelby, and that you actually return my love."

She nodded silently, simply letting the passion of her embrace speak for her.

9

SHELBY LOOKED OUT the window at the busy street below. Even on a Sunday traffic was building up, and she found herself thinking wishfully of her home in the quiet Whittier neighborhood where she had lived with her father. This was Frank's condominium, a prime location because of the beach right across the street. Since the condo was on the second floor, she could see the ocean out the window—an unobstructed view despite the row of one-story shops and businesses that lined the other side of the street.

In Puerto Vallarta she and Frank had not given a thought to where they would live once they returned home. It had not been until they were on the plane flying out of Mexico that the subject had been broached. They had laughed at overlooking such an important matter, but neither had really wanted to think of the "real world" until absolutely necessary. The two-day honeymoon in Mexico had been as close to a dreamlike existence as one could get. Indeed, nothing had existed except the two of them and their wondrous love.

Two hours before landing, the subject of the future—at least the immediate future—had to be discussed. Shelby had no problem agreeing to live in Redondo Beach at Frank's condo, in spite of the fact that she'd have a long commute to her school in Whittier. She did not need the memories her house represented. She would close up the house and perhaps think about renting it out or even selling it one day.

In fact, she felt very good about being in a new place, starting a new life. And only a short walk to the beach! Who could wish for more? It would be wonderful in the summer, lounging on the beach all day. It was not as inviting now, of course, with an overcast January sky and a chill in the air. Still, Shelby looked forward to taking a walk on the beach in the evening when Frank returned from work. It would rekindle her delightful memories of Puerto Vallarta.

She had spent the day unpacking her things and exploring the neighborhood. Now she realized with a start that it was already six o'clock. She wandered into the kitchen with the idea of seeing about dinner. She supposed Frank would want something to eat when he got home, and she didn't want them to have to go to a restaurant on their first "normal" day back. However, her intentions of being a good wife dwindled as she explored the kitchen cabinets and the refrigerator. The contents were pretty scanty. Obviously Frank was not one to cook for himself. No doubt he ate most of his meals at the restaurant.

"Anyone home?" came his voice from the living room.

"I'm in the kitchen," she called and turned toward the door just as he appeared.

They were immediately in each other's arms.

He chuckled. "Coming home was never like this before."

"I should hope not!" she said, kissing him again.

Each with an arm around the other, they walked into the living room.

"I left work early," he said.

"Early?"

"Don't you remember? I said I usually don't get away from the restaurant until ten or eleven at night."

"Oh yeah, I forgot. It makes sense, though, that you'd have to work through the dinner hour. There's still so much we don't know, isn't there?"

"It's hard to remember to talk about it all."

She leaned forward to kiss him. "Especially when there are so many better things to be doing."

He took her in his arms again and for several minutes practical things were forgotten. It was Frank who gently nudged them back to reality.

"There's a reason why I came home early," he said.

"You mean something else besides wanting to spend the evening home with your wife?" Shelby purred, leaning close to him again.

"You make it so hard to think straight . . . but . . . there are, ah, one or two other things . . . now, what were they. . . ?" He kissed her passionately, then placed his hands on her shoulders and held her at arm's length. "All right, you temptress, let me talk."

"Isn't this role reversal?" Shelby said, giggling. "The *man* wanting to talk in a situation like this."

"You make me crazy, woman!"

"Okay, what did you want to tell me?"

"About what?"

"Coming home early . . ."

"Oh yeah. Well, I hope you don't mind that I made some plans for us tonight."

"Do we get to eat dinner at your restaurant?"

"No. Actually, my grandmother would like to meet you. Are you up for that?"

"Oh yes! I've been dying to meet her."

"You're not nervous?"

"Should I be?"

"She will love you as I do. And I know you will love her, too."

Shelby was surprised at where Inez Querida—Frank's maternal grandmother—lived. It was in a simple neighborhood for the owner of a chain of five successful restaurants. Rather middle-class, but right on the edge of a San Pedro barrio where there were some very visible pockets of poverty. Frank explained that his grandmother had lived here for thirty years and, after earlier years spent living the rather nomadic life of a migrant farm worker, wasn't inclined to move even if the crime rate in her neighborhood had risen fifty percent in the last ten years.

The house was a white bungalow style with a neatly kept yard enclosed by a waist-high chain-link fence. A cocker spaniel greeted them at the gate with much yapping and jumping.

"*Siéntate, la Galleta!*" Frank said as he reached in to open the gate latch. "The dog's name is Cookie and she only understands Spanish," he explained to Shelby.

The dog continued to jump and yap as Shelby and Frank stepped into the yard. The animal leaped nearly two feet off the ground in her excitement. Shelby laughed and petted its silky reddish brown fur.

"Don't encourage her," said Frank.

"But she's so cute."

"Is that how you will spoil our children?" Frank laughed as he walked ahead down the brick pathway.

Shelby's thoughts instantly sobered. Beyond Frank showing her the photo he carried in his wallet, they hadn't discussed having a family. A million thoughts instantly jumped into her mind. How soon? How many? What about her career? Was she ready? But she quickly chased them away and forced herself to focus on the here and now. One hurdle at a time, she told herself.

As they mounted the steps to the front porch, the door swung open.

"Who says La Galleta isn't a good watch dog?" said the woman at the door in a thickly accented voice. Frank had explained to Shelby that normally the family spoke Spanish in his grandmother's presence, but in deference to Shelby they would converse in English. The older woman was adept in the language, though she chose to speak her native tongue when possible.

"Well, at least she is a one-dog hospitality committee." Frank stepped forward and gave the woman a hug and a peck on the cheek. "Hola, *Abuelita.*"

"Ah, Francisco, I'm so glad you could come. I missed you while you were gone."

She was a small woman, no more than five feet tall, and on the plump side. Her broad face was rich brown and possessed a veritable map of wrinkles that were especially pronounced around the outside corners of her eyes and the corners of her mouth. Her hair was white and pulled back in a matronly bun. She was dressed in a simple cotton housedress with practical Red Cross shoes on her feet. She was the perfect picture of a grandmother. And that "picture" suddenly jumped from its frame in pleasant animation as she directed a warm and genuine smile toward Shelby.

"My new granddaughter-in-law!" Without hesitation she embraced Shelby. Then, a little embarrassed, she stepped back and added, "I hope you don't think me too forward. I just couldn't help myself."

"Not at all," said Shelby. "You don't know how good it makes me feel to be so welcomed."

"Come in, come in, and I will really welcome you. You don't know how I have prayed for this day to come, when my Francisco would find happiness with a woman he loves."

She led them into a tastefully furnished home, mostly Victorian-era antiques that were in excellent condition and probably very expensive. On every table and shelf there were many framed photographs—graduation pictures, wedding pictures, and baby pictures—from every decade since the forties. Shelby hoped she'd have some time to study the pictures and find the ones of Frank, and she made a mental note to go by her house and pick up some of her own family albums, few though they were.

Mrs. Querida directed Shelby to sit next to her on the sofa. Frank reclined in an overstuffed chair facing them.

"Dinner will be ready soon," said Mrs. Querida, "but we have a few minutes to visit. I want to hear all about your wedding. Do you have photographs?"

"Yes," said Shelby. "I'm getting them developed now, but we have nothing formal. They're all snapshots."

"At least it is something."

Shelby nodded. "You know, Mrs. Querida, before I do anything else, I believe I have you to thank for my good fortune."

"How is that, Shelby?"

"If you hadn't asked Frank to check on your estate in Mexico, I wouldn't have met him. I am very grateful you did."

"As I recall, it was Frank who asked if he could go. He said he had to get away from the stress of his job for a while. So I think it is not me whom you must thank but rather a higher authority who knew you would be there for Francisco."

"I suppose so," said Shelby noncommittally.

"What does it matter?" said Frank. "We did meet and that's all I care about."

"Too true, *nieto!*" Mrs. Querida grinned at her grandson with obvious affection.

"Then it doesn't bother you, Mrs. Querida, that we married as we did, without telling anyone?"

Mrs. Querida shrugged. "I will not lie. I would have wanted to see my Francisco's wedding, but such things are out of my hands. I trust that our Lord, as always, was directing your ways."

"Well, uh . . ." Shelby didn't know what other response to make.

"I am sorry, does such talk make you uncomfortable?"

"I—"

Frank interjected, "I am afraid, Abuelita, that I have married a woman who possesses the same mind as I do on such matters."

"It is good for a husband and wife to be like-minded," said Mrs. Querida with a wry smile. "And I will try not to—"

"No, please, Mrs. Querida. Feel free to say what you wish. Actually,

I have an aunt who talks the same way, so I am used to it. And who knows, maybe you are right. However, I do wonder if God directs people who don't even believe in Him."

"You don't believe at all?"

"I suppose I do. I guess I just don't think of it much. I hope you can look past that, Mrs. Querida. I really want us to get along. I can tell how important you are to Frank, so it means a lot to me."

"I'm sure we can be friends." She glanced at Frank and smiled. "You've made a good choice, Francisco. I know you don't need my approval, but I still wanted to tell you so."

Frank leaned forward and took Shelby's hand in his. "One of the better choices I've made in life."

Mrs. Querida eyed her grandson with pride. "We all make mistakes, Francisco. At least you had the good sense to see yours before it was too late."

"I hope—and yes, I sometimes even pray—it is not too late."

"Ah, my nieto, you must have a more positive view of life, especially now when all seems so very good."

He nodded but his eyes remained introspective for a moment longer. Then he seemed to shake off the mood. "I'm starved, Abuelita! When do we eat?"

They had a pleasant dinner of roast beef with potatoes and green beans. "Francisco hates Mexican food," Mrs. Querida explained. That was one thing Shelby already knew about her new husband. She had hoped to learn more from Mrs. Querida, but the older woman managed to steer the conversation toward Shelby. When Shelby wasn't answering questions about herself, Mrs. Querida talked about Puerto Vallarta when it had been a sleepy village and she had spent summers there as a girl with her family.

After dinner they returned to the living room, and Shelby wandered about the room studying all the photographs. Soon Mrs. Querida was at her side giving explanations. Shelby reveled in the ones of Frank and teased him when he showed embarrassment. There were several awkward moments when they came to a photo of Frank's parents.

"And what do your mama and papa think of your new bride, Francisco?" Mrs. Querida asked.

"You know very well I haven't spoken to them," Frank replied peevishly.

"I thought perhaps you might have called them after we spoke earlier today."

"No," he said flatly.

His grandmother sighed.

"I want to meet them," Shelby offered brightly, only to shrink back when Frank glared at her. Were they about to have their first fight? But it seemed his anger wasn't really directed at her.

"Francisco, it is time you made amends with your parents," said Mrs. Querida.

"Why? And why should it be up to me? My parents turned on me, not the other way around."

"And they feel you betrayed them. Don't you see it is a vicious circle? Someone has to make the first move or it will never end."

"Then let it be them." Frank was as hard and implacable as when he had chased the intruders from the yard in Puerto Vallarta.

"I almost invited them tonight without telling you," confessed Mrs. Querida.

"Don't ever do that, Abuelita. A deception like that wouldn't be welcome." Frank's tone was so cold that his words almost sounded like a warning.

A long silence ensued until Shelby, unable to bear the tension another moment, chose a very old photograph, one she was certain predated Frank's parents, and asked, "Who is this?"

"That is my parents' wedding picture," said Mrs. Querida.

"The lace mantilla is beautiful!"

"I still have it. It's in special storage and in good condition. I had hoped my daughter or one of my granddaughters would wear it for their weddings, but so far they have all wanted American weddings. I will show it to you sometime."

They stayed for another ten minutes, but Frank was silent the entire time and Shelby and Mrs. Querida did all the talking. Frank continued to be withdrawn on the drive home. Shelby could do nothing to break through his wall. And that night, for the first time since their marriage, they slept on opposite sides of the bed, without touching. And when Shelby tried to hold him, he shrugged her away.

10

He called her at school the next day to apologize. It had been hard for her to leave in the morning while Frank still slept, the emotional distance still such an ominous presence between them, so the phone call lifted her spirits tremendously. Yet Shelby remained troubled over the drastic change in his mood the previous day.

On the phone he told her he'd take her out to dinner. Without thinking she asked if they could eat at the family restaurant, Casa del Mar, where he worked. Naturally enough, she had been curious about the place and looking forward to dining there. Shelby should have sensed by his hesitation that her request had been a mistake, but before it finally did occur to her, he was telling her to meet him there at seven.

Casa del Mar, a chain of five family-owned-and-operated restaurants in the Los Angeles area, had become successful by catering to middle-income, family-oriented customers. The walls were decorated with obvious south-of-the-border items—brightly colored woven blankets, sombreros, maracas—while recorded mariachi music played in the background. The waitresses wore peasant blouses and full red skirts. It was truly "a taste of Old Mexico," as their advertising promised. Frank's restaurant was located just a few miles from where he lived.

He was not there when Shelby arrived, but the hostess told her he'd be back soon and proceeded to seat her at the table he had reserved—obviously the best in the house in a private alcove where there were but two other tables, only one of which was presently occupied.

When Frank arrived about fifteen minutes later, he greeted Shelby with a warm embrace, and she hoped that yesterday was truly behind them. But his eyes held a serious look that she tried to ignore as a waitress came to take their order. He didn't offer his reason for being late and she did not ask. It had only been a few minutes, anyway, and Shelby decided the delay had likely been work related.

The waitress was solicitous to them, but not embarrassingly so. Actually, the young woman was fairly relaxed around Frank, as were all of the other employees they encountered, indicating to Shelby that Frank must be a good boss. It didn't surprise her at all.

They began with chips and salsa. Frank ignored the salsa and only nibbled at the chips. Shelby was starved and she attacked the appetizer with gusto. There were two varieties of the excellent salsa—hot and mild. She ate the hot. Frank eyed her with amusement.

"I think you married me only for my restaurant," he quipped. Much to her relief, the seriousness surrounding him earlier seemed to be lifting.

"It's a perfect match. I love Mexican food. But I love a certain Mexican even more."

"You always know just the right thing to say." He smiled.

"Tell me, do you dislike Mexican food because you are around it all day, or is it just out of rebellion toward your family heritage?"

His smile faded. "Let's not talk about my family."

"Who says I know the right things to say?" Shelby searched frantically for another topic of conversation as she sipped her drink. "My first day back at school was quite an event. One of my kids brought her hamster for show-and-tell. The critter escaped from its cage, and we spent the rest of the day trying to recapture it. There were a million hiding places in the classroom, and when we least expected it, the little thing would pop out and scare us to death. I'm happy to say I finally managed to return the hamster safe and sound to its cage."

"You must be a wonderful teacher," he said thoughtfully.

"I hope so. I love what I do. The kids are fabulous. Well, there are occasional bad days. The first day of school can be harrowing. This year I have a little girl who had never been away from her mother. She cried every day for three days solid. That set off a few other children who were already questioning the whole school idea. There were a couple of times I had a regular chorus of crying." She paused and sighed. "That seems so long ago, I had nearly forgotten."

"A lot has happened since September."

"I forgot to tell you what the kids think of my new name. For some reason, they have a hard time saying it. Mostly it comes out 'Stepano'— if they remember it at all. I have to confess I have had a few lapses remembering it myself."

"It hardly seems fair that a woman must change her identity when she marries and a man doesn't have to do anything."

"Spoken like a truly liberated man!" Shelby grinned.

"I try, at least."

"Well, don't worry, sweetheart, you will have your share of sacrifices to make. What about your bachelor freedom?"

"I was never truly free until I met you." The intensity of his voice contrasted sharply with her bantering tone.

"Oh, Frank . . ." She reached across the table and took his hand. But before she could say more, their meal arrived. She didn't know what she would have said anyway, knowing his words were a commentary on that inner core of sadness that seemed to haunt him.

They were halfway through their meal when three men came into the alcove. Shelby assumed they were headed for the only empty table there, but instead they stopped at Frank and Shelby's table. All three were Mexican and rather rough-looking characters. Shelby pegged them immediately as hoodlums.

"Hola, Frank!" said one, who quickly showed himself to be the leader

of the group. He was about Frank's height, well built, with wavy dark hair
and a neatly trimmed moustache over thin, taut lips. "I heard you were
dining here tonight and I had to come over to greet you. Long time no
see, amigo."

"Hello, Barcelona. I've been busy." Frank's tone was subdued, hardly
that of one meeting a friend after a long time.

"Eh, man! Now, that's no excuse." Barcelona thumped Frank on the
shoulder in a friendly manner. "We're *compadres*, eh? You and I been
through a lot together, and it hurts my feelings when you snub me like
you been doing."

"It's nothing personal."

"That's good to know. Hey, man, I hear you were down in Mexico."

"Yeah."

"We ought to get together and talk about your trip."

"There's really nothing to talk about." This statement, of course, surprised Shelby. Frank had only gotten married in Mexico.

"Used to be there was a lot to talk about when you went south of the
border." Barcelona's intonation gave Shelby the uneasy impression there
was hidden meaning in his words.

"Not anymore, Hector." Frank, too, spoke in a way that seemed to
convey something more.

Barcelona shrugged and turned his oily charm on Shelby. "And I have
been so rude to stand here and not introduce myself to your pretty com-
panion." He bowed chivalrously toward Shelby. "I am Hector Barcelona." He flashed a wolfish grin. "And these"—he gestured toward his
companions—"are my associates, Ricardo and Carlos."

"Nice to meet you. I'm Shelby Ma—that is, Stefano."

"Stefano? Frank, don't tell me—"

"My wife, Hector," Frank interjected with obvious reluctance.

"We do have a lot of catching up to do." His eyes flickered to Shelby
before returning back to Frank. "Let's get together—how about tomorrow night?"

"I'm busy."

"You're not too busy for an old friend." Oddly, Barcelona's words sounded like a demand, not a question. "I'll meet you at Lotto's club. You still know where that is, don't you? Hey, maybe you can bring Ramon along."

"I haven't talked to my brother in a couple of months."

"You got his phone number, don't you? I really want to see him. We got some unfinished business, he and I."

"I don't know. . . ."

"I won't take no for an answer. Drinks will be on me. See you then. *Adios*." He turned and strode away with his silent companions trailing behind.

Shelby watched Frank as his gaze followed Barcelona until the man disappeared. She saw that same dark mood from yesterday descend upon her husband. She wanted to say something, but she was afraid of saying the wrong thing. So, in spite of the fact that she no longer had an appetite, she lifted her fork and tried to focus her attention on her meal. In a moment, Frank brought his gaze back to her.

"We should have stayed in Puerto Vallarta," he said grimly.

"We had to return to the real world eventually."

"Why?"

She had no ready answer. Part of her deeply agreed with him. The idyllic bliss of their time in Mexico was fading as quickly as a tropical sunset.

"Let's get out of here," he said suddenly, on his feet before she could respond. She had no choice but to follow him mutely from the restaurant.

Back at Frank's condo she tried to rekindle the romance they had known in Mexico. But he shrugged her away, turned on the television, and sat on the couch. Next to him, Shelby curled her feet up under her and put her arm around him. But his distance was once again impenetrable. She desperately wanted to talk about it, but her fear of only making things worse kept her silent. If he didn't want to talk about the past, perhaps she should respect that. Yet if the past forced a wedge between them, then didn't it *need* to be talked about?

Shelby sat in confused silence for half an hour while a documentary about the life of Benjamin Disraeli droned on. She didn't see how Frank could be interested in it, but he was sitting forward, his eyes focused attentively on the screen.

"Would you like some ice cream?" she asked when the silence became more than she could bear.

"No," he said shortly.

"Frank, I can't stand this!" she blurted.

He let his body flop back against the couch, a ragged sigh on his lips. "What have I done to you, Shelby?" He pressed the Power button on the remote and the screen went black.

"I don't know what you mean, Frank, but I do know we have to talk about it."

"I should never have come back here. Meeting you and finding such happiness with you in Puerto Vallarta made me forget what I had left behind. My happiness deluded me into thinking I could truly escape." He chuckled without humor. "I feel like that hamster in your class. Tasting freedom for a few minutes—but it was only a matter of time before he was shut back up in his cage. This place is like one huge cage. I'll never get away from it!" He dropped his head into his hands, groaning softly.

"If it's so bad, Frank, then let's move away. I'll quit my job. . . ."

He looked at her and reached a hand to touch her soft cheek. "That is what I should do—run away from it all. But I shouldn't have brought you into it." He paused, shaking his head morosely. "Just hold me, Shelby. If only I can find escape in your love. Maybe that will be enough."

"Frank, can't you tell me what is troubling you so? You were such a different person in Puerto Vallarta. Oh, I saw a few hints of some deep sadness, but not like now. It's as if returning home has infected you with an awful disease. Let me share your troubles. Please! I can't promise you wisdom, but at least we can be in this together."

"Don't you see, Shelby? I don't want you to share it. I don't want you to be part of it at all. You are my escape—" Frank stopped his rush of words, obviously aware that he had said the wrong thing.

Shelby was unable to let it go. "Is that why you married me, then?"

"Is it such a terrible reason? Weren't you escaping your loneliness? There are worse reasons for marrying. It doesn't lessen the depth of my love for you. Can love really exist without an element of need?"

"Unless you conjure up love out of need."

"Do you believe that's what happened with us?"

"I hope and pray not."

Pray . . . at times like this she wished she could harness some of that prayer her aunt was always talking about. No doubt Mrs. Querida also knew something about prayer. But Shelby rebelled against the idea of turning to religion just when things were difficult. Not wanting to dwell on this line of thinking and afraid to further confront Frank's question, she jumped up from the couch and went into the kitchen. There she noticed the blinking light on the answering machine. She pressed the Message button.

"Francisco, Shelby" came the voice of Frank's grandmother, "now, don't get upset, but I've arranged a little dinner at my house Sunday—with your parents. And I want you to come. Your mother wants to meet your new wife, and she promises to be on her best behavior. Please come. Good-bye."

Since the kitchen was open to the living room, with only a counter and a dining area separating them, Shelby had no doubt Frank had heard the message. One look at him confirmed this fact. His head was back in his hands.

"Well, that's a perfect end to a perfect day," Shelby said drolly. "What are you going to do, Frank?"

"Grandma will have a fine dinner party without us," he replied with finality.

"I really want to meet them."

"Why, when you know how much I don't want to do this?"

"Because they are family. They are *my* family now." She returned to the sofa.

"Do you hope to find the mother you never had? Well, you can forget that. It's a fantasy—probably like everything else in our lives."

"I refuse to believe that, Frank. At least the part about us. I know it's hard for you, but I would like a chance to see if I could have a relationship with your parents, even if they might not be able to replace mine." Shelby didn't know why she was pressing the sensitive issue. She supposed she hoped that by getting Frank to confront some of his troubles, it might help him to solve them and perhaps bring peace back to their lives.

"Then you are welcome to visit them all you want—alone."

"Frank . . ."

He suddenly lurched to his feet. "I'm going to go out for a while."

"At this hour?"

"I need some fresh air."

"All right, Frank, you win. Forget about your parents."

He was already at the door. "We'll talk about it later."

He opened the door and left. Shelby watched, stunned. She tried hard to remember how close they had been in Mexico, but it was all so dim now. Distance was all she could feel. And that distance took on even greater proportions when she awoke the next morning and realized Frank had not come home all night.

11

SHELBY WAS TRULY THANKFUL it was Friday. The remainder of the week had passed in a rather dismal fashion. Frank had offered no explanation of where he had been all Monday night, and Shelby didn't ask. With Shelby leaving for work while Frank still slept, then often being asleep when he returned home from work at night, they had been fairly successful at avoiding tender subjects. If Shelby did manage to stay awake for his return home, they kept their discussions light and their interaction physical. No sense wasting the little time they had together dredging up problems. Perhaps over the weekend she and Frank would have a chance to redeem their frayed relationship. Shelby shuddered at that statement, knowing it sounded more like a couple trying to repair a marriage headed for divorce rather than newlyweds who had known only bliss a mere week ago. She shook her head grimly as she sat alone in her classroom after her students had left for the day. Her attempts to plan lessons for the next week were largely unsuccessful.

She still didn't know what would happen with Mrs. Querida's dinner. Shelby toyed with the idea of calling her, yet she still felt too new in her family position to take such aggressive action. She kept waiting for Frank to bring up the subject, though now that looked like a hopeless endeavor. Perhaps she had been wrong to pressure him. She should have supported him, stood by him. That's what a good wife would do—what the wife in Frank's photo would have done. But she did want to get to know his family. Perhaps Shelby could be a bridge between Frank and his parents, somehow bringing the estranged family back together.

Suddenly she put down her pen and hurried from her classroom, down the hall to the office. And before she changed her mind, she lifted the phone in the teacher's lounge. It was only then that Shelby realized she didn't even know Mrs. Querida's phone number. She had to dial information, but by the time she got the number, her resolve was wavering. Finally, after another minute, she convinced herself again of the wisdom of her decision and dialed the number.

"Hello, Mrs. Querida?" she said when the familiar voice answered.

"Yes . . ." Obviously the woman didn't yet recognize Shelby's voice, and that fact spurred her on. She wanted to know—and be known by—this sweet old lady.

"This is Shelby."

"Of course! I should have known."

"That's okay. I was just calling because of the message you left several nights ago. I'm sorry I didn't get back to you sooner."

"I can imagine Frank had to think about it first."

"Well, yes, I suppose so. . . . Anyway, I wanted to let you know we'll be there. What time would you like us?"

"I am so glad you will come! Let's say three o'clock. I would have made it sooner but I know Friday and Saturday are the busiest times at the restaurant."

Shelby hadn't even thought of that, and she fleetingly realized that her hopes of getting away with Frank on the weekend were misplaced. She said good-bye to Mrs. Querida, then packed up her things and left for home. She almost welcomed the rush-hour traffic for delaying her drive. She was afraid to face Frank. She was unsure about how couples resolved such matters. Her dad no doubt would tell her to rely on common sense, but so far that hadn't done much for Shelby. That realization was like a kick in the stomach. She knew nothing about marriage and little about male-female relationships.

What was she going to do?

However, Frank wasn't there when she got home. Why she had expected him she didn't know. She had to get used to his schedule, if nothing else. The answering machine showed there was a message. It was from Frank.

"Hi, thought you might be home," his voice said. "Guess I missed you. I'll be working late. Bye."

Deflated, Shelby plopped down in a chair and turned on the television with the remote. But her mind was in such turmoil she didn't even hear the droning of the evening news. If she and Frank worked it just right, their schedules were such that they could go forever without seeing each other. After nearly two weeks of his constant companionship and their deep emotional bonding in Mexico, Shelby felt horribly empty now—almost as bad as when her father had first died. Sudden tears filled her eyes and a sob escaped her lips. Before she knew it a full-fledged cry had overcome her.

Was her marriage over before it had even begun? How stupid and arrogant of her to think she could build a marriage without knowing the first thing about it. That was exactly what her mother would do—jump in without thinking first. Shelby had lost count of how many times her mother had been married. Sniffing loudly, she began to silently berate her mother, blaming her for Shelby's misfortunes. She used to do that when she was young, though it had never helped. It certainly didn't help now. It didn't make things right between her and Frank, and it didn't help her to know what to do.

As she sobbed and sniffed back tears, she heard the faint squeak of the front door opening. When she glanced up and saw Frank standing there, her heart skipped a beat. He dropped down before her and wrapped his arms around her.

"Shelby, I am so sorry," he murmured.

"No, it was all my fault."

"I love you so much. I don't want to hurt you."

"That's all I need to know."

He brought her hands to his lips and kissed them gently. "Believe that, Shelby. No matter what happens, always believe that."

"I do."

He looked up at her. Moisture filled his eyes also. "I wish we could go back to Mexico. Maybe you and I can go away tomorrow—someplace where we can be alone, shutting out the world for a few hours."

"I was thinking the same thing."

He smiled. "You are the best thing that's ever happened to me. You are that one shining moment in my life when I truly got it right."

Fresh tears, now of joy, filled her eyes, and she clung to him as though she'd never let go.

When they awoke the next day, the weather proved to be glorious for sailing. A clear blue sky welcomed them at the marina, the wind steady without being overpowering.

Frank's boat was a thirty-seven-foot vessel about three years old and quite luxurious, with a good deal of custom brightwork that Frank had added himself. He showed off the boat like a boasting parent. The only problem with it was that it had no name. He admitted that when he bought it he had named it after his first wife, Gloria. But their marriage had broken up shortly after—the naming had, for the most part, been a last-ditch effort to save the marriage. Shelby had noticed the name, *Gloria's Barge*, still slightly visible on the stern, though an attempt had been made to paint over it.

"They say it's bad luck to change the name of a boat," he said as he maneuvered the vessel out of the marina, "but I figured my luck couldn't get worse. Now I have a truly special name to give it."

"What might that be?" she asked coyly.

"Shelby, of course."

"I don't know . . . it doesn't sound just right."

He thought for a moment, then asked, "What is your middle name? Wait, I recall on our license that you didn't put one."

"No, I don't have one. . . ." Shelby paused, then shrugged. "Well, I don't use it. I was going to have it legally removed but just haven't gotten around to it."

"So what is it?"

She hesitated before answering, "Dawn."

"It's perfect. The *Shelby Dawn.*"

"It's my mother's name," she said flatly.

"I see." He put a comforting arm around her. "Well, we will come up with something even more perfect. No hurry."

They sat side by side in the cockpit. He steered the polished chrome wheel with one hand while holding her close with his other arm. She felt secure and happy. Truly there was no hurry; they would have a lifetime to think up names for boats and to plan a future together. And as the day progressed, the magic of Puerto Vallarta returned, confirming that it had been a reality.

Frank headed south down the coast. At times the wind propelled them along at nearly seven knots per hour. It was exhilarating, especially when Frank let Shelby steer. This was a far greater challenge than steering while motoring, for Shelby had to be constantly aware of the winds, adjusting the wheel mere fractions to get the best advantage of the combination of the wind and the sails.

Although Shelby enjoyed this, she liked best being able to sit back and watch Frank as he handled the boat. He seemed to experience a profound metamorphosis. All the tension she had seen start to consume him since their return to L.A. fell away, and he was the man she had fallen in love with that very first time she had seen him on the boat in Puerto

Vallarta. What she still didn't understand was why being home seemed to cause him such distress. Beyond the normal stresses of everyday life, Frank seemed to be tormented by something that Shelby could not identify and that he was unwilling to share.

They sailed along the coast and anchored off Point Vicente in Palos Verdes, where they had a relaxing lunch in the lee of the spectacular cliffs. Shelby decided that while he was so relaxed she would gingerly broach the subject of dinner with his parents.

"Frank, I talked with your grandmother yesterday," she said casually.

"I'm glad she called. I forgot to call her myself."

"Actually . . . uh . . . well, I called her."

"You did?"

"Well, I—"

"No, I'm glad you did. Like I said, I forgot, and if you hadn't called she would have been left hanging. How did she take it?"

"Well . . ."

"You did tell her no, didn't you?"

Shelby swallowed. A shadow began to inch over them, and the clear sky couldn't be blamed. She began to see she had made a mistake.

"Frank, please forgive me," she said earnestly. "I just couldn't bring myself to tell her no. It meant so much to her."

"And also to you?"

She nodded and a silence fell between them. Shelby could not fathom what was transpiring behind Frank's stoic visage. She feared she had ruined their beautiful day and berated herself for bringing up the sensitive subject.

But in a moment he spoke, and the tenderness in his tone dispelled all her fears. "I meant it when I said I never want to hurt you. We will go tomorrow."

"I don't want you to hurt, either, Frank. I just hope the dinner might be a way to begin to heal some of the things that seem to haunt you."

He offered her a slight smile. "Maybe you're right. Who knows, eh?"

He was quiet as they headed back to the marina. However, it wasn't the tense, dark silence she had occasionally seen him assume. This time it was thoughtful. Perhaps, as he fingered the scar on his cheek, he was considering how the dinner might go and what he could do to make it work. Shelby desperately hoped so, at least.

After securing the boat at the marina, they drove home where Frank just had time to change and leave for the restaurant. He had stolen the time off from the Saturday lunch crowd, but there was no way he could skip the dinner hour. Shelby understood and was content to have had even part of the day with him. The evening would be a good time for her to work on preparations for next week's school lessons.

She was in the middle of cutting out templates for a snowman project when there was a knock on the door. Glancing at the clock on the opposite wall, she saw it was eight o'clock. Maybe it was Christie surprising her with a visit. They hadn't seen or spoken to each other since the return from Mexico, and Shelby was eager to catch up on their lives.

Shelby's disappointment was obvious when she opened the door to two men dressed in business suits. She thought wryly that they looked like police officers. The taller man also looked like an ex-football player, quite brawny but just a bit over the hill. He had a stony expression on his handsome face, while the other man had a far more intellectual appearance and wore a stylish suit on his shorter, trimmer figure. He was certainly far less intimidating.

"Good evening, ma'am," said the shorter of the pair, sounding like a police officer, too. "I'm Detective Poole with the L.A.P.D. and this is my partner, Detective Liscom." Both men flashed badges in her face. "Would this be the residence of Frank Stefano?"

"Yes, it is. . . ."

"Is he in?"

"No, he's at work. Can I help you? I'm his wife."

"When will he be in?"

"Not for a couple of hours."

"Is his place of employment still Casa del Mar on Hawthorne Boulevard?"

"Yes. What is this about?"

"We just have a few questions we'd like to ask him." While Shelby searched for a response, Poole added, "We'll try to catch him at work. Thank you, Mrs. Stefano."

They turned and strode away, leaving Shelby standing in the doorway, shaken and confused.

12

FRANK RETURNED HOME at eleven. Shelby was in bed reading. He came into the bedroom, tossed his jacket over the back of a chair, kicked off his shoes, and loosened his necktie.

"Hi," he said, kissing her forehead. He lingered there for a moment, his dark eyes studying her intently. Then he straightened up and began to unbutton his shirt. "I'm exhausted. I guess I'm getting too old to sail all day and work all night." He shrugged out of his shirt, dropping it over the same chair that held his jacket.

Just as she was about to tell him about the visit from the police, he went into the bathroom. When he returned he started talking about his day. Because he seldom talked about work—or for that matter any of the trivial day-to-day things in his life—Shelby said nothing. She liked to listen to his deep, resonate voice and watch the expressions on his face. He made no mention of the police. No doubt they hadn't even bothered to find him at work. Whatever they had wanted had probably been unimportant.

When he had undressed down to his undershirt and shorts, Frank slipped under the covers beside her. He closed his eyes, but she noted that he didn't seem to relax. The muscles on his jaw were twitching. Realizing it was not a comfortable silence, she felt compelled to fill it. She told him about a movie she had seen while he was at work starring Gary Cooper and Rita Hayworth that she guessed was set in Puerto Vallarta or a place very much like it. She rambled on about the group of misfits looking for gold in the desert.

All at once, Frank turned toward her with eyes revealing unexpected emotion.

"The police came to the restaurant tonight," he said.

"They came here looking for you. What was it all about?"

He didn't answer her for a long moment, and when he finally did, each word came out slowly, hesitantly. "My ex-wife is dead. Her body washed up on the beach near Malibu today."

"Oh, Frank, how awful."

"Yeah. They don't know the cause of death yet. They said a missing persons report had been filed four weeks ago by a friend of hers."

"They think this happened four weeks ago?"

"There'll be an autopsy to find out. No one—not even the police— took seriously her being missing at the time the report was filed. She often took off like that, telling no one her plans. She had no regular job, no ties. I'm surprised someone even filed a report."

"I don't know what to say, Frank. I do understand that this must be difficult for you. You had feelings for her once."

"We've known each other since high school."

"I didn't realize it had gone back so far."

"We started dating seriously our junior year. It was the only thing I ever did that my parents approved of. They wanted me to marry a Mexican girl, but most of the girls at school were far beneath the social status they aspired to. Gloria's family, like my mother's family, came from noble roots in Mexico—affluent landowners. And like our family, they had, after coming to America, climbed the social ladder. Her father is a well-to-do lawyer. Gloria was a charmer. My mother never knew what a wild one she was. You can't imagine my mother's elation when we became engaged the summer after our last year of high school. I think she was more in love with Gloria than I was."

"And were you?"

"Believe me, I would never have married just to please my parents."

"Oh." Shelby knew it was too much to expect him to say he had never loved her, though she recalled him having hinted at that once in Puerto Vallarta. It sounded like there was *something* between them, but Shelby was too afraid to probe him.

"We married that Christmas following graduation. Actually, she graduated, but I never did—didn't have enough credits. Anyway, she was only eighteen, I was nineteen. Our marriage lasted six years . . . six stormy, miserable years. I got this condo to get away from her—she never lived here," he added as if to reassure Shelby, and it did. He continued, "I don't know why we even let it go that long. She was very Catholic and still had some convictions about divorce. Finally, though, even she had to admit it was a bust. I should have told you all this before."

"It wouldn't have mattered."

"Shelby, I—" He stopped and focused his eyes on the ceiling, obviously unable to face her. "I wish I hadn't dragged you into all this."

"I don't understand."

"The police don't think her death was an accident or suicide. They have no proof, but it's only a matter of time . . ."

"They certainly don't think you are involved."

He rubbed his hands over his face. "Who can tell what they will think? It could get hairy, that's all. She was mixed up in a lot of things—things that at one time involved me."

"What kind of things?"

"Illegal things. I should have told you about all this before," he repeated, as if somehow saying it over and over would repair his mistake.

"I didn't want to know."

"And I was so afraid of losing you."

"It's all in the past. It doesn't matter." She reached out a hand, but when she touched him she felt his body tense.

"Yes . . . in the past."

"Frank. . . ?"

"I told you before how hard it is to escape the past. I tried . . . but it keeps reaching out at me." He stopped and took a deep, shuddering breath. "I gotta get some sleep," he said, then turned over, his back to her.

His abruptness left Shelby stunned. Wasn't there more to talk about? He was obviously still distressed. And she still had questions. But perhaps it was just as well the conversation had ended before she could ask the question that weighed heaviest on her mind. *Was* he involved?

But no, it was impossible. He was only distraught because someone he knew was dead. That was only natural. Shelby reached up and turned out her light. Then, in the darkness, she scooted close to her husband and held him even though he made no response to her gesture.

Somehow she fell asleep that night, but she awoke the next morning alone in the bed. Fearing he had spent the night somewhere else again, Shelby was relieved when she found Frank in the kitchen pouring himself a cup of coffee. He looked terrible, as if he'd had a night that included little if any sleep. His uncombed hair stuck out in several untidy directions, there were bags under his eyes, and he still wore only his undershirt and shorts, both very rumpled.

"Coffee?" he asked.

She poured herself a cup and sat down at the kitchen table with him.

"You don't look like you slept well," she said.

"Let's not talk about it anymore."

"I'm here when you do want to talk."

"Okay."

"Are you hungry?"

Frank took a breath. "Sure. What do we have?" Resolve echoed in his tone.

She got up and opened the refrigerator. The offerings were slim.

Shelby still had not found the time to do more than shop for a few necessities. It was hard to believe they had been home from Mexico only a week.

"How does toast sound? I see a jar of jam."

When he nodded she went about fixing the toast. They ate in silence. She simply could not dredge up small talk when there was so much of consequence to discuss. Frank was not only silent but distant, as well. He had turned entirely inward, leaving nothing of the Frank she loved exposed for her to touch. Finally, completely frustrated and her scanty meal half eaten, she jumped up and without a word went into the bedroom to dress. He was still in the kitchen, hunched over a cold cup of coffee, when she returned.

"I really have to go shopping," she said, "and this may be the only chance I'll get." She had to get away from Frank before she exploded at him, making things worse than they already were. Grocery shopping was as good an excuse as any.

"Okay," he replied dully.

"You're welcome to come," she relented.

"No . . . I'll just hang out here."

She grabbed her purse and left, ignoring another topic that needed to be faced. How did their plans for dinner stand now? With Frank in his present mood, it hardly seemed a good time to jump into another potentially volatile situation. She would be home long before they were expected at Mrs. Querida's, so they could discuss it then. Maybe in a couple of hours Frank would have overcome his—what was it? Last night she had thought it natural for him to be in shock over the death of his ex-wife. But his mood had grown morose and dismal since then. It was as if he were devastated. It was as if someone he loved dearly had died. Yet last night he had told her how terrible their marriage had been. His misery now seemed out of proportion to those words. Did he still have feelings for Gloria, then? Feelings, perhaps, he couldn't even admit to himself . . . much less to Shelby.

Two hours later, carrying a bag of groceries, she returned to the condo. There were three more bags in the car, which she had hoped Frank could carry in. She opened the door and headed toward the kitchen to unload her burden. On the way she noted Frank wasn't in the living room watching television. Had he gone back to bed? Then she heard his voice from the kitchen.

"Where've you been, Ray?"

He must have been on the phone because there was no response to his question. Instead, he spoke again.

"I don't worry about you. It's merely curiosity. Did you hear about Gloria?" Pause. "That doesn't make it any easier. She didn't deserve to be murdered. . . ." Pause. "Well, they don't know. It's just . . . not hard to assume, that's all. You know what I mean."

Suddenly feeling guilty about eavesdropping, Shelby made noise by jiggling the shopping bag and shaking her car keys.

"I gotta go," Frank said quickly. "Yeah. When? That's not good. . . . Later . . . okay."

Shelby ventured into the kitchen just as Frank was hanging up the telephone receiver.

"I thought you were talking to yourself," she said lightly.

"That was my brother. Are there more grocery bags?"

She nodded, setting down her bag.

"I'll go get them." He was dressed now in Levi's and a T-shirt. He hadn't showered, though, and his hair was still disheveled even after an obvious attempt to comb it. He looked so unlike his usual self, so much more needy, that she wanted to run to him and embrace him, soothing his emotions. But he had turned and was exiting the kitchen before she could follow her impulse.

When he returned he set the bags on the counter, and Shelby began putting things away. She took as a good sign the fact that he remained in the kitchen with her. He probably really did want to talk but just didn't know how to begin. She wasn't sure where to begin, either. But instinctively, after her previous errors, she knew the best path would not be to jump right into the middle of a sensitive area.

"I should have made a list before I went to the store," she said, "and asked for ideas from you. I tried to get things I thought you'd like, but I wasn't certain."

"I'll like whatever you bought."

"Except tortillas and salsa."

He smiled.

"What *is* your favorite food, Frank?" The question seemed so inane in view of all that had happened in the last two days. But Shelby thought it was a wonderful thing to ask. Suddenly the ordinary was very appealing.

"Pizza. Now it's my turn. Do you cook?"

She burst out laughing. And he joined her, laughing as she had seldom seen him do. He looked so good, the corners of his eyes crinkling and his lips parted in a welcome smile.

"We have got to get a normal life," she declared.

"I have another question," he said, seeming to warm to the frivolous bent of the exchange. "What's your favorite color?"

"Blue. What's yours?"

"I don't have one."

"Oh, come on. Everyone has a favorite color."

He thought a moment, then replied, "Then I guess it's blue, also— the color of the sea."

"Of course, I should have known." She put her hand to her mouth in thought. "Here's a good question: What political party are you?"

"Independent."

"That's cheating."

"No, I really am. All sailors tend to be rebels at heart."

"Okay—" Before Shelby could finish, the phone rang. Frank answered it and had a brief conversation before hanging up.

"That was my grandmother," he said. "She isn't feeling well and wondered if we'd mind having dinner at my parents' house. She'll be there, but she just doesn't feel up to cooking."

"How do you feel about that?"

"No doubt my mother manipulated this so we could meet on her turf. Grandma buckled under in the interest of bringing us together."

"We don't have to go." Shelby couldn't hide the slight disappointment in her voice. Yet, all things considered, this still wasn't the best time for a family dinner.

"Let's just get it over with." All the lightness of a few moments ago disappeared. The cute crinkles around his eyes were gone and his lips formed a thin, taut line.

The walls were closing in once again. When they tried to recapture the previous banter, it was forced and the smiles were manufactured. Shelby thought, as she had many times of late, of the sun-washed beaches of Puerto Vallarta and wished her dreams could transport them there.

13

THE SPRAWLING SPANISH-STYLE HOME of Tomas and Dolores Stefano, located in the hills of the Palos Verdes Peninsula, had its charms—though it was mixed oddly with the bizarre. The white stucco of the house, the red-tiled roof, and the tiled portico were as elegant as the resort in Puerto Vallarta. The gardens surrounding the house, however, spoke of refined beauty gone slightly awry. And Shelby was hard-pressed to tell if this was by design or by accident. The trees needed trimming, as did the shrubbery, Bougainvillea, Azaleas, and Fuchsias. Even in January, when they should have been more subdued, they seemed wild, out of control. The garden must be an absolute riot in the summer.

But it was not the house nor the plants that lent the most surreal quality to the place. Rather it was the statues all about the yard. Shelby was not entirely familiar with Catholic saints, but all the statues—she counted ten in the front yard—had a definite religious ambiance. One was certainly St. Francis, with birds perched on his hands and a rabbit and doe at his feet, and another statue was obviously of the Madonna. Shelby could not put names to the rest, but many held crucifixes or books of Scriptures. It was one of the strangest sights Shelby had ever seen.

Frank leaned toward her. "You have now entered the Twilight Zone," he murmured wryly.

"It's very interesting. But . . . why?"

"Don't you know that the more symbols of religion you possess the better your chances of getting into heaven?"

"This should be quite an experience."

"Don't say I didn't warn you."

They reached the door and Frank knocked. Shelby expected a maid to answer the door. The house was in a very exclusive neighborhood, where the *crème de la crème* of Southern California resided. But Dolores Stefano herself answered the door. Shelby did not doubt her identity for a minute because of her strong resemblance to Frank. A trim woman, she was several inches taller than Shelby. She was truly what might be called a handsome woman, but not beautiful or even pretty. Her dark hair was cut short and permed in tight curls, and her makeup was sparse, with only lipstick and blush and an obvious line of eyebrow pencil extending her thick, dark brows. She was dressed in beige slacks and a purple silk blouse, and several expensive-looking gold chains adorned her neck. Three fingers on each of her hands displayed large, jewel-encrusted rings. One of these hands she now held out, rather limply, to Shelby.

"I'm happy to meet you, Shelby," she said after Frank had made introductions. She spoke with a very slight accent.

"And I am glad to meet you, Mrs. Stefano." Shelby wished she could say something like, "Frank has spoken so highly of you." But all would know that was a lie.

Except for a terse but civil greeting, Dolores all but ignored Frank. "Everyone else is already here." There was an edge to her tone that Shelby could not identify. Glancing at Frank, Shelby noticed him rolling his eyes covertly. Was the woman rebuking them, then, for their tardiness? And what did she mean by everyone? It would only be them, Mr. and Mrs. Stefano, and Mrs. Querida, wouldn't it?

They followed Mrs. Stefano across a marble foyer, where Shelby noticed more crucifixes and religious paintings on the wall. Arriving at a tastefully decorated living room with lavish, hand-carved hardwood trim and ornately patterned hardwood floors, Shelby was taken aback to find a group larger than she had expected. Was she to be presented, without warning, to all of their friends and family? She now regretted not following Frank's initial instinct to refuse the invitation.

Mrs. Stefano, quite in command of the room, made introductions. Besides Mrs. Querida, there were Frank's two sisters, both older than him, and their husbands. The sisters were Maria and Carla, but Shelby quickly forgot the husbands' names. There was another couple, old friends of the family, whose names also fled from Shelby's mind the minute she heard them. Finally, there was Tomas Stefano. He was a little man, at least five inches shorter than his son and half that of his wife. Though not fat, he was definitely of a husky build, with a round face that sported a thick moustache. He seemed to be a quiet man, speaking little. If Frank had inherited his mother's physical appearance, Shelby was certain he had gotten his stoic personality from his father.

Hors d'oeuvres were laid out on a table along with several varieties of beverages. Mrs. Stefano saw to it that Shelby and Frank had something to drink and a sampling of the appetizers, then directed them to chairs. After the flurry of introductions and such, the conversation died away to silence. Shelby sipped from her glass uncomfortably, afraid to look at Frank, knowing she couldn't count on him to rescue the situation. After all, this was the last place he wanted to be.

"You have a lovely home," Shelby finally said, even if it did sound lame.

"We'll show you around if you like, after dinner," said Mrs. Stefano. "We had it built especially for us ten years ago. We are quite proud of it."

"And of all it represents," Frank murmured dryly.

Shelby tensed. Was it all going to explode this soon? But Frank was ignored, and the conversation continued cordially.

"Mama says you are from Whittier," Mrs. Stefano said to Shelby.

"Yes. I lived there almost all my life."

"And your father has passed on?"

"Two months ago."

"I remember reading about it in the newspaper," offered Maria.

"You must be proud of him," said Mrs. Stefano. "And what about your mother?"

"She's gone, too."

"Passed on?"

"No . . . my parents divorced when I was quite young."

"That's too bad. But your father raised you? How unusual. Do you see your mother at all?"

"No . . ."

"Papa," Frank broke in quickly, "what do you think of that new Mexican restaurant that opened a mile from our Torrance place?" Shelby wanted to kiss Frank for saving her.

"A flash in the pan," said the elder Stefano. "How many restaurants have been in that location in the last five years? At least three."

"That's true. But I hear the food is good."

"Not better than ours," said Mrs. Stefano.

"There is no Mexican food better than ours," put in Mrs. Querida with a grin. "You aren't worried about that new place, are you, Francisco?"

"No one likes competition."

"You just keep running that restaurant the way it should be run," said Mr. Stefano, "and business will not be affected. We have a name and a reputation—and that's what counts."

The conversation focused on the restaurant for a few minutes, and Shelby's attention wandered to several photographs in frames on the baby grand piano near where she was seated. There were four eight-by-tens, two that were obviously Maria's and Carla's senior pictures. Another was an eight-by-ten of a young man, fifteen or sixteen years old, and Shelby wondered if that might be Ramon. There was no individual photo of Frank, which was disturbing enough, but the final photo proved even more so. It was a wedding photo—of Frank and Gloria. It was a close-up, and their smiling faces were all too apparent. Regardless of what Frank had told her, he did look very much in love—or he was quite a good actor.

Shelby didn't know what to make of Gloria. She was very beautiful, with rich, dark hair and deep, penetrating eyes that, despite the smile on her lips, were rather cold. She seemed to resemble an ice carving rather than a living being. And probably because of that analogy, Shelby shivered. Probably also because an image flashed through her mind of that same exquisitely beautiful woman cold and dead and washed up on a lonely beach.

"On that note," Mrs. Stefano's voice drew Shelby's attention back to the present, "let's move into the dining room so we can have our dinner. Shelby, we thought you would like *real* home-cooked Mexican food. I do hope you have a better appreciation for it than my son."

"I love Mexican food. I'm sure this will be wonderful." She didn't look at Frank, but she felt like she was walking a narrow bridge over a precipice.

They moved into the dining room, and everyone was seated according to Mrs. Stefano's directions, who, once her guests were settled, went into the kitchen. A few moments later she returned, followed by another woman who was obviously a servant—although Mrs. Stefano made it clear that she and her daughters had done all the cooking. Before the maid brought out the first course, Mrs. Stefano looked at her husband.

"Please offer the blessing, Tomas."

Stefano nodded at his wife. "Let us pray. Bless us, O Lord, and these thy gifts which we are about to receive from thy bounty, through Christ our Lord. Amen."

Everyone at the table except Shelby repeated "Amen" and crossed themselves. Even Frank joined in the ritual, surprising Shelby. She had thought he did not accede to his family's religious ways. Perhaps he hoped to keep peace by not flaunting his rebellion. Nevertheless, Shelby felt awkward, which was not helped by Mrs. Stefano's next comment.

"You're not Catholic, Shelby?"

"No . . . I don't really follow any particular faith."

"Don't tell me you are an atheist?" Mrs. Stefano was clearly appalled by the idea.

"No. I believe in God. I'm just not a member of a church."

There was an uncomfortable silence for a brief moment, and then the maid began serving salad and a relish tray with several different kinds of fresh vegetables and an assortment of hot and spicy peppers.

Any reprieve the serving of the meal brought was short-lived.

"Ah, it is good to have the whole family together," Mr. Stefano began in an obvious attempt at congenial conversation.

"Not the *whole* family," Mrs. Stefano put in sharply.

"Dolores, you promised . . ." pleaded Mrs. Querida.

"Well, I just can't help it!" Dolores Stefano's lips were pursed as if ready for battle. "How can I ignore that one of my children is so obviously missing? It's just not right." Her eyes jerked accusingly toward Frank.

"You can't blame Francisco—" Mrs. Querida began.

"And why not?"

Frank cut in before his grandmother could reply. "I don't control Ray's life. If you invited him, I certainly didn't tell him not to come. If he's not here, it's of his own choosing."

"You turned him against us," accused Mrs. Stefano.

Shelby watched in shock at how quickly the heat rose around the table, proving how close to the surface the tension had been smoldering. She wanted to rise in Frank's defense, yet she felt too much of an outsider to become involved. Not to mention her dread of having Dolores Stefano's ire focused upon her. What could she say anyway? That Frank was a gentle, loving man who would never seek to hurt his family? All Mrs. Stefano would say to that was, "What do you know? You've known him less than a month." How could Shelby argue with that? And deep down, Shelby felt as if she knew him less now than when they had first met.

The phone jarred the silence, and Shelby felt relief. Dolores Stefano excused herself to answer the phone, but when she returned her face was white with shock.

"I've just had terrible news," she gasped. "That was a friend from church who wondered if I'd heard about Gloria. . . ."

Frank let out an involuntary groan.

"Did you know, Frank?" asked Mrs. Stefano.

Frank nodded. Then his father asked, "What is it?"

"Gloria is dead. She drowned in the ocean." There were several moments of shocked response around the table before Mrs. Stefano continued. "Why didn't you tell us, Frank?"

"I didn't want to spoil your dinner."

"I can't believe you would still come to a dinner party after such news. This is horrible! I would think you'd be devastated."

"Gloria and I were divorced." Frank's tone was matter-of-fact, but his eyes were dark, smoldering.

"Yes, you were," Mrs. Stefano said harshly. "Another slap in your family's face."

"Yes, Mother, I lay awake at night trying to think of ways to shame you. It's my goal in life. I wonder what I'll do next—"

"Stop it! Show some respect for a poor dead girl."

Frank threw his napkin on the table and pushed back his chair. "I'm not going to sit here and listen to this. Shelby—"

"Francisco . . ." said Mrs. Querida, again pleading. "Please don't leave."

"I'm only here because of you, Abuelita. And Shelby. I keep trying to do what I must to be a good son, but it'll never be enough. I will never stop paying for the past. There's nothing I can do. . . ."

"You've done enough," retorted Mrs. Stefano. Shelby didn't know how the woman could so cruelly ignore her son's obvious pain.

Frank jumped up. "Good, I'm glad that's out. I'm sorry for even trying to make things better. I can see it's a wasted effort." He turned to Shelby. "Come on, Shelby, let's go."

"Please, Francisco," said his grandmother.

"I'm sorry, Abuelita. This is not going to happen." He strode toward the doorway, a shaken Shelby in tow.

14

ON MONDAY SHELBY WENT TO WORK as usual, but instead of staying to plan the next day's lessons, she left at two so she could spend some time at her house in Whittier. She needed to check on the place, and there were several things she wanted to pack and move over to her new home. She had also called Christie after the disastrous dinner with the Stefanos in hopes of getting together with her. They made tentative plans for dinner that evening.

Shelby supposed her real reason for coming to her old house was a growing need within her to reconnect with her other life—her life before Frank. She felt as if she was losing her identity in him. At first that had been blissful, but now that reality was setting in, she needed to touch the part of her that had represented such security. She couldn't bring back her father, the foundation of that security, but perhaps just being where they had shared such a good life would help.

As she opened the door of the house, she expected to be confronted with the musty smells of disuse. But all was normal, reminding her that it hadn't been very long since all the changes had occurred. She walked around the three-bedroom, 1940s-era house just to fill herself with the pleasant ambiance of the past. She paused in her father's room, noting that all was as he had left it the day before he died. Even the Tom Clancy thriller he had been reading still lay face down on the nightstand.

Shelby was glad she hadn't changed anything. Soon, she supposed, she would have to sort through his things and probably even pack up the whole house and sell it, but now she needed it just as it was. There were, however, a few things that had to be done. The refrigerator needed to be cleaned out. Food in the cupboards could be packed up and used at the condo. And she needed the rest of her clothes. These things, though, wouldn't affect what was most important in the house.

Going through the kitchen items stirred welcome memories. There were at least a dozen cans of Chef Boyardee ravioli, for which her father had had a decided weakness. She also found several packages of chocolate pudding mix—Shelby's weakness—that her father had found on sale and brought home to her triumphantly. The packing boxes filled up quickly, and only half of them would fit into her Mustang. Surprisingly, she realized she looked forward to a return trip. It felt good to be here—alone and in a familiar place. Which must mean it felt good to be away from Frank. But Shelby wasn't ready to admit that. It was merely refreshing to be temporarily away from the present tensions in his life.

She was standing on a chair, reaching into the top shelf of a cupboard, when she thought she heard a knock on the front door. Pausing, she wondered if it had been her imagination—after all, no one but Christie knew she'd be here. She was about to ignore it when the doorbell sounded. A salesperson? Or a neighbor? As the bell rang again, Shelby got off the chair and went to answer it.

The person who greeted her was the last face she had expected. It was her mother.

"Hi, Shelby," Dawn said, sounding like a cross between a perky cheerleader and a helpless puppy.

"How did you—?"

"I happened to call your friend Christie this morning. I had to drag it out of her that you'd be here. I've been trying to get ahold of you, but I never got an answer here. I was starting to worry."

Shelby bit back a cutting remark about why Dawn should suddenly start to worry after all these years. "Well, I've been very busy."

"It seems that way. Can I . . . come in?"

"Yeah, I guess."

"I won't stay long."

"I wasn't going to be here much longer myself." Shelby stepped aside and let Dawn in. "Have a seat," she said, gesturing toward the living room sofa.

Noting the stack of boxes, Dawn said, "You're not moving, are you?"

"I've already moved—to Redondo Beach." She rebuked herself for naming the location. This might have been her perfect opportunity to escape Dawn completely.

"My, that is a surprise."

"I'm married," Shelby added bluntly, thinking she'd feel more pleasure than she did in dropping this bombshell on her mother.

"Whoa! You're kidding. Married? Who? When? I didn't even know you were serious about anyone."

"There's a lot you don't know about me, Dawn."

"I guess so. I'd still love to hear all about it." There was such eager entreaty in the woman's tone. Would she never give up?

"Well, I—" Shelby glanced at her watch. "It's a long story and I really don't have a lot of time."

"I know I shouldn't have just barged in on you like this," said Dawn. "I didn't know what else to do. Shelby, I am your mother, no matter how much you want to deny it. I care about you—I can't help it. Would you just let me into your life a little? I won't expect much . . . just a little."

"There's really not much to tell." Shelby didn't realize she was contradicting her earlier excuse. "I met someone in Mexico, fell in love, and we got married. His name is Frank Stefano."

"He's Mexican?"

"Does that matter?" Shelby replied defensively.

"I'm just curious."

JUDITH PELLA

"He's Mexican-American."

"Are you happy...? What am I saying? You must be deliriously happy. A newlywed, in love . . . how wonderful."

"I am happy." She was—deliriously so. Wasn't she? Well, Shelby wouldn't admit anything less to Dawn. "I really have to get finished here."

"Let me at least help you with those boxes."

"You don't have to—"

"I want to," Dawn said with uncharacteristic firmness.

They began carrying out boxes, but after a couple trips they were out of breath.

Dawn giggled. "Boy, am I out of shape."

"Me too," said Shelby. "But I can handle the rest. I don't want you to hurt yourself."

"Don't worry, I won't sue you. But I could use a glass of water before we carry out the others."

"Do you want a Pepsi? There were a couple of cans in the frig and they're nice and cold."

"Sounds good."

Shelby popped open the cans and brought them to the living room. "I hope you don't mind drinking out of a can. I want to avoid dirtying dishes."

"It's the best way to drink soda, except out of bottles. But you can hardly find bottles anymore." Dawn perched on the sofa and sipped her drink. "Shelby, I know you don't want to talk to me, and maybe you are in a hurry, but there's something I want to share with you. I wanted to tell you at Mike's funeral, but that didn't work out. It won't take long."

Suddenly feeling slightly embarrassed about her behavior, Shelby sat at the other end of the sofa, facing Dawn. "Go ahead, Dawn. I'm sorry if I've been rude."

"I never gave it a thought." Dawn paused. She took another swallow of Pepsi, obviously hesitant to proceed. "Well, here goes. In more ways than one, Shelby, I really haven't had a right to keep asking you to tell me about your life. For one thing, I've never told you much about mine. But that was mostly because I haven't been too proud of it. I had three marriages that went sour after your father. There were also a couple of serious relationships that ended before there could be a marriage. I don't know how much your father told you about me, but knowing him, I'm sure he didn't make a big point of the bad stuff."

Shelby nodded agreement with this, and Dawn continued. "There were a lot of bad times. One of my husbands was a drug dealer and I got hooked on heroin. I did rehab and beat it, but it was rough going. I don't want you to feel sorry for me, it just seems that this is the only way to lead up to what I really want to tell you. I got out of rehab seven months ago. That wasn't my first time in treatment. Through the years I've been on and off drugs and alcohol many times. But this last time was the hardest because it finally hit me—here I am a middle-aged woman who could practically be a grandmother, and I was worse off than many teenagers."

"I didn't know all that, Dawn—about rehab and all."

"Mike was such a good man. Still protecting me after all these years. But I suppose he was protecting you really, not me. Well, anyway, that's my life story in a nutshell. Since I got out of rehab this last time, I've been living with your aunt Lynn. You know what a religious fanatic she can be, at least that's what I always thought. She's been trying for years to convert me."

Shelby smiled. "She's been working on me, too."

"Well, it finally took with me." Dawn gave her a weak grin. "That's what I wanted to tell you. I just . . . I guess I just wanted you to know. But more than that, I just feel so much better since I did it. I go to church now and to a Bible study for beginners—new Christians, that is. Don't worry, I won't be as fanatical as Lynn. I figure I can barely take care of myself—much less try to convert others."

"I'm glad you found something that makes you happy, Dawn."

"Looks like we both have." Dawn paused, but Shelby could tell she had more to say. "I don't want you to think that just because I've found faith in God, I think you should accept me. It's not that at all, it's just that now I think I can be . . . I don't know . . . a better mother to you. Maybe just a better friend. I know I don't deserve it, but I needed to ask you if maybe you could . . . let me see you more, talk to you more. I won't try to be your mother, I only want to know you better."

How could Shelby refuse that earnest, almost pleading tone? Yet the years of resentment were difficult to shed.

"I understand what you're saying," Shelby replied evenly, "and I guess it wouldn't hurt for me to be more accepting. I just can't promise that I'm going to suddenly be the daughter you're looking for. I've got a lot to deal with now, adjusting to my new marriage and Dad's death. I don't know if I can give what you want."

"I won't demand much from you. Maybe I can just call you once in a while, or you can call me."

"That doesn't sound too hard."

"Good! Really, that is so wonderful!" Dawn grinned, looking pretty and childlike. She jumped up. "I've kept you long enough. Let me finish helping you with those boxes, and I'll be out of your way."

Ten minutes later, when the boxes were loaded into Shelby's car, Dawn was halfway down the walkway when Shelby called after her, "Dawn, you didn't get my phone number." Shelby surprised even herself that she reminded Dawn. Had she not said anything she would have been off the hook. But the pleased expression on Dawn's face made the small gesture worth it. Shelby wrote Frank's phone number and address on a piece of scrap paper. As she handed it to her mother, she thought fleetingly that if Dawn were true to form she'd lose the paper and Shelby would still be off the hook.

Somehow that thought wasn't as pleasing to Shelby as she expected it to be.

15

FRANK SAT AT HIS DESK in a back room of the Casa del Mar. He left the door open so the late-afternoon sounds of voices and clattering dishes could drift in. He had no appreciation right now for silence. Unfortunately it was Monday—a slow day in the restaurant business. He tried to refocus his attention on the ledgers before him, wishing once again his parents would agree to computerize the accounts.

He squeezed his head between his hands. His parents were the last thing he wanted to think about.

He concentrated on the columns of figures, then turned to his calculator and began entering the totals. His thoughts drifted again, this time to Shelby. He wondered if he could leave for home now, forgetting the rest of the accounts. They had spoken very little after the disastrous dinner at his parents'. She had been more than willing to talk, but he wanted to simply forget it had all happened. That had been a lot easier to do before he married Shelby. In the past he had been in his own little world—ignoring what he wished, embracing the things that made him feel good. Puerto Vallarta had been the ultimate extension of this philosophy. He had successfully forgotten his life in California—and had totally and completely embraced Shelby. What he hadn't considered in his ecstasy was that Shelby would want to be part of *all* his life, not just what he deemed acceptable.

Shelby thought she was being a good wife for wanting this. She had no idea of the danger of digging too deep. She ought to be happy with the surface of things. He didn't want to see her tainted—or worse yet, hurt by the dark side of the life he had tried to forget in Puerto Vallarta.

Maybe he was a fool for thinking that could be possible.

His fingers had paused over the keys of the calculator, but all at once he willed them back into motion. He made himself think only of the figures, of profit and loss. And when the figures balanced he turned to a stack of invoices, his mind almost in a fever pitch to keep from thinking of anything else. But his escape in work was suddenly cut off as, from the corner of his eye, he noted a man standing in the open doorway. He looked up and inwardly groaned.

"Barcelona," he said in a far from welcoming tone.

"Hola, Frank. *Que paso*, man?"

"I'm busy, Hector. What do you want?"

"You are always busy, amigo. I guess you were too busy to meet me at Lotto's the other night. I was very disappointed."

"Sorry." Frank obviously didn't mean it. "I've got a lot of responsibilities now."

"Oh yeah." Barcelona stepped into the office and closed the door behind him. "Like a new wife? You old dog!" He slapped Frank on the back. "And a pretty gringo girl, too." He chuckled, a leering look on his face.

"What do you want, Hector? I no longer have any business with you."

"I thought maybe since you were in Mexico—"

"I told you I'm through with that!"

"Don't get so touchy, amigo. It's not why I'm here anyway. I came to offer my condolences about poor Gloria."

"All right, consider them offered. Now leave me alone."

"What a waste, eh? Such a great woman she was, full of life and all that. There'll be a lot of men mourning her—"

"Get out, Barcelona!"

"There might even be a few men glad about her untimely demise. I'm not one of them, mind you, but I could probably name a few. Your name would top my list."

"I don't know what you're talking about."

"The police came to visit me today—"

"What did you tell them?"

"I make it a point never to tell the police anything. But you know, if they begin to put on the pressure, I will have to look out for myself. Anyway, they were bound to find out eventually that you and Gloria had a less than congenial marriage and an even worse parting."

"I ask you again, Barcelona. What do you want?"

"Let's forget about Gloria, okay? I don't know nothing, and I really don't care. What I do care about is debts owed me. Isn't everything about money? You used to care about money, too. Remember all those sweet deals we used to have? Ray has tried to fill your shoes, but he isn't as smart as you, man. He gets in over his head sometimes."

"And. . . ?"

"Then he forgets who his friends are. There are people you can cheat and people who are sacred. Do you get my drift, Frank?"

"I think so. Ray owes you some money."

"And every time I try to collect, he slips away from me. He ain't smart, but he is slippery."

"How do I fit in?"

"I probably know more about you and Gloria than anyone, except maybe Ray."

"But you'll keep all you know to yourself if I deliver Ray?"

"Now you're getting the picture."

"How much does Ray owe you?"

"Twenty thousand."

Frank shook his head. Any thought of paying Barcelona off himself ended with that figure. There was no way Frank had that kind of cash on hand. Maybe if he sold a few things. For the first time in a year, he began to regret turning from the profitable lifestyle he had once maintained.

"I'll see what I can do," Frank said slowly. "But I need to warn you that I don't have any control over Ray."

"Come on, man, you're his big bro. He worships the ground you walk on."

"That was in the past."

"Let's hope not, man. I don't know how deep you are involved in this thing with Gloria, but I figure you got a lot riding on this."

"You're crazy, Hector."

"I'll tell you who's crazy—it's Ray. He's loco if he thinks he can mess with me and get away with it." For the first time, Barcelona's tone betrayed emotion. His voice shook as he leaned across the desk and leveled his ominously dark eyes at Frank.

"I'll not argue with that." Frank did not flinch as he kept his tone and gaze steady.

"You're getting real high-and-mighty these days, Frank. Don't you forget—I could cut you off at the knees. One word to the cops and I could finish you."

"Get out, Hector."

"I've had it with you Stefano boys." Barcelona strode to the door, paused, and added, "You'll learn not to fool with me."

Frank watched Barcelona go, waited until his footsteps died away, then lifted his phone receiver. He hesitated. This was not a call he wanted to make, because in making it, he would be stepping backward, back into the past, into the world that had almost destroyed him and was still destroying his brother. But Barcelona was right about one thing; Ray still looked up to Frank, though he acted arrogant and disdainful of Frank for turning to an honest life. For that reason alone, Frank had to make the call.

His thoughts wandered back several years to the first time he had enticed his little brother into crime. Ray had been fifteen, a sophomore in high school and a good student. Frank had been eighteen and had dropped out of high school before his senior year ended. He probably would have been kicked out anyway. He had been a terrible student, coming to school stoned half the time. He started experimenting with drugs in eighth grade, though he had never liked the hard stuff. Marijuana was all he did, along with a little cocaine at parties. It was the dealing of drugs that he had found far more exciting. And excitement was what it had all been about. He never really needed the money because his family's restaurants had successfully taken off before his first year of high school. It had always been for the thrill and for the chance to impress Gloria. He had been obsessed with her and with the image having a beautiful girl like that gave him. She had given him his first taste of the drug culture and had connected him with Barcelona, a distant cousin of hers.

Ray had wanted to be a doctor, and he'd had the grades for such aspirations. But Frank had wanted to be a big shot.

"Ray, you gotta try this. Grass is cool, man. It'll heighten your senses, probably give you even better grades."

"I don't know. . . . Mom and Dad are ready to kick you out, Frank, if you don't quit. I don't want to get in trouble."

"I'm ready to leave anyway. I'm sick of them trying to control my life. That's what it's all about for them—for Mom, especially. Control, man. If you don't stand up to her now, you're gonna end up a mama's boy." Frank knew that was the ultimate insult to a young Mexican.

"I want to get into a good college."

"Don't you know nearly all college students do grass? Hey, but if you're chicken, man . . ."

"I'm not afraid!"

"It's not like this is speed or coke. Just a little grass . . ."

Of course, Ray could not let his big brother think he was a coward. He took the marijuana and soon became a very good customer. Within a year, however, Ray was looking for cocaine. Frank could never understand how Ray had gone so out of control. Maybe he had some physical defect that made him more susceptible. Frank didn't like to admit that the reason was more because Ray was drawn to the camaraderie the drug bond had created between the brothers. For a while they had had a good time together—getting stoned, going to wild parties, listening to hardcore music.

Then Frank and Barcelona decided to smuggle in their own supply of drugs directly from Mexico. Dealing was a dangerous business because of the more extensive contacts necessary, while smuggling was more insulated and a bit safer. And, of course, the money was better. Frank's connections in Puerto Vallarta were quite useful. They bought a sailing vessel—not the most efficient method of transportation, but it offered the perfect cover. And by anchoring in out-of-the-way coves to make pickups and drops, they were able to effectively avoid border patrols. Frank had learned how to sail on family vacations to Puerto Vallarta, so he could make the runs himself, eliminating middle men.

Then Ray wanted to be part of the action. Frank never forced him, never twisted his arm as their mother contended. Ray had *begged* to join the venture.

After that everything spiraled downward. The money rolled in and the excitement never let up, but the price was a deeper involvement in the drug underworld, not to mention with the law. Somehow Frank managed to avoid arrest, though he'd had a few close calls. Ray's juvenile status allowed him to do the more risky jobs, since the legal consequences for him would not have been as great. He had to appear in juvenile court a few times, much to their parents' disgrace, and he spent a few weeks in juvenile hall. But nearly two years ago, when Ray was twenty-two, he was arrested as an adult for possession with intent to sell. He got a hard-nosed judge who gave Ray a year in San Quentin. And because Ray refused to turn in his partners, he served the full year.

The arrest did little to curb Ray's criminal activities, but it proved to be a turning point for Frank. Seeing his brother go off to prison—knowing, even without his mother's accusations, that it was his fault—had been extremely daunting for Frank. By then he was wearying of the criminal life anyway, having seen far too much of its dark underside. Ray's arrest, his mother's scathing accusations, and his disastrous marriage to Gloria all converged to open his eyes to the depravity of what he was doing.

Ray thought he was a sucker for quitting when profits were at an all-time high.

"You're not responsible for me, bro," Ray had told Frank through the screen of the prison visiting room. "I'm my own man. No one controls me."

How Frank wanted to believe that. He'd told his mother those very words many times. But he knew they weren't true. He *was* responsible. But he was helpless to do anything about it except clean up his own life and hope, maybe even pray, that Ray would eventually follow him on that path as he had the other.

Now, however, that seemed a slim hope. Even Frank's pathetic attempt to go straight was blowing up in his face. The past was not going to let him go. He looked at the phone receiver as if willing it to tell him differently. He knew he did not have a choice. In death, as in life, Gloria still wielded tremendous power over him. He had been a fool to hope all that had ended with her death.

He keyed in his brother's pager number, then keyed in their private code. Hopefully Ray was only laying low from Barcelona. He hung up the receiver, continuing to stare at it, hoping it would ring right away, yet at the same time dreading the conversation.

When the phone did ring a few moments later, he jumped. But it wasn't his brother. It was Detective Poole asking him if he would come to the precinct station to help them with a few more details regarding the death of Gloria Herrera. Frank didn't like the sound of the "request." Nevertheless, he couldn't very well refuse.

16

"WE'RE GLAD YOU COULD COME down here," said Detective Poole from behind his desk. "Believe me, we appreciate your cooperation. Have a seat."

Frank sat in a chair next to Poole's desk while Liscom, his partner, stood on the other side with one foot propped up on a chair. This appeared to Frank—who was not unfamiliar with police tactics—as a carefully staged effort to appear casual. They probably didn't want to spook their prime suspect. Frank immediately went on his guard.

"This has been a rather tedious process since we discovered the body a week ago," Poole began.

"A week ago?" Frank repeated.

"Didn't we mention that when we spoke the other day? Yes, that's right. She was a Jane Doe for a couple days while we matched dental records. A body that has been in the water any length of time can be next to impossible to identify."

"The coroner estimates her body was floating around for a couple weeks before it washed up on the beach and was finally discovered," put in Liscom. "By then it was pretty chewed up. Crabs and small feeder fish had done away with much of the soft tissue—nose, lips, ears, eyelids were pretty much history. Decomposition is four times faster in the water. Did you know that? Her hair, also, was torn away by the wave action, and what was left of her body was bloated—I'm sorry, Mr. Stefano, that was really thoughtless of me. You okay?"

Frank licked his lips. He wasn't okay. His stomach churned in a sick knot, and the blood had drained from his face. Liscom's apology was full of mockery, and Frank knew the man's intent had been to create that very effect. Frank only nodded because he was afraid of what his voice would sound like if he spoke just then.

"Anyway," said Poole, "you can see why our investigation is proceeding slowly. We did just get in a preliminary report from the coroner's office. It appears that she went into the water about the time the missing persons report was filed. Also, the body was traumatized before entering the water."

"Traumatized?"

"Fractured skull."

"Couldn't that have come from smashing up against rocks?"

"A killer might hope it would be confused with that, but there are ways to determine the difference."

"So you are saying Gloria was killed before she . . . entered the water?"

"That is the sad thing," answered Liscom. "There's enough water in her lungs to indicate otherwise. The poor woman was not only smashed on the head and dumped into the sea, but she also had to suffer drowning. It is very possible that her initial contact with the cold water revived her enough from the head injury so that she suffered terribly before finally suffocating."

"A horrible death," said Poole mournfully.

Frank rubbed his hand over his mouth and shook his head slowly, miserably. Oh, Gloria! Why did it have to be like that?

"What do you want from me?" Frank said as evenly as he could.

"Even though you are divorced, we understand you still had contact with Ms. Herrera?"

"We'd known each other a long time and still had many friends in common, so we occasionally saw each other in social situations. Weddings, christenings, that sort of thing."

"And that's all?"

"Yeah . . . well, I was still paying her alimony, and we'd had a few discussions about that recently."

"You were behind?"

"I just thought it was time to end the payments."

"What ex-husband doesn't?" said Poole with a chuckle. Frank didn't laugh. "Did you fight over this?" Poole asked more seriously.

"No, of course not."

"You fought a lot in your marriage, though, didn't you?"

"Never anything physical. But, yeah, we did argue a lot. Which is why the marriage fell apart."

Liscom removed his foot from the chair and plopped his hefty frame into the seat. Rubbing his chin he asked, "Did you see her four weeks ago?"

"Am I a suspect?" Frank asked, trying to quell his anxiety.

Poole answered in his friendly, congenial way. "You are just a concerned citizen helping out the police."

"It doesn't sound that way."

"We want to keep this a friendly discussion, Mr. Stefano."

"I think I need a lawyer."

"No way," said Poole soothingly, "I haven't even read you your rights. We have no suspects at this time. We are merely trying to pull together a few facts about the deceased. We are questioning everyone who knew her. You have no reason to be nervous."

"Do you?" added Liscom, leaning forward with a piercing look in his eyes.

"No." Frank returned the look unflinchingly.

"Then you don't mind answering a few questions? I'm sure, like everyone, you want to get to the bottom of this terrible tragedy." Poole again was the cajoler. The "good cop."

"I was in Mexico four weeks ago," Frank said, trying to calm down.

"Oh yeah," said Liscom, "that was convenient, wasn't it?"

"Hey, Marv," Poole said sharply, "cool it, okay? Stefano is cooperating with us. Those kinds of comments are way out of line."

"I guess you better handle this, Ed," said Liscom. "I just can't help losing it when pretty young women are found all chewed up on a beach." Liscom lurched to his feet and walked away.

"You gotta forgive Liscom," said Poole. "He has a daughter about the same age as Ms. Herrera."

Frank shrugged. Liscom was probably childless but a very good actor.

"So," Poole continued, "you were in Mexico four weeks ago. Was that for business or pleasure?"

"A little of both. I go to Puerto Vallarta periodically to check on my grandmother's estate."

"Exactly what date did you leave L.A.?"

"December sixteenth."

Poole shuffled through some papers on his desk. "The missing persons report was filed on the seventeenth."

"I saw her the day before I left," Frank said. He tried to hide his trembling hands from the detective. "She was okay then."

"You might very well have been the last person to see her alive—except, of course, for her murderer. You said she was okay. She wasn't behaving in an unusual manner? Depressed? Nervous?"

"I don't think Gloria was ever depressed or nervous. She was a very cool number."

"What did you see her about?"

"I'm not a suspect, right?"

"You seem very concerned about that."

"I saw her the day before she disappeared. We did not have the most friendly relationship. You might start to draw conclusions."

"I deal in facts, Mr. Stefano, not unfounded conclusions. And I have no physical evidence to link you to any crime. But if you feel uncomfortable with the direction of these questions, I cannot make you cooperate at this time."

"I feel very uncomfortable with these questions. Not because I'm guilty, but rather because of all the implications."

"Then you don't wish to answer any more questions?"

"No."

"I guess you are free to go, then. But I will ask that you not make any trips out of town for a while. I may have to speak with you again."

"I'm not going anywhere," said Frank, rising.

He walked away from Poole's desk and had reached the squad room door when Liscom strode up to him, placing himself ominously between Frank and the door.

"We never could nail you in the past, Stefano, but I'll tell you, I'm gonna nail that girl's killer. I'm gonna see him pay."

"Then we agree on something," Frank replied evenly.

"You're one cool spic—"

"Is that an ethnic slur, Detective?"

"Just a slip of the tongue. I meant, 'one cool Hispanic-American.' "

"Are you going to let me leave?"

Liscom stepped aside. "Adios amigo," he said snidely.

Frank shoved past him, saying nothing. He just wanted to get out of there. He was more worried than ever. The way they were playing him didn't look good. Did they have evidence or were they just fishing? The way Liscom was acting, it didn't seem as if hard evidence was going to matter much. Nor would Frank's guilt or innocence. They knew about his past, and in their eyes that was enough to point the finger of accusation right at him. But how much evidence *did* they have? Did they know that he and Gloria had fought that last night? Might the neighbors have heard . . . and would they be eager to tell the police about it if questioned? Did they know that Gloria was still very much involved in drug trafficking? The police would no doubt assume that Frank was also still involved. Liscom wanted him. It wouldn't take much.

A tangle of nerves, Frank climbed into his Ford Ranger, started the engine, and pulled into traffic. It was now seven in the evening. He wanted desperately to be with Shelby but knew he couldn't face her like this. She'd see right through him, and the last thing he needed now was for her to interrogate him, too. So he drove around for an hour. Once, almost unconsciously, he drove by Ray's apartment building, but there were no lights on in his window and his car was gone from its parking spot. Had he tried to answer Frank's page? Now more than ever Frank needed to see him. He had to know if the police had questioned him yet. Maybe not, since the detectives had said nothing to Frank about Ray. But they would find and talk to Ray sooner or later. Then what?

Frank drove down Hermosa Boulevard, but instead of going to his place, he parked a couple of blocks away and walked to the beach. There was nothing more soothing than the sound of waves crashing against the sandy shore. Fifteen minutes later he was ready to go home.

Liscom plopped back down in the chair next to Poole's desk.

"I'm sick of pussyfooting around," he said. "Let's nail that sucker."

"I want to be sure the arrest is gonna stick, Marv. I'm just not convinced we have enough for probable cause."

"I don't like the way you're playing him like some fancy violin. 'You're just a concerned citizen, Mr. Stefano.' 'We want to keep this a friendly discussion, Mr. Stefano,'" Liscom mimicked his partner.

"We don't want to scare him off by revealing all we have. What do we have, anyway, Marv? Witnesses who heard them arguing. A neighbor who saw him return later that same night to argue again, with some crashing sounds added in."

"We have a witness who says Stefano threatened her the previous day—in fact, several witnesses heard them in a bar. He even made a physical move then—"

"He grabbed her arm."

"Nevertheless, prior threats are extremely damaging to him. And what about her appointment book that says Stefano was going to come see her that night? If you ask me, that's very compelling evidence."

"We need some physical evidence."

"What about the police report we located?"

"That's five years old."

"It still proves what the man is capable of. The photos of a very battered Gloria Herrera don't lie."

"Charges were never pressed."

"Blast it, Ed! You sound like his defense attorney."

"I just want a solid case. Give me some physical evidence and I'll happily lock the man up."

17

SHELBY WAS CURLED UP on the sofa in front of the television when Frank came home. At her surprise, he explained that it had been a slow day at the restaurant. She smiled as he came and sat beside her. It almost seemed like what a normal evening should be. Shelby asked him how his day went, and though he said little, she decided not to make an issue of it.

"Well, I had an interesting day," she said. "I went to my old house to pack up a few things, and guess what? My mother came by. The most amazing thing was that it wasn't horrible. She really wants to have a relationship."

"That's good. Do you think you'll give her a chance?"

"I gave her our phone number. But . . . I don't know. She told me that she's started going to church and is trying to get her life in order. She's been a drug addict and an alcoholic all these years. I never really knew that. Once when she came to see me, I'm pretty sure she was drunk. But I was too young to think much of it, and my father never said anything."

"So do you feel sorry for her now?"

"I don't want to. She made her own choices."

"When someone becomes an addict, I think the drugs start to make their choices for them."

"Were you a drug addict, Frank?"

He suddenly looked uncomfortable, and Shelby regretted her question.

"No," he answered slowly, "but I've been around enough of them."

"What do you think I should do about my mother?"

"I'm the last person to give advice on family matters."

"I want so much to hate her. But she can appear so vulnerable that it's awfully hard to do. And I have to say there was something about her today that was different. It makes me wonder if she really has changed."

"My grandmother would say that was probably because God has come into her life. In fact, you ought to talk to my grandmother about this. She'd give you good advice."

"I might just do that."

Much to Shelby's disappointment, a knock at the door interrupted them. Frank rose and answered it. He didn't open the door enough for her to see or hear who it was, and after a moment he stepped outside. A few minutes later he came back in alone.

"I'm going out for a little while," he said.

"Who was at the door?" she asked.

He hesitated a moment before replying, "My brother."

"Is he still here? I'd really like to meet him."

"He's kind of in a hurry—" Before Frank could finish, the door opened and Ramon Stefano came in.

Shelby would have known him to be a Stefano immediately, but more from his resemblance to their father than to Frank. He was about Frank's same build, though perhaps an inch shorter. His moustache made him look like a younger version of his father. He had small, sharp eyes and a ready grin, friendly and warm, which he focused immediately upon Shelby.

"Frank, I don't care what you say. I'm gonna meet your wife." Ray stepped toward Shelby, his hand outstretched. "Hi, sis. Glad to meet you!"

Shelby smiled and took his hand. "I'm glad to meet you, too. Are you sure you can't stay for a few minutes?"

"We have to run an errand," Frank answered quickly.

"All we need to do is talk," said Ray, taking a seat in a chair facing Shelby.

"I can fix some coffee," Shelby suggested. "And I brought home some chocolate cake from the freezer in my old place."

"No, we have to go," said Frank.

"If you want privacy . . ." Shelby began.

"I won't be long." Frank bent down and brushed Shelby's cheek with a kiss. "Come on, Ray."

Ray shrugged. "He can be a real tyrant sometimes."

"Well, I'd love for you to come for a longer visit soon," said Shelby.

Shelby watched, slightly bemused, as Ray rose and the two brothers left. How could things between she and Frank dissolve so quickly? Since returning from Mexico, it always seemed to be that way. One minute they'd be having such a marvelous time, then one wrongly spoken word, or a phone call, or a knock on the door . . . and everything would fall to pieces. The catalyst always seemed to relate to Frank's family. And the frustrating fact was that his family wasn't going to go away. Frank was never going to be able to completely avoid them. And that was going to continually affect their relationship. Shelby wondered how much she could take of Frank's mercurial moods, never knowing when one would strike, leaving her tattered emotions in its wake.

She decided it was time to talk to someone about this. She simply could not stand bearing it alone. She lifted her phone and dialed Christie's number. Their previous dinner plans had fallen through because Christie had to meet with a client, but perhaps she'd be free by now. Shelby was pleased when Christie answered and agreed to get together. They arranged to meet at a coffee shop located halfway between Whittier and Redondo Beach.

Frank and Ramon drove in Frank's truck to a nightclub in San Pedro. They used to hang out there in their younger days but hadn't been there in a long time, and Ray thought it would be a good place to talk without running into anyone familiar. The place was not busy on a Monday night, but it was still noisy with loud, poor-quality taped music. The brothers found a table in an isolated corner and ordered glasses of Pacifico beer.

"So, que paso, bro?" said Ray, sipping a Mexican beer. "You haven't paged me in a long time. What's going on?"

"You have to ask? Gloria's dead and Barcelona is looking for your hide. Where do you want to start?"

Ray shrugged nonchalantly. Frank could tell he was high by the slightly glazed look in his eyes and the imperturbable attitude.

"What do you plan to do about Barcelona?" Frank asked, grimacing when his brother shrugged again.

"He doesn't worry me. I got a deal cooking now that will take care of him and leave me sitting pretty."

"You're setting up your own deals now? No wonder Barcelona's ticked off."

"Hey, it's a free country. I met a guy in prison who's connected to Cali—"

"Ray, I didn't think you were that stupid," Frank cut in.

"Give me some credit. Anyway, we been dealing with the Columbians all along, way down at the bottom of the chain of command. Now I just have a more direct route."

"Over Barcelona's head."

"My guy doesn't want to include anyone else in the deal. Cuts down on the profits and makes us more vulnerable to the law. He wants to keep things simple. He trusts me because we did time together. He trusts very few others. He guarantees I'll make a million in six months. And I'm willing to cut you in, Frank."

"You know better. I'm finished with all that." Frank shifted uncomfortably, knowing now why Ray had bothered to answer his page. Lately Ray only sought Frank out when he wanted something.

"All right, I'll be straight with you, bro. I need you. I can't make this deal happen with Hector breathing down my neck. If you can help me pay him off, I can proceed more freely. And like I said, I could pay you back in a matter of months—with a very high rate of interest."

"Even if I did agree to help you, where did you think I would come up with twenty thousand? I don't have that kind of money anymore."

"I'll never understand why you gave it all away. It was bad enough to quit the business, but then to let yourself exist on the salary of a restaurant manager . . ." Ray shook his head incredulously. "And our parents' restaurant to boot. You are crazy, Frank. You had it all, man, and you flushed it down the toilet like a good line of cocaine. For what? Me? I thought you had more sense than that."

"The point is, Ray, I don't have twenty thousand to give you," Frank replied, trying hard to ignore his brother's words and the painful truth they exposed.

The song "La Bamba" blared over the speakers, and Ray closed his eyes a moment before speaking. "That's a great song, isn't it, bro?" He drummed his hands on the table to the beat of the music. "Makes me proud to be a Mexican." He said nothing more until the song ended, then pushed back his chair. "I need to visit the rest room. Order me another beer, will ya?" But as he started to rise, Frank laid his hand heavily over Ray's arm, restraining him.

"Let's finish this conversation first," said Frank. "Then you can do whatever you want in the rest room."

"Come on, man! I just want a quick snort—you know, to clear my head. Then we can finish—"

"If you leave, the conversation is over." Frank knew that in making that threat he was committing himself to listen to his brother's proposition—but the old guilt crept in again, forcing him to stay.

Ramon relaxed back in his seat and called a waitress over to order another beer. Then he said, "Okay, man, here's the deal. You don't have to come up with twenty grand. All I need is five to make a buy down in Mexico. I'll be able to sell it up here easily for the twenty grand, and then some. That'll get Hector off my back so I can proceed with the other deal."

"Only five?"

"I've got a couple of grand of my own to throw in."

"I have two thousand in the bank."

Ramon shook his head with pity. "What about Shelby?"

The idea of borrowing money from Shelby was totally repulsive. Yet perhaps in the long run it was a small price to pay to get rid of the threat of Barcelona. The true price, however, was far greater than having to humble himself by asking his wife for money. Not only would it put him, for all practical purposes, back in the drug business—it would also encourage his brother. Maybe the best thing to do would be to let Ramon take his chances with Barcelona. Someday Frank had to quit protecting his brother. But was now really the best time for that? If Frank walked away from Ramon, it could well mean they would both be destroyed. Frank thought longingly of Shelby and the wonderful, normal life he hoped to have with her. Could he throw that away? At least by helping his brother there was still a chance to come away unharmed. It wouldn't be a sure thing, and at best it was a precarious juggling act, but it seemed his chances were better with Ramon than with Liscom and Poole.

"That's it? Five grand is all?" Frank asked, knowing nothing was as easy as it might appear on the surface.

"Well . . . I'll need your help to make the pickup in Mexico."

Frank felt himself being helplessly sucked into a horrible vortex. "The boat?"

"I got it all figured out, Frank. It'll be a piece of cake."

"You know, of course, that the police are almost certainly watching our every move?"

"I have a plan."

"What plan?" Frank hated to ask.

"Next weekend is the Four Winds Yacht Club's regatta down in San Diego." Ray spoke with confidence and enthusiasm. Frank hoped it was from more than his brother's last hit of cocaine. "You go every year, so it won't seem unusual for you to go this time—especially if you bring your wife."

"I won't do that."

"You've got to, bro. It's the only way to make it appear innocent. If just you and I go, it'll look suspicious. Listen to my plan, and you'll see there won't be any danger to Shelby. It'll be a piece of cake. There's an opening race on Saturday afternoon. We do the race just like normal. We dock at the yacht club marina, then after dark we come up with some excuse to go back out into the bay, maybe to watch the sunset or something. The Coast Guard isn't gonna worry about a boat leaving the harbor—it's the ones coming in that are under scrutiny. Anyway, while we're out, we'll head south—all under the cover of darkness. We can make the run to that little hidden cove . . . you know, between Tijuana and Ensenada. We'll get back to San Diego in time for the race on Sunday morning—no sweat. We just show up at the starting line, and no one will think anything of it."

Frank had used similar scenarios before with good success. But he wanted to find a way to shoot down the plan. "And what if someone notices that our slip in San Diego is empty all night?"

"Who's gonna notice? There will be fifty extra boats there for the regatta—the place will be a zoo. Joe Franklin will be there. He'll cover for us—you know, take our slip by accident so we can say we had to dock somewhere else. Happens all the time."

"And where will Shelby be all this time?"

"Do I have to figure everything out? You were always the brains of the outfit. I'm sure you'll think of something."

Ignoring the problem of Shelby, Frank asked, "Who are you dealing with in Mexico?"

"Manuel."

"Then you're buying marijuana?"

"Yeah. Barcelona hasn't dealt with our pot contacts in over a year, since he's gone completely into the cocaine and heroin business. So there's no chance of fouling him with this deal. Manuel's cool with everything. He never liked Hector anyway."

"He still in good with the *Federales*?"

"Very good. No problem there."

"I've got to think about this."

"There isn't much time. I have to make all the arrangements before Friday."

"You're asking a lot of me, Ray."

"I wouldn't if I wasn't desperate."

"I don't like involving Shelby."

"If Gloria were still alive, she could go with us." Ramon smiled as if at a pleasant memory. "No one ever suspected her."

"So you don't think that's what got her killed?"

"How would I know? I figured you'd know more about that than me."

"Why would you think that?" Frank asked defensively.

"You've been talking to the police, haven't you?"

Frank shifted uneasily in his chair. "Yeah, and they think I killed her."

"But they don't have any evidence, or you'd be in jail."

"Smuggling a boatload of pot won't help my case if I get caught."

"You're not going to get caught," Ray replied with empty, drug-induced confidence. "You never got caught before."

"I didn't care before. Now it's different. I have a wife I love and a chance to realize my dreams. I'll be looking over my shoulder, nervous, afraid."

"You can do this, Frank. One more time, that's all. Then go have your wife and that straight life you seem to want so much. I'll never bother you again. I promise."

"I'll think about it, that's all. No promises from me, you got it?"

"I need to know within a couple days so I have time to set up everything."

"Okay." Frank's stomach pitched as he spoke. He wondered if he could still run away from it all. Glancing at his brother who was getting fidgety, drumming his fingers on the table as his need for a fix increased, Frank knew he could not leave Ray now. He had to save him, even if it meant the ultimate sacrifice.

18

CHRISTIE DIDN'T HAVE any great wisdom to offer, but after several cups of decaf latté and lots of laughter, Shelby felt much better. Maybe it was because Christie was part of Shelby's past—a life she didn't want to lose. Maybe it was simply that for a few moments she was able to forget her troubles with Frank.

When it was time to part, Christie apologized for not being much help, but Shelby could not have had better therapy. They vowed not to let their friendship drift simply because a few more miles separated them.

It was almost midnight when Shelby drove into the condo's underground garage. She parked, got out of her Mustang, and was walking to the elevator when she heard footsteps behind her. She turned to find Hector Barcelona and his two companions from the other evening. An involuntary chill coursed up Shelby's spine, which she tried vainly to ignore.

"Hello . . . Hector, isn't it?" she said as casually as she could muster.

"You have a good memory, Shelby," Barcelona said in a smooth, almost slippery tone.

Shelby glanced around the parking area, noting that Frank's truck was gone. "Frank's not here."

"Maybe that'll give us a chance to get to know each other better," Barcelona said with a leering grin that could have only one interpretation.

"Sometime, when it's not so late, Frank and I will have you over."

"But I'm here now." He moved so close to her that she took a step back. "What's the matter, *amante*?"

Shelby knew that the Spanish word meant the equivalent of sweet-heart; sometimes Frank called her that—at least he had in Mexico. It made her cringe to hear it from Barcelona's lips.

Barcelona continued. "Why don't you want to be friendly with me? In the past Frank and I used to share our women. Gloria and I—"

"Please," Shelby said, "why don't you come back when Frank is here?"

"Maybe it's not Frank I want." He grinned again and kept moving until he had backed her up against the brick wall of the garage. He was pressed up against her with a hand on her shoulder, fingering her hair. "You got such pretty pale hair." He leaned in and put her hair to his nose. "It smells like coconut."

"Leave me alone!" Her voice was shaking and hardly had any power.

Barcelona only grinned more. "You realize, of course, that I could have you now if I wanted," he said, taunting her.

"Frank would kill you." She didn't know why she said that. She had no idea how Frank would react.

"Sí, he has that in him, doesn't he? Maybe he would kill you, too, eh? I mean, why wouldn't he think you were completely willing? What woman wouldn't want to be with a macho specimen like yours truly?"

He began kissing her ear and neck, and when she tried to push him away, he took her hands and pinned them against the wall over her head. As she tried to kick him, his two companions made their presence more obvious by stepping closer.

"Why fight," Barcelona taunted in a menacing tone, "when all I want to do is show you a good time. Frank's no fun since he got religion—I'll bet you wouldn't mind a little fun."

"Please—!"

He laughed. "Now she is begging for my attentions. I knew you'd change your tune."

Suddenly Shelby was wrenched away from the wall. Momentarily disoriented, she was certain Barcelona's amorous intentions had suddenly turned violent. Then, as she crumbled to the ground, she realized Frank had come and yanked Barcelona away. Relief washed over her, but at that same moment she realized Frank's peril.

Barcelona's companions had been momentarily taken off guard by the suddenness of Frank's attack, but they were quickly back in form and rushing toward where Frank and Barcelona were struggling on the pavement. "Frank!" Shelby screamed, but her warning was too late.

It didn't take long for the two hoodlums to neutralize Frank's advantage over Barcelona. It did, however, take both men to pull Frank off his prey. He fought mightily and continued to struggle even after they were each able to get a good hold of his arms, preventing further resistance.

Barcelona jumped up and brushed off his rumpled and torn clothes. Spots of blood ringed a tear on the elbow, and more blood trickled from his lip, dripping on his silk shirt.

"Now, look," said Barcelona with a pout, "you've gone and ruined my new Armani suit. Why'd you do that, Frank? I thought we were friends."

"Not anymore, Barcelona. You've gone too far."

"Time was you didn't mind sharing with me, amigo."

"Did I ever have a choice?"

"Do you have a choice now?"

"What's your point?"

"I can take whatever I want. I'm the *man*, you got that?"

"What do you want?" Frank spat, glaring at his adversary.

"I could want this pretty little woman of yours." But as Barcelona advanced once more on Shelby, Frank fought so hard against his captors that one of the men lost his hold. Frank lurched toward Barcelona, but the bodyguards caught him once again, this time yanking his arms behind him with such force he cried out in pain.

"Okay, okay," said Barcelona with an easy smile. "Maybe I don't want her that bad. But I *could*, couldn't I? If I wanted. You know that, right?"

"You are a pig, Barcelona!"

"Let me teach him some manners, Hector," said one of the guards.

Barcelona gave the man a nod, and with the other guard firmly holding Frank, he delivered three punches to Frank's stomach that would have left him doubled over in agony had his captor not forced him to remain upright.

Shelby jumped up and ran toward them, oblivious to the fact that she was hardly a threat. But she couldn't just sit there.

"Don't, Shelby!" Frank gasped.

But before she reached the two henchmen, Barcelona caught Shelby. "You're a spirited gringo girl, eh?" He held her firmly against him, then nodded to Ricardo, who delivered another punishing blow to Frank. "If you don't relax, woman, your dear esposo will only suffer more."

Shelby forced herself to ease her struggling, but she in no way relaxed, especially as Barcelona continued to tightly hold her.

"Now, Francisco, don't spoil my good mood," said Barcelona smoothly. "I don't want to hurt you. We are compadres. So let's talk like friends, eh? You asked what I want. I told you before. I want Ramon."

"And I said before that has nothing to do with me." Frank's words came through gritted teeth, pain, anger, and even fear mingling in his voice.

"You been around gringos too much, Frank. With our people, families stick together. One brother's problems belong to the other brother. Ray's problems are yours, too."

"What do you want me to do, hit him over the head and drag him unconscious to you?"

"You gotta do what you gotta do, eh? It worked with Gloria. . . ."

"What do you mean?"

"I heard that she was killed by a blow to the head before she was dumped into the water. If that's the only way to get someone to cooperate . . ."

"Ray can't pay you if he's dead."

"He ain't doing much good alive."

"Give him some more time. How about if he pays you ten percent now and the rest in a month? That's better than getting nothing."

"I ain't no bank, amigo. When I want my money, I want my money."

"Be reasonable."

Barcelona shook his head with an indulgent sigh. "All right, two grand now, and then you got two weeks to come up with the rest."

"Two weeks!"

"Who knows what's gonna happen after that? The police are going to start locking up suspects in Gloria's murder. Then where will I be if you or Ray ain't around to pay?"

"You seem pretty certain the police will be after us."

Barcelona shrugged. "You gotta admit that you must be number one on their list."

"What about you, Hector? Maybe she owed you money."

"I got an iron-tight alibi. Do you, Frank?"

Frank licked his lips. "I'll bring you the money tomorrow morning."

Barcelona motioned for his men to unhand Frank, then gave Shelby a harsh shove before the three strode away. Although a bit unsteady on his feet, Frank hurried over to her.

"Are you all right?" he asked.

"I think so. What about you?"

He nodded, though he still walked slightly bent. "Shelby, I'm sorry. . . ."

"Frank, don't—"

He shook his head, halting her words. "You would never have become involved if it wasn't for me."

"Please . . . please tell me what's going on. It seems I *am* involved, but I need to hear about it from you."

"Maybe you're right . . . I don't know . . ."

It was almost like Puerto Vallarta with the lovely sound of breaking waves and the fragrant smell of salt in the air. Shelby and Frank took off their shoes and walked on the wet sand, waves lapping against their bare feet. They looked like two lovers on a romantic midnight stroll. Looks could be so deceiving.

"We were drug smugglers," Frank said flatly.

"You and Barcelona?" Shelby asked in a tightly controlled voice.

"And Ray . . . and even Gloria. Our own little drug cartel."

Shelby struggled to get her spinning thoughts under control while Frank focused his gaze on the horizon at the water's edge.

"It's time you stop being naïve, Shelby. You didn't want to hear about my past. You may want to think what I did was just kid stuff. But it wasn't. We put the drugs on the street for the kids to use. I wasn't just some punk selling dope to eighth graders behind the junior high. I smuggled hundreds of thousands of dollars of marijuana and cocaine into the country. I made lots of money. Did you ever wonder how a twenty-seven-year-old restaurant manager can afford a condo across from the beach? Or a yacht—even a small one? No, of course you didn't." His tone made her wince. "I'm the guy your dad always warned you about. You didn't listen to him and now you'll pay. You should have asked more questions, Shelby. Why didn't you? Why—"

"Stop it, Frank! I didn't ask because I loved you."

"And now. . . ? No, don't answer that. You'll still try to play the innocent, believing love heals all. It doesn't. Not this. You'll still want to think I was some foolish kid who got sucked into a bad crowd. That's not true, either. I sucked other people in. I got Ray hooked." He stopped walking and turned to face her, daring her with his eyes to cling to her little fairy tales.

"Oh, Frank . . ." Shelby did not want to admit how confused she felt. She *had* been naïve. Frank had been a drug dealer; he had sold drugs to his own brother and turned him into an addict. Shelby could hardly think of anything more reprehensible. This was not the man she fell in love with on a sun-washed Mexican beach. This was not the man who offered his own love with such tenderness. But was it possible for a man to change so radically? Shelby's aunt Lynn often told her that faith in God would change a person's heart. But she didn't think Frank had such faith. Suddenly she thought of something Barcelona had said. *"Frank's no fun since he got religion."* What had he meant? She began to ask Frank but stopped. Maybe she was just grasping at straws. Maybe she was still being naïve.

"I don't blame you," Frank was saying in response to her silence. "It's repulsive, sickening. No one would blame you for despising me."

She wanted desperately to deny all he was saying. She wanted to declare her undying love and devotion. But when she uttered the words, they seemed hollow in her ears. "I can't despise you. I don't know who that other man was, but it isn't the man with me now. It isn't the man I married."

He paused, then shook his head. "I'm wrong putting blame on you. Deep down, I wanted to deceive you in Puerto Vallarta. I didn't say anything because I was afraid of losing you." He fingered his scar as if willing it to remind him of the past. "I am a shame not only to my family, but to my people, as well. Perhaps that's the worst of my sins. . . . But now I have deceived you, the woman I vowed to love."

"Do you want me to hate you?"

"Don't you see? I destroyed Ray, and now I'll destroy you. You *should* hate me. And you should run while you can."

Yes, she wanted to run away. This man had destroyed lives. Not only his brother's, but countless others—young kids with so much to offer. He had robbed them of their youth. How could she still love him? Yet even now, Shelby felt so right being next to Frank, feeling his presence though they made no physical contact. He was a part of her, and even the specter of that other Frank could not dull what she felt. People did change. Why not Frank?

"I won't lie to you, Frank. This confuses me. There is only one thing I am certain of: I don't hate you. I can't turn off my love so easily. Somehow we'll just find a way to deal with the rest."

"Somehow . . ." he murmured but said no more.

They walked in silence for a time.

"What made you change, Frank?" she asked after several minutes.

"About two years ago, Ray was convicted of possession with intent to sell. The DA offered him a plea bargain if he turned the rest of us in. They really wanted Barcelona and me—we were the leaders of the ring. But Ray wouldn't budge. He spent a year in San Quentin. That's what finally made me realize what I had done. I was in terrible despair. My grandmother told me about God's forgiveness and how only that could give me the strength to go on with life. I already told you how I'd fought religion all my life. But even I could see what she was saying was different. She showed me a God who wanted only to give to me. All the 'Thou Shalt Not' sermons of my parents' religion were not there. It sounded so good."

"And you did what my mother did? You became a Christian?"

"I wanted to, but it was just too easy."

"You didn't think you deserved to get off that easily?"

"Not with my brother doing time because of me. But I couldn't go on dealing drugs, either. I had begun to hate the business anyway. Pot was bad enough, but the cocaine business made that look like selling candy. I was already on the edge, and Ray's arrest just gave me the final push. So I quit the business. My grandmother made my parents give me the job at the restaurant."

"And that is what matters. You are through with it."

"I can quit it, but it won't quit me. Don't you see?"

"Why didn't you just leave California and never come back?"

"I couldn't desert Ray. I guess I am my brother's keeper."

She reached out for his hand, but when she grasped it, he pulled away.

"What are you doing, Frank?"

"I'm making it easy for you."

"Let's go home."

"I'll walk you back. Then I'll spend the night on the boat."

Maybe Frank was right. She needed time to take it all in, to wade through her confusion. And there were so many other questions left unanswered. They had not even broached the subject of Gloria. Shelby knew she was afraid of that topic. She didn't want to know what Barcelona had meant with all his veiled statements, but the questions flooded in. Why had he been so certain Frank would be a suspect in Gloria's death? And why had Frank denied nothing? Why was he so willing to pay off Barcelona to keep him from talking to the police? And why did Frank become so distraught whenever Gloria was mentioned?

Instinctively, Shelby knew these were subjects best avoided. Yet she was just as certain they could no more be avoided than an oncoming train. For now she let Frank walk her home and did not argue when he gathered a change of clothes and left. Perhaps he had been right all along with his earlier desire to escape from it all. How she wished she had heeded him then!

19

SHELBY WENT TO WORK the next day only because of the sure distraction it provided, but afterward she drove to San Pedro and to Mrs. Querida's house. Why she ran to her instead of Christie, Shelby didn't know. She had never known her own grandparents—her father's parents had died years ago and her mother's lived in Florida and had little to do with her. With no real-life examples, Shelby had always had a rather idealized concept of what grandparents should be—paragons of wisdom and such. She had a feeling Mrs. Querida would come close to that ideal.

The older woman did not mind at all that Shelby dropped by without calling first.

"I'm happy you felt comfortable to do so," she said with a smile. "I'll put on a pot of coffee. You do drink coffee, don't you? But of course, I remember you do."

They sat in her kitchen, a bright and cheery room with the afternoon sun pouring in through the large sliding glass doors that led out to a small backyard. They drank from lovely china cups, and there was a tray of homemade cookies on the table. Mrs. Querida was indeed everything Shelby envisioned in a grandmother.

"I talked to Dolores yesterday," said Mrs. Querida.

"Was she still upset?"

"That is a woman who can hold a grudge better than anyone I know. It makes me wonder where I went wrong in raising her. Then I remind myself that in spite of her shortcomings, she is a good person at heart—and I hope that isn't just an indulgent mama speaking. She volunteers three days a week at a children's hospital, and she is chairperson for the fundraising committee of an East L.A. hospice. She also raises money to fund D.A.R.E. programs in several barrio schools. She fought to escape the barrio, but she hasn't forgotten those she left behind."

"I never thought she was anything but a good person. I imagine she suffered a lot over . . . her children's problems."

"I never believed you thought ill of Dolores, Shelby. I suppose I was merely relating her accomplishments for my benefit. I'm as proud of her as I am at times angry. And it does upset me how she treats poor Francisco."

"He is very special to you?"

Mrs. Querida nodded and sipped her coffee thoughtfully. "I like to think I love all my grandchildren equally, but he and I do have a special bond that only grew deeper with his mother's treatment of him. Yet that's not how it began. Francisco is very much like my husband, Arturo, who died when Francisco was a boy. Arturo was quite a rebel—that's why he was forced out of Mexico in the first place. But first he married me, daughter to his family's political rivals." She shook her head, smiling slightly at the memory. "We were the Mexican Romeo and Juliet. But the political intrigue of the Mexican government makes those in Verona seem tame. My family's party was in power at the time of our forbidden marriage. Soon after, Arturo's family staged a coup and forced us out, seizing the property of the most ardent supporters of the deposed regime, including my family. We were allowed to exile to our estate in Puerto Vallarta. But Arturo was furious at how we were treated—he had futilely hoped that my family would be spared because of our union. Anyway, he became involved in a counter-coup that failed and was finally forced to flee the country."

"What an exciting story!" Shelby exclaimed, only to be suddenly embarrassed at her enthusiasm over an account that could well be painful to the older woman. "I'm sorry . . . I'm sure it was a very hard thing for you both."

Mrs. Querida grinned. "We were young, and though it was hard, I suppose it was rather exciting, as well. Especially going to a new country and living for some time as illegals. It was humbling, too. We had been of the elite class in Mexico, but in America we had to start at the bottom with everyone else. The only work my husband could find was in the fields of the Central Valley. My Arturo had never done a stitch of manual labor in Mexico, but he worked hard in the fields and never complained—except about the abuse of the owners toward the workers. It wasn't long before he became involved in organizing workers. When Caesar Chevez came, Arturo eagerly joined his ranks. The rebel all the way."

"Yes, and from what he's told me, I can certainly see that attribute in Frank. He rebelled against his parents' social climb by continuing to identify with his barrio friends. He rebelled against their morals by getting involved with gangs and drugs. The difference seems that his rebelling was more self-destructive than his grandfather's."

"That is true." Mrs. Querida sighed heavily.

"I wasn't certain if I could talk with you about Frank," said Shelby, feeling more and more at ease with her new grandmother-in-law, "because I didn't know how much you knew about his . . . activities."

"Everyone has tried hard to spare me the whole truth. As if the frail old lady might not have the strength to bear it." Her lips parted again in a warm smile. "They still don't realize that I have a source of strength greater than they could ever imagine. Despite their attempts to protect me, I think I have a very good idea of everything. Ramon did not spend time in prison for selling candy. Yes, I know Francisco was involved in some very bad things and that Dolores is not imagining it when she accuses him of involving Ramon."

"But still you never rejected him yourself? You continued to love him?"

"I knew he needed my love even more because of all those things. But certainly that shouldn't surprise you, Shelby. You loved him anyway, too." Shelby frowned and Mrs. Querida added, "You didn't know about these things before you married?"

"Nothing specific. He wanted to tell me," Shelby added quickly, as if to defend Frank. "I didn't want to know about his past."

"Why is that?"

"I suppose I just . . ." But no ready response came to her mind except what Frank had told her. "Maybe I was just naïve."

"But now you know and are confused?"

"It doesn't change my feelings. It's just that there are times when he seems changed—nervous, tense, angry. Mrs. Querida, are you sure . . ." Shelby lifted her eyes to meet the older woman's with a searching gaze, ". . . he really has changed? That he is no longer involved in those other things?"

"We can only know by what we see. It is God who knows his heart."

"God . . ." Shelby murmured unconsciously. "I mentioned before, Mrs. Querida, that I've never been a very religious person. But lately I've been hearing a lot about God. The other day my mother told me she had started going to church—she said she'd 'become a Christian.' I guess I always thought everyone was Christian—well, in America, at least, except for Jews and Buddhists and such. But not everyone talks like you or she does. It's almost as if you know something the rest of us don't know."

Mrs. Querida smiled benignly. "Perhaps it is because we are getting to know God in a more personal way. Like a friend . . . an amigo."

"If you don't mind me saying, I especially haven't heard of Catholics talking the way you do. I thought it was all liturgy and ceremony."

"For some, yes. It is even so for some Protestants."

"Yes, I can believe that."

"I have been a Catholic all my life. And I myself at one time stood in mass and recited the prayers, or went to confession, or took communion entirely by rote—never thinking about what I was doing or what it all meant."

"Then what happened?"

"It was nothing spectacular, really. I think I began to draw closer to God because of Francisco—years ago when he first started getting into trouble. He was almost thirteen, failing school, getting suspended. I started praying for him, and I discovered that God was accessible to me without the intercession of a priest. God knew me and heard my prayers, and it was only a matter of time before I began to know Him."

"But God didn't answer your prayers. Frank only got in worse trouble and then involved his brother in trouble. That would have made me really wonder about God."

Mrs. Querida nodded, a slight smile still on her face. For a moment her gaze seemed not to focus on Shelby but elsewhere, perhaps inwardly, perhaps on the God she said resided there. "You would think so," she said at length. "But oddly, I was able to focus not on what I could see but rather on the hope God put into my heart. It is a hard thing to explain unless you've experienced it yourself."

Suddenly Shelby was uncomfortable with the subject. She began to fear Mrs. Querida would ask her if she wanted to experience it, if she wanted to become a Christian. Spiritual conversations with Aunt Lynn always ended that way. And Shelby would then slink away, feeling like a rotten sinner because she never saw the point in becoming a Christian. So now Shelby braced herself for the same scenario with her grandmother-in-law.

She was pleasantly disappointed.

"Would you like more coffee?" asked Mrs. Querida.

"What?" said Shelby, unable to mask her surprise.

"Coffee? I think it's still warm."

"Okay."

Mrs. Querida rose, got the coffee carafe, and brought it back to the table. As she refilled their cups, she asked, "When we are finished, would you like to see my wedding mantilla?"

"I'd love to."

Five minutes later, Mrs. Querida led Shelby to her bedroom. Here the furnishings were heavy, ornate mahogany with a definite Spanish flavor, and they seemed to predate the Queridas' arrival in America by many decades. Of course, the furniture could have been purchased from an antique shop recently, but Shelby thought otherwise.

"What wonderful furnishings," she said. "They seem quite old."

"This bedroom set has been in my family for a century and a half. We have been very lucky to preserve it through all the times of upheaval in our history. The pieces have always been passed on to the firstborn daughter as a wedding gift. I thought I would lose it when we came to America, but because it had been kept on the Puerto Vallarta estate, we were able to ship it here, though it was years before we could afford to do so." She ran her hand along the intricately turned rail of the footboard. "But my children preferred to have new American things, especially when they had the money to buy them."

Mrs. Querida went to a large chest that looked as old as the other bedroom furnishings and was of a style that Shelby could easily picture being on a Spanish galleon full of doubloons and treasure. When it was opened, Shelby saw it was filled with treasure of a different sort—mementos of a lifetime that had spanned seventy years. There were photo albums, trinkets made by childish hands, old clothes, and a couple of cigar boxes filled with more little treasures such as coins, matchbooks, and ticket stubs. Mrs. Querida lovingly set aside several items until she came to a box that was about the size of a coat box from a department store. She lifted this out and opened the lid. Inside was a plastic bag that, with Shelby's help, she took from the box and spread out on top of the bed. The mantilla was in the plastic and, though a bit yellowed, was marvelously preserved.

"I wish I could take it out of the bag for you," said Mrs. Querida, "but several years ago I noticed it was aging, so I had it sealed in this air-tight bag."

"That's okay. I'm pleased I can see it just like this. Is it handmade?"

"My grandmother made it for my mother's wedding." Mrs. Querida ran her hand lovingly across the plastic. "I did not have a big wedding myself because, as I said before, our families did not approve. Arturo and I had to go to Mexico City before we could find a priest to perform the ceremony. But before I left, my mother came into my room one night and told me that though she could not give her blessing to my plans, she loved me too much to let her only daughter go off without some token from her. And she gave me the mantilla, which I wore in our wedding. I have a picture. . . ." She turned to the dresser and lifted a framed photograph, handing it to Shelby.

"What a handsome couple," said Shelby, then looked closer at the photo. "Frank does favor your husband quite a bit." She handed back the picture. "Frank and I happened upon a wedding while in Mismaloya. I didn't get to see the bride because they were still in church and it was too crowded for us to get in. That's when Frank and I decided to get married."

"Do you wish you would have had a big wedding?"

"Maybe a gown would have been nice, but I have no family I cared about being there and only a few close friends. I suppose even if we had waited it would have been a small wedding—except, of course, for Frank's family. I don't know how many of you would have wanted to come."

"It's hard to say. Despite all the tensions, the family still gathers together for special occasions—Christmas, Easter, and such. They are not always happy gatherings, but Dolores insists on them because of how it would appear to others if her family did not do these things."

"Does Frank attend?"

"He makes an appearance, as does Ramon, but they never stay long."

"Mrs. Querida, did—" Shelby stopped, wondering about the wisdom of asking the question upon her lips. But her curiosity took over. "Did

Frank and Gloria have a big wedding?"

"Oh yes. Three hundred guests, as I recall. I don't think Gloria's father really approved of the match because he thought Francisco was a wild one, but Gloria was his only daughter and he spoiled her rotten, gave her anything she wanted."

"And she wanted Frank?"

"They wanted each other. But, Shelby, you must remember that was a long time ago."

"Frank said Mrs. Stefano was thrilled with the marriage."

"Gloria won her over completely."

"And you?"

"I mostly feared for them. Frank was a rebel and Gloria was so spoiled. I wouldn't let her wear the mantilla, though. She wanted to, and Dolores was furious at me, but . . . I just could not bear to do it." Mrs. Querida rubbed her chin thoughtfully. "It is a shame how it all turned out. So tragic. Gloria's life was always lived so much on the edge, as they say. In a way, I am not surprised that it ended in an untimely way."

"Frank has been very distraught by her death."

"Are you worried, dear, that he still loves her?"

"In my most insecure moments."

Mrs. Querida smiled and laid her hand on Shelby's arm. "Let me ease your mind about that."

"Are you going to tell me their marriage was stormy? Sometimes that is the strongest indicator of love."

"No, I wasn't going to say that—though it is true. What I was going to say was that I have seen Francisco look at you, Shelby, and I have never before seen such tender love in his eyes. You have no cause to worry."

As Shelby left Mrs. Querida, she clung to those words. It was almost as if the promise of his love was a lifeboat in the midst of a turbulent sea. And she feared what would happen if she ever let go.

20

She did not see Frank all the next day. Was he really going to continue to stay on the boat? How could they work through this if he stayed away? At one point she actually thought about praying for him to come back. But she didn't even know where to begin. Maybe Mrs. Querida was praying, because on Wednesday evening, as Shelby was thinking about facing another lonely dinner in a home that wasn't hers, she heard a sound at the door. She left the kitchen, where she had been idly rummaging through a cupboard, just as the door opened and Frank came in. She couldn't help the relieved smile that curved her lips. She would have run right into his arms, but his hands were full.

"Have you had dinner yet?" he asked, holding out the two bags in his hands.

Shelby shook her head, trying to calm the emotion she seemed to be feeling more than him. "There was nothing interesting in the kitchen."

"How about Chinese?"

"I love Chinese."

"Not as well as Mexican, though."

"Well enough. What have you got?"

"I brought a variety because I wasn't sure what you'd like. Sweet and sour pork, Szechuan beef, hot and sour soup, and shrimp fried rice."

"That ought to keep us fed for a couple days."

"Us. . . ?"

"Of course us." Shelby wasn't going to even entertain the thought that it might be otherwise.

"What about the other day?"

"All I know is that I miss you, Frank. You belong here—with me. Now, let's eat while it's hot."

They went to the kitchen, and Shelby got plates while Frank opened up all the little boxes. The conversation was kept purposefully light as they ate. There seemed to be no need to rehash everything that had already been said. Somehow they would work it out—and they would do it together. Shelby kept thinking about what Mrs. Querida had said. Wasn't the love they had for each other all that really mattered anyway?

"Shelby," Frank said as they ate, "I have to ask you something. I hate this, I really do, but I haven't got a choice."

"What is it, Frank?"

"I need some money."

"For Barcelona?" His pained nod told her this was extremely hard for him. "Don't stress over this, Frank. That's what marriage is about—sharing and being there for the other person."

"Several months ago I had some extensive work done on my boat. I was putting aside money in the bank to begin making payments to the boatyard. Now the owner of the boatyard has hit some hard times and needs me to pay him everything now. He's been patient with me all this time and—"

"Frank, you don't have to explain. What is mine is yours."

"I haven't told you how much I need."

"We haven't discussed money much," Shelby said. "There's been so much else to think about. But I have quite a bit of money from my father's insurance, social security, and various other funds from the fire department. How much do you need?"

"Five thousand."

The amount surprised her but she made a concerted—and she hoped successful—effort not to show it. Nevertheless, five thousand would not be difficult to get. "That's no problem at all."

"I'll pay you back."

"You don't have to—"

He shook his head adamantly. "I will pay you back. A man doesn't borrow money from his wife. I hate doing this."

"I'm not going to expect it, but if you feel like you must, I won't argue. Maybe someday we ought to sit down and discuss finances. Joint bank accounts or separate? Who pays the bills? Fifty-fifty or—"

Suddenly the doorbell intruded harshly. Shelby cringed. She could not recall a welcome interruption to any pleasant time they'd had together. She got up and answered it, knowing the moment the door was open that this time would be no different. It was the two detectives who had come before. As they were asking for Frank, he came into the room.

"I'm glad we could track you down, Mr. Stefano," said the one named Poole. "We'd just like a minute of your time."

"What is it?" Frank asked stiffly.

"Would it be possible for us to have a look at your boat?"

"Why?" An edge of hostility was now apparent in Frank's tone.

"We just want to check out the possibility that your ex-wife's body was taken out to sea to be disposed of rather than washing out from the shore."

"And the first place you want to look is my boat?"

"Well, it does seem logical. You never mentioned owning a boat."

"It didn't seem important."

"Well, it is now," said Liscom harshly.

"Do you have a warrant?" countered Frank.

"Now, don't start getting defensive again, Mr. Stefano. We just figured you'd want to cooperate. Have you considered the fact that someone might have stolen your boat for this purpose—while you were down in Mexico, perhaps."

"That's what you think?"

"We haven't formed any definite opinions at this time."

"Get a search warrant," Frank said and put his hand on the door to close it.

"We have a warrant," said Poole. "Nevertheless, your cooperation will mean a *lot* to us."

"I don't really care—"

"Frank," Shelby broke in, unable to keep silent any longer, "don't you think—"

"Be quiet, Shelby!" Frank snapped. "Don't interfere in this."

"I think you ought to listen to your wife," said Liscom, stepping ominously forward. "If we have to break down the doors and such, we could become very difficult to deal with later on."

"I'm not going deal with you—now or later."

"Frank, please!" said Shelby.

Frank glared at her and was silent for a long, tense moment before speaking. "Okay, what do I care? Search the boat. You won't find anything." He dug in his pocket and took out a ring of keys. "Do I need to go with you?"

"That's your choice, but it's not necessary," said Poole.

Frank handed him two keys from the ring. "Those will get you into the cabin and the lockers."

"We appreciate this," said Poole.

"How long will this take? I might use the boat in a couple days."

"We'll get the keys back to you in the morning."

After Frank closed the door behind the detectives, he and Shelby stood silently for a very long minute. Then he faced her.

"I'm sorry for yelling at you," he said quietly.

"It was a very stressful situation."

He nodded, then suddenly grabbed her and pulled her roughly to him, holding her so tightly it was uncomfortable. But Shelby said nothing. She could feel his arms trembling.

"The last thing I want to do is push you away," he murmured. "I need you so."

"And I need you."

"What's going to happen?"

"I'm afraid, too, Frank. We just have to keep remembering what we have—what we had in Mexico. I know now why it all happened like it did. It had to be so powerful to get us through what is happening now."

She felt his arms relax, though he still held her firmly. "I love you."

"That's all I need." Tears rose to her eyes.

"Dear God, I pray that is so." His voice trembled over the words.

Then there was a quiet knock at the door. This time it was Ray.

"Was that the cops?" he asked, his words quick and breathless. "Man, they're really hounding you, aren't they?" He walked with quick, hurried steps all the way into the living room. He seemed agitated or just in a big hurry. Shelby supposed that was to be expected, considering he probably was not on good terms with the police. "What'd they want? No, never mind—just nagging you about Gloria. What jerks! They've questioned me, too. I just couldn't avoid them any longer without looking suspicious. I keep telling you, Frank, it just ain't no use—they'll never give a guy credit for cleaning up his life."

"What do you want, Ray?" Frank broke into his brother's nervous chatter.

"I told you I needed to know about this weekend." Ray paced around the room, pausing to pick up random items and setting them down after barely taking note of them. Shelby wondered if he was high on drugs, though she'd had very little experience with addicts.

"What's happening this weekend?" Shelby asked.

"Haven't you even told her?" Ray asked, perturbed. "I thought that's why you needed time. I gotta know now."

"Nothing," Frank said to Shelby. "Ray and I were just talking about going to a regatta, that's all."

"What's a regatta?"

"It's when a lot of boats get together for a race or a series of races. No big deal."

"Sounds like fun," said Shelby.

"It's a blast," said Ray. "It'll be all weekend—sailing, partying. And I hear the weather will be perfect."

"Where is it?" Shelby was certain she and Frank needed a fun weekend.

"San Diego," said Ray. "We sail down on Friday and Saturday and come back Sunday and Monday. You gotta go, Shelby. You'll love it."

"No, you won't," said Frank. "You'll be bored. We just race—it's nothing like a relaxing sail."

"Sure it is!" encouraged Ray. "Oh, there are some die-hard racers there, but for the most part everyone is pretty laid back."

"It sounds like fun. I want to go," said Shelby.

"You'll have to miss school—"

"It's Martin Luther King's birthday. We get Monday off. That's probably why they planned the regatta this weekend. I can leave school right after class on Friday—"

"I tell you, you won't like it!" Frank's tone was hard, almost angry.

"Come on, Frank," snapped Ray. "Don't be such a wet blanket. She wants to go. We'll have a great time."

"I said—"

"If you don't want my company, Frank, just say it," Shelby cut in, tears of a different sort now filling her eyes.

"It's not that, it's just . . ."

"Maybe this marriage *is* a lost cause if you don't even want to spend a weekend with me!" Shelby said through a sob, then turned and fled down the hall to the bedroom.

Just as she stepped inside and closed the door behind her she heard Frank curse at his brother. Giving the door a firm shove she ran to the bed and threw herself on it, tears streaming from her eyes.

Five minutes later there was a soft knock on the door followed by

Frank's voice asking to talk to her. He must have taken her silence for assent, because a moment later he was sitting on the edge of the bed.

"Shelby . . ." He laid a hand gently on her back. "If you want to go, I suppose it'll be okay."

With her face buried in her pillow, her shaky voice was muffled. "I don't want to barge in where I am not wanted."

"It's not that. . . . It's hard to explain."

"Forget it, Frank. Don't even try. We both know what it is. No matter how often you tell me you love me and swear you need me, it's obvious you regret our marriage."

"That's the furthermost thing from the truth!" His tone was so intensely sincere. How could he not mean it? He leaned down and pressed his cheek against the back of her head. "I don't know what got into me. I guess I know too many men whose wives won't sail with them because of a bad experience, and I want so much for us to share my love for sailing. This will be a long sail, a big commitment for a novice."

"I know how much sailing means to you, and I want to share it with you, too. I don't want your boat to be the 'other woman.'" She turned her head and gazed into his dark, brooding eyes.

He smoothed damp strands of hair away from her face. "That would never happen. You are everything to me. And I want you to come with us to San Diego."

"Are you sure?"

He hesitated only slightly before answering. "Yes."

21

On Friday Shelby left school at twelve-thirty, as soon as the last child was gone. She drove directly to the boat, where Frank and Ray were stowing away their gear for the weekend. In the cabin, Shelby changed into jeans and a T-shirt. It was sixty-five degrees outside and the sky was clear and sunny, a perfect day for January. Ray's weather prediction seemed right on target.

The sail down the coast to Newport would take six hours, with another eight-hour sail on Saturday to reach San Diego in time for the afternoon race.

Shelby settled on the deck to enjoy the sail and discovered she was quickly growing to love Frank's hobby. Even Ray was good company, though he made frequent trips to the small lavatory below. Eventually Shelby realized the reason for these trips, especially after overhearing a heated exchange between Ray and Frank.

"You better not louse up this deal," Frank had said in a low, barely controlled growl.

"Don't worry about me," Ray had replied defensively. "My head is clear. I can do five grams a day and still be sharper than you ever were."

"You're going to fry your brain."

"My brain is just fine. What really worries me is that you've lost the

179

killer instinct—and that's what's gonna blow this thing."

"I told you—"

"Never mind," Ray countered sharply. "I'll cut back if that makes you feel better."

"It makes me feel better."

Shelby thought this must be the cause of Frank's tension, though she was surprised at their fierce drive to win the sailing competition. She hoped Frank would soon relax, as he always seemed to do when at the helm of his boat. Shelby decided to leave him to himself as much as possible, hoping this would help him regroup his frayed emotions. Also, since he hadn't been enthusiastic about her coming, she wanted to show she could be a good passenger and that her presence would not cramp his style.

When they were a few hours out of King's Harbor, Ray climbed to the upper deck where Shelby was leaning against the mast reading a paperback romance. He held out her sweat shirt.

"Wind's picking up," he said. "Thought you might want this."

"Thanks. I was just debating if I was cold enough to leave my comfy little nook." She took the sweat shirt and slipped it on.

"Mind some company?" he asked.

"Not at all." Shelby scooted over, and Ray sat down beside her. It was the first time since their voyage had begun that she remembered him sitting still. When he wasn't making his excursions to the bathroom, he was pacing the decks, pausing occasionally to make quick comments and small talk. As they sat, Shelby positioned herself so she could watch Frank as he steered the boat from the cockpit. He was facing them but not really looking at them, and there was enough distance between them so that he could not hear their quiet conversation. He certainly didn't appear interested in it, even if he could hear.

"Frank tells me you're a schoolteacher," Ray said.

"Kindergarten."

"Wow, that must be a kick. I don't think I could handle two dozen screaming kids all day long."

"I love it. I suppose I must have a knack for it. What do you do, Ray?"

He gave her a surprised look, then grinned. "You don't know?"

"Well . . ."

"Oh, you mean besides that." He laughed. "I don't have to do anything else. I've got so much money stashed away, I won't have to work for the rest of my life."

"I guess I had the impression that you owed—" Shelby caught herself before finishing, then added awkwardly, "I'm sorry, it's none of my business."

"Okay, so I talk big. I would have that kind of money, but I've made a few bad investments lately. I'll get back my stash before long." He began to fidget, picking up a nearby line and twisting it in his hands. "It isn't the most stable business, that's for sure."

"I guess that's why Frank got out."

"Frank lost his nerve—I'm sorry, I don't mean to put him down. I suppose you are the straight-arrow type?"

She nodded.

"You ever do anything?"

Shelby knew he meant drugs. She shook her head.

"None at all?"

"I never saw the point."

"Because you never tried." Ray reached into his pocket and took out a small plastic bag. "Have a little snort. You'll see how nice it is. It makes everything sharp and gives you incredible energy. There's nothing better." He thrust the bag toward her.

"No, thanks. I have quite enough energy."

"Well, if you change your mind, you know where to come. Of course, it's free for family."

"I'm really not interested."

Ray shrugged and stuffed the bag back into his pocket. He jumped up. "I don't know what my brother sees in this sailing thing. It makes me claustrophobic. Nowhere to go but a few feet of deck. I should have driven down to San Diego and met him there." He waked to the bow, then back again, sitting down next to Shelby once more. "I'm gonna drive back, even if I have to rent a car."

"I thought you were really into this regatta thing," said Shelby, confused.

"Oh . . . well, yeah. The regatta itself is a blast, it's just this long ride back and forth."

"I'm enjoying it," Shelby said. "It is so incredibly peaceful on the water."

"I guess, if you're into peace." He jumped up again. "I'll be right back," he said and went below.

Shelby turned her gaze on Frank. At that moment he was wearing a frown as he watched his brother duck into the cabin. Then he seemed to realize she was watching him and he turned his gaze toward her, smiling.

"Is Ramon keeping you entertained?" he called lightly.

"I sense he's getting restless. I hope he doesn't jump ship."

"I'm going to rent him a car for the trip back."

"I don't think he'll have any argument with that. Are you enjoying yourself, Frank?"

"I'm trying to unwind."

"I hope you can. I'll make sure not to bug you."

He made a few adjustments to the autopilot, then came up and sat next to her. "You'll never bug me, Shelby."

"I'll bet after a few years together we might occasionally bug one another," she teased.

"Never."

"You really are an idealist," she commented with some surprise.

"Only regarding you."

He took her into his arms and kissed her with more passion than she'd felt from him in a long time. Perhaps the sea air was helping after all. But the sound of Ray politely clearing his throat made them break apart.

"Okay, none of that," scolded Ray playfully. "I'm gonna get all red in the face and embarrassed."

"Oh, go below and have another snort!" Frank replied, only feigning anger this time.

Ray laughed. "Well, maybe you're finally loosening up." But before he turned to go, he added, "Give me a signal when it's safe to come up."

"It's never safe, bro."

"That's right, you're newlyweds."

They all tried to keep up the light banter for the rest of the sail. And they seemed to relax, though whether it was real or just an incredibly good cover-up, Shelby did not know nor did she care. She kept telling herself that fun was what they needed, and it didn't really matter how they achieved it. Well, she didn't care for Ramon's idea of "fun," but she tried to ignore that.

They spent the night on the boat in Newport. Ray was up all night, and his stirring around the cabin kept Shelby awake. Frank slept well and was in a good mood when he kissed Shelby an hour before dawn, slipped from the birth in the master quarters, and went up on deck to prepare the boat for departure. Ray had a pot of coffee going, and Shelby grabbed a cup from him like a lifeline after she staggered from her bed. Two cups later she felt human enough to join Frank on deck.

"Would you like breakfast?" she asked.

"I'll have something after we get underway."

"This is exciting," Shelby said, hugging her knees to her in the morning chill as she sat on the cockpit bench. "It'll make a great story to tell my class. How long till we reach San Diego?"

"We'll get there around two or three. They're forecasting a nice breeze out of the northwest that should give us a broad reach on a starboard tack most of the way down."

"I love your sailor lingo!" She grinned.

"I'm glad you're here, Shelby."

The winds were light through most of the morning and Frank had to start up the engine, but around noon the winds freshened and Frank raised the sails, keeping up a steady speed of five knots an hour most of the way. It turned into a clear but chilly day. Shelby spent a lot of time perched on the bow of the boat, watching the sea. A couple of dolphins appeared at the bow and swam with them for a time. Then, off the port bow, Shelby saw a marvelous sight. A flying fish ascended from the water and soared into the sky, spreading its magnificent wings. It traveled over a hundred feet before descending back into the water. Shelby ran below and got her camera in hopes of a repeat performance and was rewarded about half an hour later.

Frank set the autopilot and joined her. "I've got an idea, Shelby. Since you didn't sleep well last night, why don't we get a hotel room for tonight? We'll have a real shower and a bed that doesn't move, and best of all, Ray can stay on the boat. It'll be just you and me."

It sounded like a wonderful idea to her.

They sailed into the San Diego harbor around three o'clock and headed for the docks at the Four Winds Yacht Club, which was sponsoring the regatta. Several other boats were ahead of them, and it took a while for them to register and get a slip assignment. Most of the docks were full of activity. Everyone seemed to know one another and, as Ramon had said, there was a definite party atmosphere all over the marina. Many sailors called out friendly greetings to them as they docked, and one man on the dock helped them tie off the boat.

"You still don't have a name for this old scow," he said good-naturedly.

"Good things take time," said Frank. "How you doing, Joe?"

"Great. Long time, no see."

"Been busy," said Frank.

"He sure has been busy," Ramon added. "Got himself hitched."

"Well, congrats!" said Joe. Then to Shelby, "You must be the bride."

Frank made the introductions.

"Make sure you take good care of her," Joe stated. "She looks like a keeper."

"You bet she is," Frank said, and he put an arm proudly around Shelby.

Shelby sighed with contentment. This was how it should be—so normal, so fun.

The inaugural race was to begin at four or, in sailor's terms, sixteen hundred hours, and would end just before sunset. It was quite a sight to watch all the boats gather, their sails spread out against the blue sky. Unfortunately, the wind had died down to a faint breeze, and all the sails flapped rather loosely. Though Shelby thought it was a fine afternoon, Frank and the other sailors seemed concerned, and several suggested canceling the race.

"Can't race if we're dead in the water," Frank explained to Shelby.

"What about your motor?" asked Shelby innocently.

Frank laughed. "That would disqualify us."

"Not if everyone motored," offered Ramon. "I think it's a terrific idea. Anyway, we're up a creek if they cancel the race."

"What do you mean?" asked Shelby, now thoroughly confused.

"He doesn't mean a thing," Frank replied. "I think the wind will pick up."

The race started off slowly. The traditional jockeying for position was awkward and frustrating in the light air. Two boats collided and were spared serious damage only because there was so little wind. These conditions, however, gave the slower vessels a bit of an edge, and Frank took full advantage of this, managing to capture a good position when the pistol shot sounded the start of the race.

It was obvious Frank was pleased with his performance once the race was underway. Though he said it had been a while since he had raced, Frank gained ground on normally faster boats that were stalled in dead air. Shelby felt like an integral part of the race crew as she adjusted the spinnaker sheets with every shift of the wind. At the finish line, Frank praised her and said he couldn't have done it without her. And Ray, too, of course. Out of a field of fifty boats, when handicaps were figured, Frank came in sixth.

After the race they took off immediately for their hotel room, which Frank had reserved before the race. They had a great view at the San Diego Hilton, looking out on the beach. With visions of a passionate evening dancing in her head, Shelby turned from the window to embrace her husband, only to have him brush her aside as he began searching for the TV remote.

"What's the matter, sweetheart?" she asked tenderly, though unable to hide the surprise from her voice.

"Long day."

"I thought you were having such a good time it wouldn't matter."

He shrugged. "I don't know what it is."

"Why not let me give you a nice back rub."

"It's not my back," he said shortly.

"I have an idea. Let's order room service. We can have a quiet, relaxing dinner here, and then we can . . . see what happens." Shelby grinned mischievously.

"Tonight?" he said.

"Isn't that what getting a hotel room was all about? You know, a little romance?"

"You could be a little more sensitive. I'm exhausted."

"The room was your idea—"

"Yeah, so we could get some rest."

"I'm really confused, Frank."

He shook his head with frustration. "It's simple. Once again, we are on two different wavelengths."

"I didn't—"

"Look, I'm too exhausted to start sparring with you. I'm going back to the boat—maybe I can get some rest there."

"This is utterly ridiculous!" she exploded with as much frustration as anger. "I can't believe you are going to leave."

"Do you have to argue about everything?" he snapped. "You always have to get your way!"

"I . . . I just . . ." His outburst hit so suddenly she had no ready response.

"You're just a spoiled brat!" he added heatedly.

"That's not true. I just don't see the problem."

"The problem is you refuse to give me some space. Can't you back off a little?"

Tears replaced words as Shelby stared blankly at him. Maybe he was right. She thought marriage meant togetherness, but she must have blown it again. The idea of marriage had seemed so simple in lazy, balmy Puerto Vallarta. But in reality it was the hardest thing she'd ever attempted.

She watched in silence as he grabbed his duffel bag and left, slamming the door behind him.

22

FRANK'S MOOD WAS DEFINITELY SOUR as he stomped around the boat, barking orders at his brother, yanking harshly at lines, and nearly pulling winches out of their fittings.

"Get a grip, bro," Ramon said at one point.

"Shut up and bring in those fenders."

"What'd I do, man?"

"Because of you I had to pick a fight with my wife. She may never speak to me again."

"Ah, you know women. You'll buy her some flowers—heck, you can get her a nice diamond bracelet or something with the profits from this deal—and before you know it, she'll be eating out of your hand."

"You don't have a clue, Ray."

"What you need is to loosen up." Ramon took a Baggie from his pocket. "A little blow always did you good before."

Frank stared at the bag of cocaine. For a brief instant he was tempted. How else was he going to get through this night? For that matter, how was he going to make it through everything that was coming down—Barcelona's threats, the investigation of Gloria's death, not to mention the steadily growing discord in his marriage? A little coke might numb him just enough. . . .

Ramon chose that moment to open his bag, pinch some of the powder between his fingers, and inhale it—no need to hide his usage in the lavatory anymore. He grinned and thrust the bag out to his brother. Frank thought of his jumpy nerves and the prospect of having to meet drug dealers on a secluded Mexican beach in the middle of the night. He remembered his days of drug use and the sure escape it had provided. A couple of snorts now wasn't going to turn him into an addict, and it might just get him through a nightmare situation.

Then, as Frank's fingers closed on the bag, Ramon said, "I can't believe Shelby's never done anything, not even pot. How'd you ever hook up with a straight like that?"

Frank knew the answer to that question was also his best reason for not accepting Ray's offer. Shelby represented everything he so desperately wanted in life. He would never have found, much less attracted, a woman like her had he still been in the drug scene. And getting back into that scene would be the surest way of losing her. He had to help Ramon tonight, but he didn't have to get in any deeper. He had to keep believing there was still a way out for him—a way to have that normal life.

Frank clasped the bag in his hand and in a single quick motion, flung it into the water.

"Hey!" Ramon gasped. "Are you *loco*? That was five hundred dollars' worth of high grade—"

"I don't care. If you want my help, there's not going to be any more of that tonight."

"Gloria was right about you!"

"What do you mean?"

"She said you would hold me back and I was better off without you."

"Gloria was always right, wasn't she?"

"She was right in dumping you."

"And in turning around and snaring you." Frank faced his brother squarely. They had never spoken before of their individual relationships with Gloria. Yet Frank knew that as soon as Ray had been released from prison, he had started sleeping with Gloria. Frank had helplessly watched as Gloria manipulated and used Ray, just as she had used him. That's why he had gone to see her that last night—to make her let Ray go.

"You'll never let yourself see her as she truly was," Ray said.

"No, we split up because I finally did see what she was. I can't believe you are defending her, Ray." Did Ray truly think she had ever been faithful to him?

"Why shouldn't I?" Ray retorted defensively. "I loved her, man." Ray looked at the water, toward where the Baggie was being swallowed up by the swells. "And now she's dead. . . ."

"Do you know what happened to her, Ray?"

"How should I know? It's you the police are hounding."

"What's that supposed to mean? Do you think I killed her?"

"She's gone . . . so does it matter anymore?"

"It'll matter to me if I get arrested."

Ray jerked his head toward Frank. "They'll never arrest you. I mean, if you're innocent, how can they?"

Frank laughed at his brother's incredible naïveté. "You're kidding, right?"

Ray shrugged. "I'll never let it happen, bro."

"What can you do about it, Ray?"

The two brothers locked eyes, studying one another for a long moment until Ray shrugged again. "I'll find the real killer, that's what I'll do! It's probably the Columbians, maybe even Barcelona. I won't let you fry, man."

"Ray," Frank said softly but earnestly, "if I get arrested, I don't want you to do anything stupid, okay? Just let it be. I'll deal with it."

"You think you're the only one who can protect his brother?"

"Ray, just let it be!" Frank said more emphatically.

"Okay, bro," Ray finally said, "it's cool between us."

"We've got far more important things to think of anyway."

Frank gazed out at the dark horizon. The sky was full of stars and the half-moon was up. The gentle breeze didn't bother him because they were motoring. They would reach the rendezvous point in Mexico in another couple of hours. Yes, there was a great deal to think about—especially the fact that he was once again in the drug business.

As drug exchanges went, the upcoming deal with Manuel would probably be a cinch. Frank had been involved in many deals in which his primary goal had been to merely survive with his life. There was always the fear of either getting ripped off or, even worse, getting in the middle of a police sting. Every dealer had elaborate setups to prevent ever putting the drugs and the money together, for that only increased the potential for getting cheated and probably killed, as well. It was those very risks that had once appealed to Frank.

Manuel was a different case. Frank and Ray had dealt with him many times. There was a foundation of trust between them. There had been times, especially in the beginning before the money had started pouring in, that Manuel had given them pot on consignment until Frank had marketed the stuff in the States. Thus, as Frank motored into the hidden cove north of Ensenada, he had little reason for worry. He expected his anxiety to begin when they attempted to bring the drugs back into San Diego.

It was about one o'clock in the morning and very dark and chilly when Frank anchored in the cove and Ray lowered the dinghy into the water. The row to the beach would be short and easy. He and Ray left the dinghy's outboard motor on the boat not only to cut down on noise, but also to cut down on weight. As it was, the load of marijuana would fill the dinghy to capacity.

The beach looked deserted, but he expected Manuel and his men would keep out of sight until they were sure the approaching boat was their contact. With his flashlight, Ray gave the pre-arranged signal—two short flashes, a long one, and another short. In a few moments the response came—a long flash, a short one, and two more longs. Frank maneuvered the dinghy through the surf, a wet and rocky ride, and hoped the dope was wrapped well so it wouldn't get soaked on the row back.

He and Ray were dragging the boat up onto the beach when several figures began to appear on the beach. Manuel was leading the others and was recognizable even in the dark because he was a little man, just over five feet tall and wiry like a spider. He wore a heavy, drooping moustache that completely hid his mouth, so it was always hard to know if he was smiling or grimacing. But it was neither his moustache nor his expression that concerned Frank as he drew near to Manuel and his men. What worried him far more was the fact that the men were all heavily armed. Several carried M–16s with bandoliers of ammunition criss-crossing their chests and automatic pistols tucked into their belts; others had Uzis and rifles. One man had a very intimidating automatic shotgun. Some weaponry was to be expected; even Frank was carrying a little nine millimeter pistol, and Ramon had a hefty 357 Magnum under his belt. After all, they were breaking the law, and it was prudent to be prepared for anything. But Manuel's men appeared to be ready for guerrilla warfare.

"Que paso, amigo?" Frank called, and the conversation proceeded in Spanish, the only language Manuel was comfortable with.

"Hola, amigos!" said Manuel, and he shook hands warmly with Frank and Ramon, a rather unsettling gesture with an M–16 slung over his shoulder.

"Hey, Manuel," said Ramon, "what's with all the hardware?"

"You know this is a dangerous business," Manuel replied, and though he was trying to sound casual, Frank detected an edge to his tone. "The government is under a lot of pressure from the States to crack down on the trade."

"You assured my brother that the Federales were taken care of," said Frank.

"Yes, of course." There was an awkward pause before Manuel continued. "Well, then, let's get on with the exchange." He called over his shoulder, "Pablo, bring out the—"

"Hold on, Manuel!" Ramon interrupted. "What's the hurry?" In the past the men would often share a bottle of tequila before a deal.

"Tight schedule this time, that's all."

Frank never knew a Mexican to be pressed for time. *"Mañana"* time was more the rule south of the border.

Manuel told Pablo and several others to bring down the merchandise, and after they did so, he paused, his eyes scanning the rocks and crevices behind them. Something was definitely wrong, and Frank also turned his gaze toward the terrain surrounding the cove. He saw nothing, but a knot began to form in his stomach, nevertheless.

The kilos, all carefully wrapped in several layers of plastic, were brought down to the beach, where Ramon looked them over rather casually. With Manuel, there wasn't the need for the more exacting inspection. Frank felt no need to inspect them at all until he noted some packages that looked decidedly different.

"What's this?" he asked, picking up a bundle and looking it over.

"It's the coke. Thirty kilos, like we agreed," said Manuel.

Frank glanced at his brother, who squirmed a moment before responding defensively. "He's fronting the whole thirty keys—I couldn't pass the deal up."

Frank shook his head with frustration. What did it really matter? He was already in over his head. A little cocaine wasn't going to change things that much.

Manuel ordered his men to load up the dinghy, and the men responded double time.

"Look, Manuel," Frank said, "something's going on and I want to know what it is. Your men are behaving like scared jack rabbits."

"Like I said—"

"I thought we could trust you, but this is starting to look like a setup."

"No, Frank, it's nothing like that. We are compadres, you can trust me."

"Then what is it? I haven't dealt with you in a while, but things couldn't have changed this much in such a short time."

"I tell you, we've just got to get back to town. . . ."

"You never were a good liar, Manuel. Did the police get to you?"

"I swear, no! But . . ." Manuel's gaze scanned the hills again. "So much talk! We must hurry." He paused, fingered his moustache thoughtfully, then began again with resolve. "We were followed part of the way up here by the Federales."

"What!" exclaimed Frank and Ray in unison.

"We lost them. Not to worry." But the words were small comfort in view of Manuel's skittishness. "They don't even begin to know these hills like me and my men. They will never pick up our trail."

"Then why are you so nervous?"

"No sense in tempting fate, eh?"

"But you said you'd bought the Feds."

"Maybe someone gave them more."

"Who?"

Manuel shrugged. "Do you think I stopped to ask them? But I will tell you, I saw Ricardo Perez in town yesterday."

"Barcelona," breathed Frank.

"It's possible, but I don't want to waste more time with talk. We must be on our way. Where is the money?"

Ramon handed Manuel an envelope. The Mexican drug dealer took it, quickly checked the contents, then said, "We'll be in touch in two weeks to settle for the cocaine." Then he turned to his men. "*Ándele,* muchachos!"

The men needed little more encouragement than that before they turned and jogged away. Manuel said his good-byes and quickly followed. Frank and Ramon also lost no time in shoving off. It was slow moving in the loaded dinghy, and the last thing Frank wanted was to be caught by the Federales in such a vulnerable position. The ocean was rougher on the trip back to the boat, and the swells made it difficult to come alongside the boat, much less load their cargo. It took nearly an hour before all was loaded and the dinghy was secured aboard. Frank pushed the boat's engine to its limit to motor out of the cove.

Their clean getaway, however, did not ease his tension. When they were out to sea with the autopilot engaged, Frank turned to his brother and found him looking rather self-satisfied.

"You know this isn't the end of it," Frank said. "Barcelona could easily find out before we get to San Diego that his attempt to intercept us failed. That means we could be walking into anything when we dock."

"Why would he do this? He's just screwing himself. He's gotta know what I make from this deal will go toward paying him off."

"Maybe he doesn't want you to pay him off. Maybe he's looking for an excuse to kill you. Maybe he found out about your deal with the Columbians."

"So . . . now what?"

"We just have to stay one step ahead of him."

23

SHELBY SPENT A MISERABLE NIGHT in the hotel room. She kept thinking Frank would come back since the argument had been so petty. And though she was dead on her feet from the long day, she hadn't expected to sleep at all with her mind so full of worry and confusion. However, she finally did fall asleep a couple of hours before sunrise.

She was hardly refreshed when she awoke, but two cups of strong coffee seemed to clear away the cobwebs. It did little, however, for her emotions. She puzzled for a long time about what to do and finally decided to go to the marina and make the first move toward making up with Frank.

Shelby took a taxi to the marina and walked out to the dock only to find Frank's slip empty. It was seven in the morning and all the other slips were occupied. There was little activity since the second race would not start until ten. No doubt the boaters, having partied late last night, were still sleeping. Except Frank. Why had he left so early? Or had he gone out last night and stayed out? A sudden panic gripped her. What if something had happened to him out there? She hoped Joe might know Frank's whereabouts, but all was quiet at Joe's boat.

Shelby walked to the public marina adjacent to the yacht club, where there was a coffee shop. After getting something to eat, she mentally chewed on the awful way her life was turning out. Was her marriage over? What Frank had said about her not giving him space kept replaying in her mind. Earlier she had been afraid of just the opposite—the fact that with their different schedules they hardly saw each other. Now she was more confused than ever. Perhaps he suddenly realized he had made a mistake and was just looking for a good excuse to end the marriage. Demoralized, she shook her head. Even her mother's four marriages had lasted longer than a few weeks.

Shelby walked around the marina for a long time, trying to sort it all out. When she finally returned to Joe's boat at about eight-thirty, her mind was not a bit clearer.

Joe was reclining in the cockpit, his hand wrapped around a cup of coffee.

"Hi," he said in a friendly manner, though there was a slightly perplexed look in his eyes.

Shelby realized how this must look. Frank was gone and here she was still at the dock. She tried to think of some excuse but drew a blank. Anyway, why be coy? If Joe knew what Frank was doing, she wanted to know.

"You wouldn't by any chance know where Frank is?" It was a difficult question to ask of a stranger.

"I noticed his slip was empty," said Joe. Maybe he also noticed her woeful expression and felt sorry for her, for he asked, "You want some coffee?"

"I've already had four cups this morning—way over my limit. You'll be scraping me off the walls if I have more."

"You're welcome to hang out here until Frank comes back. My wife will be up any minute."

Shelby climbed aboard and visited with Joe a few minutes until their conversation was interrupted by static from Joe's VHF radio.

"Four Winds Yacht Club, this is sailing vessel *Gloria's Barge*. . . ."

Joe ducked into his cabin and turned up the radio. Frank's voice called the yacht club twice more before there was a response.

"Four Winds Yacht Club here. Switch over to channel twenty-two."

Joe switched his channel so they could hear the exchange.

"This is Frank Stefano. Is there someone on the race committee I can talk to?" Frank's voice asked.

"I'm on the committee, Frank. This is Wayne Sullivan" came the reply from the yacht club. "How can I help you?"

"I anchored out in the bay last night," said Frank, "and now I've overslept. Can I forgo the skipper's meeting for the race and just connect out in the water?"

"Sure, Frank. You know the drill since you've done it a few times before. See you out there."

"Thanks, Wayne. Out."

Joe turned down the radio. "Well, there's a mystery solved."

"Well, I'm glad he's okay" was all the response Shelby could muster. Maybe she had made more of the situation than was there. Perhaps he was truly okay, in every way. Maybe their marriage wasn't over. She tried to ignore the fact that he'd used the boat's old name. He probably had no choice.

"I've gotta get moving, too, to make it for the race," Joe said. "Do you want to come with us?"

"I'd probably just be in the way."

"We can always use ballast."

Shelby laughed. "At least I'm good for something." She couldn't help feeling slightly pleased at joining up with Frank's competition. She saw herself waving gaily at her husband as Joe sailed first across the finish line. It was a petty and immature image, but satisfying nonetheless.

Joe finished tenth. Frank was among the last finishers. Shelby waited for him on the dock by his slip. She saw him come into the marina waters and was wondering what she would say to him when two men and a woman in coast guard uniforms walked up to her on the dock.

"Hello, ma'am," said the woman. "Are you waiting for vessel number CF109873?"

"Well, I don't know its number."

"The owner is Frank Stefano."

"Yes. Is there something wrong?"

"Just a routine inspection, ma'am."

That did not ease Shelby's mind, especially since this was the second time in less than a week that someone wanted to "inspect" Frank's boat. But Frank did not look concerned as he eased his boat into the slip. In fact, he gave Shelby a grin that should have made all her fears vanish. She wanted to rush into his arms and put the weekend fiasco behind them.

Frank tossed a line to one of the guards, then when the boat was secured he cut the engine.

"Are you Mr. Stefano?" asked one of the men.

"Yes. What can I do for you?" asked Frank.

"We'd like to board and inspect your boat."

"Is this a safety inspection?"

"We'd just like to board, sir."

Frank shrugged. "Okay, no problem."

The guards boarded, but Frank jumped off and went directly to Shelby.

"I'm a jerk," he said. "A rotten, lousy jerk. I don't deserve to be forgiven, but I swear I will make all this up to you someday." She could tell he wanted to embrace her, but he was holding back, no doubt to allow her a chance to make the first move.

And of course she did. Shelby reached out to him, and that was all the encouragement he needed before gathering her to him and holding her with incredible intensity, even for him. But the coast guards had no respect for their reunion. The woman jumped onto the dock.

"You're from King's Harbor?" she asked.

"Yes, I'm here for the regatta."

"Have you taken your boat anywhere else in the last twenty-four hours?"

"No, of course not. This isn't just a safety inspection, is it?"

"We received an anonymous call that your boat was carrying contraband."

"Contraband?"

"Specifically, controlled substances."

"Drugs? That's ridiculous."

"Well, we have to follow up such tips. We are sorry if it is inconvenient for you."

Several minutes later the other two coast guards came ashore.

"It's clean," said one.

The other added, "Did you come from King's Harbor without any kind of lifeboat or dinghy?"

"I had a dinghy, but we hit some rough waters on our way down the coast and lost it."

"I suggest you replace it before you head back. Your insurance will probably cover it."

"My thought exactly," Frank replied. "Anything else, officer?"

"That's all," said the woman. "Again, we apologize for the inconvenience."

The coast guards left, and Frank helped Shelby board. He immediately sat down on a bench, stretched out his legs, and leaned his head back against a forestay. He looked exhausted. Shelby sat next to him.

"Frank, I hadn't even realized the dinghy was gone. Are you sure everything's—wait a minute! Where's Ray?"

"I didn't want to get into it all with the coast guard," he sighed. "Ray and I anchored out in the bay last night, and then we had a fight. He took the dinghy to shore. If you haven't seen him, I don't know where he is. He was so mad I wouldn't doubt if he scuttled the dinghy. But I don't care about Ray. I'm glad he's gone. Now you and I can enjoy the rest of the day and sail alone back to King's Harbor."

Shelby wasn't concerned about Ray, either. It might have been his presence that had been the catalyst for all Frank's tension. She was feeling more and more certain that life would be so much better if family were left out of their relationship.

24

ON WEDNESDAY, FRANK'S SISTER CARLA had called and said it would mean a lot to her if Frank and Shelby came to her daughter Susie's *quinceañera* celebration. Shelby was not surprised Frank had ignored the upcoming event, which was planned for Saturday, a week after the regatta. She, too, would rather not attend, since no family gathering thus far had been pleasant. But this time there was more to it. On Friday there was also to be a luncheon for ladies only to honor Susie, and Carla really wanted Shelby to come.

"The quinceañera is a really big deal in the Mexican culture," Frank explained to Shelby. "And as Americanized as my family is, there are still cultural traditions we cling to—the older folks especially. I'm sure this is as much for my mother's and grandmother's benefit as it is for Susie's. She's the first grandchild to turn fifteen."

"So this is sort of a birthday party?" asked Shelby.

"That and an old-fashioned coming-out party all rolled into one. In the old days, of course, it was to let everyone know you had a daughter of marrying age and to display her before husband material. Now it's just . . . tradition. Carla would have a coronary if Susie married at fifteen or even eighteen. It's just an excuse for a party."

"And I'm always saying we need to have more fun."

He smiled. "But I bet this wasn't what you had in mind."

"Not exactly. Still, maybe if we keep working at this family thing, we'll get it right eventually."

Frank's smile faded, but he kissed her and told her how much he appreciated her.

On Friday, Shelby arranged to leave school after the last child was dismissed. She was grateful to work for a principal who allowed fairly flexible hours for her teachers who often put in hours over and above their contracts.

Shelby was hurrying to her Mustang with just enough time to get to the restaurant in Malibu. She opened the car door and was about to get in when she heard her name called.

"Shelby, I'm glad I didn't miss you."

"Dawn. What a surprise!"

Dawn smiled a warm, disarming smile. "I guess I didn't call ahead again. Sometimes I tend to be a little impulsive."

That, of course, was an understatement, but Shelby had the grace not to state that fact. Instead, she said, "That's okay, but it is really a bad time. I have to be in Malibu in an hour."

"I was hoping we could have lunch or something. Maybe another time."

"Why don't we schedule something right now."

"You mean plan ahead?" Dawn giggled. "That'd be novel. When?"

"How about . . ." Suddenly Shelby had a totally impulsive idea herself—after all, she was Dawn's daughter. Despite everything, she had to admit Dawn was her mother and could very well act as an ally, especially in a situation in which Shelby expected to be little more than a stranger. "Dawn, would you like to join me now? I'm on my way to have lunch with all the ladies in my husband's family."

"All of them, huh? It sounds like you aren't looking forward to it."

"Well . . . some of them—specifically my mother-in-law—can be pretty intimidating. I guess it would be nice to have someone there on my side. I mean, that is, if you . . ." She regretted the presumption of her words. She had been hostile to Dawn all her life. To invite her into her life not only felt strange but also seemed a bit self-serving.

Dawn only grinned. "I'm glad I can finally do you some good, Shelby. Let's go!"

Dawn followed Shelby in her rather worn Honda to the upscale Malibu restaurant. It was a trendy place that Shelby later found out had been Susie's choice. Shelby hoped the family would be gracious about receiving an uninvited guest and was nervous as the hostess led them to the private room where the luncheon was being held.

Carla, whom Shelby remembered from that ill-fated dinner at Mrs. Stefano's, came to greet them at the arched doorway.

"I'm so glad you came," she said and really seemed to mean it.

"I hope you don't mind that I brought a guest," said Shelby.

"I popped in on her unexpectedly," put in Dawn.

"Carla, this is my mother, Dawn—" Shelby was about to say her mother's last name, then suddenly realized she didn't know, after four marriages, what surname her mother was using these days.

"Your mother! How wonderful. We're all family now, aren't we? Come in and sit down. We have an extra place." Carla turned to the group already gathered and introduced Shelby and her mother.

There were about twenty women of varying ages seated around the large table. Two of the women were nuns, several were Susie's cousins and friends, and the rest were eventually introduced as various aunts, great-aunts, and second cousins. Mrs. Querida gave Shelby a welcoming smile, while Mrs. Stefano gave her a brief glance and a stiff, perfunctory smile. Shelby wondered what Frank's mother thought of Dawn as they studied each other after being formally introduced. The stately, somewhat matronly Dolores could not have been too many years older than Dawn, yet Dawn almost fit in better with Susie's teenage friends.

What a crowd! Shelby thought ruefully as she sat down next to her mother, determined to have a good time—or at the very least, survive the afternoon.

The chatter around the table during lunch was lively, with half a dozen conversations vying for space. Shelby, seated between her mother and Tomas's sister-in-law, joined in whatever discussion happened to catch her attention, limited mostly to the women nearby. Tomas's sister-in-law insisted Shelby call her Aunt Bev, then asked politely about Shelby and Frank's wedding. Relieved she had brought along photos, Shelby got them from her purse but realized her mistake too late.

"Guess what, everyone? Shelby brought pictures of her and Frank's wedding," Bev announced, drawing the attention of the whole group.

Shelby cringed, not wanting her photos—or herself—to be in the spotlight. This was Susie's day, not hers. But the damage was done.

The photos went around the table, and when they reached Mrs. Stefano, Shelby simply could not keep from looking in her direction to note her reaction. She gave them as perfunctory a perusal as she had given Shelby herself.

"Too bad you didn't wait for a big wedding," Dolores commented.

"I've never cared much to have a big to-do made over me," Shelby said.

"Oh, but not even a decent gown!" Dolores sighed. "All my married children had nothing but the finest weddings. Carla's gown cost fifteen hundred dollars. Maria's gown was less because she wanted a honeymoon trip to Europe."

"But the dress still cost at least a thousand dollars," boasted Maria, "and there were two hundred guests at the reception with a sit-down dinner and champagne flowing like water. A day I'll never forget!"

"But even I have to admit my daughters' weddings were a shadow compared to Frank and Gloria's wedding," continued Dolores. "You would have thought she was royalty for all her father spent."

"Didn't her gown cost five thousand dollars?" said Aunt Bev.

"At least," said Dolores. "They had it designed especially for her—"

"Mother," broke in Carla, "I don't think Shelby wants to hear about Gloria's wedding."

"Nonsense!" said Dolores. "I'm sure she is secure enough in her marriage not to be bothered. Aren't you, Shelby?"

"Of course," answered Shelby, knowing her response was a lie. She only hoped no one else noted the lack of confidence echoed in her words. She kept thinking of the wedding photo she'd seen . . . that breathtakingly beautiful woman had once been Frank's wife. And she remembered the loving look on Frank's face in that photo and how distraught he had been over the news of Gloria's death.

"Well, I don't know this Gloria person," said Dawn with a pointed look at Dolores, "but even in a simple embroidered peasant dress, Shelby is stunning. I suppose some people need more froufrou than others."

Shelby wanted to hug her mother.

But Dolores was responding. "You certainly didn't know Gloria. She was the most beautiful girl I've known. Why, she could have been a model. Even my daughters, as lovely as they are, would have to admit that. Surely you wouldn't speak so of a woman who has so recently died."

"I didn't know that," said Dawn apologetically. "I didn't mean to offend, but—"

"The waiter wants to know if we are ready for dessert," broke in Carla, much to Shelby's—and no doubt everyone's—relief.

After the orders were taken Shelby seized the opportunity to excuse herself to the rest room. Hopefully when she returned the women would have forgotten weddings and would be chasing after mundane topics that had nothing at all to do with Shelby.

In the rest room, Shelby took a couple of deep breaths, then ran a comb through her hair. Her reflection in the mirror made her think once again of Gloria's image in the photograph. Shelby's father had raised her not to put great stock in physical appearance, and she had never been overly consumed with her looks. She was attractive, Shelby knew that, but not stunning as her mother had tried to convince everyone. Nevertheless, it was something she had given little thought to until now. She was absolutely plain compared to Gloria, who was the kind of beauty that turned heads—both of men and women.

And Frank had cared for her, held her, kissed her with those full, desirable lips—

"There you are!"

Shelby gasped and dropped her comb in the sink. "Hi, Mrs. Stefano," she said weakly.

"Carla thought I should come and talk to you. She thought I might have hurt your feelings."

"Oh no, not at all. . . ."

"Well, that wasn't my intention," Dolores continued, ignoring Shelby's stammered denial. "It's just that . . . well, it's so hard, you know, dealing with Gloria's death. She meant so much to me. I can honestly say she had become like a daughter. She was such a delightful girl."

"I'm sure she was."

"I was so happy when she married Frank. I think if they had stayed together longer she might have been able to straighten him out. But then, I can't blame her for leaving. . . ."

"She left him?" Shelby had just assumed because of Frank's comments that he had never loved Gloria, that he'd ended the marriage.

"Oh yes. She simply could not take the drugs and all the . . . you know, criminal activity. She married him thinking he had quit all that. But he had fooled her."

"Fooled her. . . ?" A lump swelled in Shelby's throat. This was not at all how she'd imagined it.

"I know he's my son, but I have had to accept the fact that he is simply no good. I'm sorry if that disturbs you. I hope for your sake it isn't true. But I think you ought to realize you might have gotten into something you may regret. At least Gloria was smart enough to end it. I just hope it didn't destroy her anyway."

"What do you mean?"

"There are rumors, you know, that her death wasn't an accident."

"It might have been suicide—"

Dolores's sharp laughter cut Shelby off. "She would never have killed herself. Never."

For a long, awkward moment the two women just stood there and stared at each other.

Then Dolores said, "Anyway, I just wanted you to know how I felt. Forgive me if I sounded rude before. Perhaps someday I will feel for you as I did for Gloria, but I doubt it. Truly, it has nothing to do with you. I simply don't think you will be around long enough. I believe you will see my son for what he is, and then you will get out. That is, if you are lucky."

"How can you say such things about your own son, Mrs. Stefano?" Shelby shook her head in disbelief. "You must feel some affection for him."

"He killed my feelings when he destroyed my baby, my Ramon. Take my advice, Shelby, and leave him. Don't wait as long as Gloria did. Her faith kept her in the marriage because as a Catholic she believed divorce was wrong, but you don't have that to hold you. I guess being a heathen has its merits."

"I . . . I . . ." Shelby was too stunned to say anything that made sense. How could two people have such a completely different perspective of the same person? And even more mind-boggling, how could a mother so spitefully reject her son? What was wrong with the woman? What was wrong with that family? Or was it Shelby that was wrong—in her perception of the man she loved?

The rest room door opened again, and this time it was Dawn. Shelby instinctively knew her mother had come to rescue her.

"Busy place," said Dawn brightly.

"I was just leaving," Dolores said, quickly exiting.

"You okay?" Dawn asked when they were alone.

"Yeah . . . I guess so."

"I see you weren't exaggerating about your mother-in-law."

"You only know the half of it, Dawn."

"Do you want to leave?"

"No," Shelby replied with such conviction it surprised even her. "I won't be bullied."

"Good for you!"

Shelby managed a tentative smile. "I really appreciate you sticking up for me."

"That's what I'm here for. But you ought to know, you aren't completely alone in your new family. Carla was furious with the old bag—I mean your mother-in-law. She made her come in and apologize."

"I hope there wasn't a scene."

"Not much. Although Mrs. Stefano didn't look very apologetic when I came in."

"She wasn't, really. Maybe we can talk about it later. I want to return to the party. I just hope it's not ruined for poor Susie."

25

SHELBY INVITED DAWN to her place after the luncheon. Perhaps of all the unbelievable events of the day, this was the most. She actually *wanted* to spend more time with her mother. It still was a bit hard to admit, and even harder to discover, that Dawn wasn't such a horrible person after all.

"This is a nice place," Dawn said as she sat on the sofa. "No wonder you decided to live here instead of Whittier."

"It was good for me to get away from the memories."

"I hope you don't forget the memories altogether, Shelby."

"I won't. It's just that it was pretty hard being so close to Dad's things when I miss him so much."

"He was a good man. One of the best. You wouldn't have turned out so well if he hadn't been."

Shelby smiled awkwardly. "Would you like something to drink?"

"Sure."

"How about some juice?"

"Perfect."

Shelby went to the kitchen. "Do you want to come in here?" she called. "I've got to mix some up."

"Don't go to any trouble," Dawn said, joining her.

"It'll only take a minute. Have a seat." Shelby got a can of frozen juice from the freezer and a pitcher from a cupboard, glad for something to do as they talked. "Dawn," Shelby asked after a few moments of silence, "what really happened between you and Dad? You don't seem to hate him, and he never—well, almost never—spoke ill of you."

"That was so long ago," Dawn replied slowly, thoughtfully. "I think your dad and I got together for all the wrong reasons. He was this stud fireman and I didn't look too bad, either. We made a beautiful couple. That's what we were looking for. People envied us. But not long after we married, I realized I did not like the life of a fireman's wife—the risks he took, his long hours. I was just too self-centered to handle not being the center of Mike's life. I started drinking and partying. Then I had this one-night stand. It meant nothing to me, but, of course, he was pretty upset about it when he found out. We were going to separate when I found out I was pregnant with you."

"Dawn," Shelby said with a terrible knot in her stomach, "are you sure he's really my dad?"

"I'm sure. You don't have to worry about that. I didn't really go off the deep end until after you were born. Mike and I stayed together because of you. Mike made sure I didn't drink or anything while I was pregnant. He was a real macho guy, but I think his maternal instincts were greater than mine. But . . . you need to understand, Shelby, I was so immature, such a baby myself. I was barely nineteen when you were born. Mike was gone a lot with his job, and I was stuck at home. I couldn't handle it. He spent a lot of nights at the fire station, and while he was gone, I'd slip out and party, leaving you alone. I got into drugs and men and everything. But that didn't get to Mike as much as me leaving you alone. Wow! Was he furious when he found out. He kicked me out."

"He did?"

"Who could blame him? I deserved it. And deep down that's what I wanted—I didn't have the nerve to walk out on my own. But Mike didn't force me to stay away. He would have let me see you. I couldn't, though. You scared me. Being a mother scared me. Sometimes it still does."

Shelby filled two glasses with ice. A month ago she would not have understood how a relationship could deteriorate, nor how a person could be too scared to face life's responsibilities. Now she could actually sympathize with Dawn. Shelby's problems with Frank were of an entirely different sort, but they had still shaken her black-and-white perspective of life. Suddenly love was not all a relationship needed to survive. Shelby sighed as she poured juice into the glasses and carried them over to the table.

"You loved Dad, didn't you?" Shelby asked as she sat at the table opposite Dawn.

"Yes."

"I think he still loved you. That's why he never remarried."

Dawn let an ironic smile play at the corners of her lips. "People can be so stupid sometimes." She sipped her juice. "I mentioned the last time we spoke that I'd become a Christian. Well, I've often wondered how things might have turned out if I'd looked to God sooner. Do you think Mike and I would have stayed together and raised you?"

"I'm the last person to know answers to questions about God," said Shelby. "Maybe that's the problem with my marriage," she added without thinking.

"Oh, Shelby . . ." Dawn reached across the table and patted Shelby's hand.

"I wasn't going to say anything. I don't even want to think about it." Shelby lifted her eyes and met her mother's, finding such understanding and real concern that sudden tears rose in her eyes. "I don't know what's happening. . . ." The tears spilled down her cheeks, and she brushed them away with the back of her hand. Before she knew it, she was telling Dawn everything—Frank's family and all that Mrs. Stefano had said in the rest room, Frank's moods, and the arguments that seemed to spring from nowhere. And about Shelby's fear that, though dead, Gloria was still a part of Frank's life.

"What have I done wrong?" Shelby asked tearfully when she finished.

"It sounds to me like you are doing as well as anyone could."

"Is it Frank, then? Did I make a mistake? Did I misjudge him terribly?"

"I don't know, Shelby."

"Here's the strange part. I still feel so sure we are right. That it wasn't a mistake. But I do waver when his own mother tells me what a horrible person he is. Sometimes I think I've married two men, like good and evil twins. Wouldn't that be a hoot!" A tearful giggle escaped her lips.

Dawn smiled, too. "If only it could be so simple, huh?"

"Isn't there something religious to say about all this? Aunt Lynn would think of something."

"Yes, she would," said Dawn with a slight smile. "Me, on the other hand . . ." She shook her head. "I can barely keep my own head above water. I wish I could give you some answers. I guess I'm about as good a Christian as I am a mother."

"That's okay, Dawn. I love Aunt Lynn, but sometimes her answers were just a bit simplistic."

"That's the beauty of faith—it is simple. It couldn't have appealed to someone like me otherwise."

"Why do they have stores full of books on the subject, then?"

"If you really are interested in all this, Shelby . . ." Dawn faltered, looking embarrassed.

"What, Dawn?"

"I told you I wouldn't try and convert you, and I mean it. That's not my thing. But . . . well, if you're interested . . ."

"Yes?" Shelby could have cut off what she knew was coming, but she didn't. Maybe she *was* interested.

"I go to a great church, and maybe sometime . . . you might want to come with me. Only if you want to."

"I don't know about going to church," Shelby hedged. "I'd feel so weird."

"I felt that way, too, at first, but now I enjoy going. It's just that I can't answer your questions, but I know someone at church could."

"Can you tell me one thing, Dawn?" Shelby sipped her juice as her mother nodded. "What made you become a Christian? I know you said before that your life was messed up and all, but why not some other religion?"

"I'm not a philosopher or anything," Dawn answered. "I don't know a lot about other religions, but I did have a boyfriend who was into all that Eastern stuff. It went way over my head, you know, philosophically. On the other hand, Christianity is simple. Oh, it can be complex, too, but the bottom line of Christianity is so very easy. 'God so loved the world that he gave his only son that whoever believes in him shall be saved.'" Dawn paused and blushed. "That's a verse I memorized. Shelby, God's unconditional love is what it all means to me. I don't have many friends. Women are threatened by me because of my looks, and men use me. I was always alone even when I was with people. I've found a friend in Jesus who has no agenda with me except to be there for me, to love me. I'm not alone anymore." She smiled, and Shelby could see that what Dawn was saying was truly more than mere words to her.

"You sound a lot like Frank's grandmother," Shelby said, her voice full of the affection she felt for Mrs. Querida.

"It was nice to meet her today. I'd really like to meet Frank, too."

"Hey! I have an idea. Why don't we go to Frank's restaurant now? You could meet him, and maybe we could have dinner while we are there."

"I'd love to, but I have to go to work tonight. Let's do it another time."

"Okay. Where do you work, Dawn?"

"I'm a waitress at a steak house. I never did finish high school. I'll tell you, Shelby, I was never prouder than when I watched you graduate from college."

"You were there?"

"Yeah. I was going to say hello, but you and your dad were hugging, and I just didn't feel I belonged. I had no right sharing the spotlight since

I'd had no part in it. But I was still proud."

"I'm sorry."

"It's in the past. I know we can never forget it, but . . ."

"We don't have to dwell on it anymore," Shelby finished for her mother.

Dawn smiled. "I hope so." She rose. "Thanks for a wonderful day."

"I had a great time, too. Let's do it again."

Shelby walked her mother to the door. Then, completely on impulse, she leaned toward Dawn and gave her a hug.

"Oh my!" Dawn said, tears welling in her eyes. "Thank you."

Shelby watched her mother walk away. Sometimes her impulses did pay off. Sighing, she wondered about the last big impulse of her life—her hasty marriage. Would it come out all right in the end? Would she and Frank have many long years together and have children and grand-children? Was it truly possible for them to be like the family in Frank's photo?

Even as she clutched at the hope of that happening, she recalled Mrs. Stefano's ominous words. *"I believe you will see my son for what he is, and then you will get out."*

Sighing, Shelby plopped down on the sofa. What are you, Frank? Are you the man I thought I was marrying in Puerto Vallarta? Are you the man that my heart loves? Or is my heart too blind to see the truth?

"Oh, God, I don't know if I have a right to pray to you. . . . I suppose I have to repent first. I'm not ready to do that. But if I could just ask you one thing—" Shelby stopped and shook her head. "Never mind . . ."

It was a silly notion, asking favors of someone she didn't know—and she didn't know God. It was foolish to think He'd listen to her, especially if she was unwilling to make any commitment to Him. Yet if there was anything she needed now, it was a friend like the one her mother spoke of, whose friendship and love were completely unconditional. Unfortunately, Shelby wasn't quite ready to give so freely of herself.

26

THE STEFANO FAMILY MIGHT NOT get along with one another, but they did know how to throw a party. The quinceañero for Frank's niece was an affair every bit as lavish as a wedding. It was held in the ballroom of the Hyatt Regency, and there were about seventy-five guests, an equal mix of Mexicans and gringos, teenagers and older folks. Susie's friends came as couples and were decked out as if for a prom. She wore a white satin sheath-style gown, completely unadorned except for rhinestone spaghetti shoulder straps. She looked very grown-up. As in a wedding, she had attendants, six of them, wearing identical burgundy gowns and carrying bouquets of gardenias. They arrived at the hotel in limousines. The music performed by the live band ranged from south-of-the-border to '60s rock 'n' roll to rap. The dancing was kicked off with a traditional waltz with Susie and her father. When Shelby commented on how well Susie handled the waltz, Frank said there had no doubt been several rehearsals prior to the event to assure all would come off perfectly.

After the first dance, everyone joined in. Even Mrs. Querida waltzed with Frank and Tomas. And there was no major discord during the evening. Ramon even made an appearance, breezing into the party like a five-minute hurricane, then leaving before anyone could react. Frank and his mother were able to avoid each other without drawing attention to the fact. Frank even relaxed a bit—though that might have been due to the free-flowing champagne and tequila. Nevertheless, he seemed far more his true self.

Tomas Stefano also had more than his share of alcohol. He didn't become obnoxious, but he did laugh a lot, which Frank commented was quite unusual for the normally stoic man. At one point he asked Shelby to dance with him to "Yesterday" and showed himself to be quite a good dancer, even with a partner who was unrehearsed and untrained. When the song was over, he took Shelby's hand and led her toward the refreshment table.

"I'm parched," Tomas said. "Let me buy you a glass of champagne." He grinned at this because as one of the hosts of the party, he was buying all the champagne.

Shelby followed him across the crowded dance floor. She wasn't especially thirsty, but she certainly was not going to refuse any invitation from her father-in-law. She glanced back at Frank, but he only smiled and nodded, making no move to join her. Was he actually encouraging her to bond with his father? Maybe his attitude toward his family wasn't as hardened as she feared.

Tomas snatched two glasses of champagne from the tray of a passing waiter and handed one to Shelby.

"This is quite a day," he said. "The first grandchild to come of age. Should make me feel old, but I feel pretty good." He laughed and held up his glass. "Maybe this has something to do with it. But Dolores told me to have a good time, and I always obey my wife."

"It is a very nice party," Shelby said lamely.

Tomas drained his glass and within moments had replaced it with a fresh one. "So, Shelby, are you going to be adding to my brood of grandchildren? Six between my two daughters, you know."

"Well . . . uh . . ." She took a swallow from her glass.

Tomas laughed again. "Too soon to tell, eh?"

"I'm sure we'll want to eventually."

"Of course you will. Who wouldn't? Children are a joy. Oh, they can be a royal pain, too, but that's the way with life in general. Nothing's completely good and nothing's completely bad. At least that's the way I look at it. You gotta do the best you can no matter what hand is dealt to you."

"Frank didn't tell me what a philosopher you are. You make a lot of sense, Mr. Stefano."

"Can I give you more of my great wisdom?"

"Sure."

Mr. Stefano turned his head, and Shelby followed his gaze across the room to his wife. She was speaking animatedly to a small group of people who looked to be her age.

"Those people with Dolores are all benefactors of her various charities. No doubt she is cajoling more money from them." He smiled affectionately. "She's a good woman in her own way. She does have one fault, though. Dolores loves her children too much."

"Even Frank?" Shelby said before realizing the potential danger in her words.

"Don't you see, Shelby? She loved Frank more than the rest because he was her first son, arriving nine long years after Carla. She didn't think she'd have more children, and then God blessed her with Frank. And also, Frank is the most like Dolores, though neither of them will admit it. Can you see why the things he did hurt her so much?"

"I'm sure he didn't want to hurt her. He didn't want to hurt Ramon, either. He is very distraught about Ray's life."

"Dolores can't see that. In her mind the damage has been done and she cannot forgive it."

"Do you forgive him, Mr. Stefano?"

"In my heart, yes. But I must stand by my wife. I have to live with her; I don't have to live with Frank." He grinned and gulped down the rest of his champagne. "You know what they say, 'Hell hath no fury like that of a woman scorned.' "

"I'm glad we had this talk, Mr. Stefano. I hope we, at least, can be friends."

He patted her arm, a lopsided but warm smile on his face. "As long as the old señora doesn't find out."

After staying at the party a respectable length of time, Frank and Shelby said their good-byes and left.

As they were driving home, Frank said, "That ought to fulfill our family obligations until Easter."

"I thought it went fairly well. I had a nice little visit with your father. Did you know he doesn't hold anything against you?"

Frank snorted derisively. "That man gives Mexican machismo a bad name."

"I think he's sweet."

"That's his problem. He's too sweet to stand up to his wife. You say he holds nothing against me, yet he still won't give me the time of day."

"He has to think of his marriage, I suppose."

"It's not right."

"You're hardly a domineering husband yourself, Frank—not that I'm complaining." Shelby grinned, trying to keep the conversation light.

"So you don't think I'm macho, eh?" His dancing eyes belied the mock seriousness of his tone.

She put her hands around his firm biceps. "Very macho! But sweet, too. And gentle."

"Well, I'd be crazy to argue with that."

"Does it ever just hit you, Frank? That we are married? That someday we will be old married people like your parents, with babies and grand-babies. . . ."

"I hope and pray we do," he answered fervently.

They were silent for a while, then Frank added, "You know when it hits me most—that I am married? When we are in bed—"

"How typical." She rolled her eyes mockingly. "A one-track mind."

"No, not that. It's when I wake up and you are asleep next to me. And I realize I am not alone anymore. That my life is finally complete. Yet there is always a fear mixed with my happiness. Is it possible we will actually go on forever?"

"I can't predict the future, Frank. But I can say I am deeply committed to you and to our marriage. Still, I can see that it is harder for you having had a failed marriage, wondering if I will leave you like Gloria did. All I can say is I can't see myself doing that. I love you too much."

"What gave you the idea Gloria left me?"

"Your mother . . ."

"Haven't you realized by now that woman is living in a fantasy world?"

"You left Gloria?" Shelby's tone had such relief in it she must have sounded silly.

"Yes."

"What happened?"

"It's not important. I wish you hadn't mentioned her. I don't want to spoil the day."

"Subject closed," Shelby said without any hesitation. She didn't want to think of Gloria, either. "Let's go back to another subject. Babies."

"Are you ready to have babies?"

"We've never really talked about it. I assumed you wanted some because of your photograph. I want them, too. Timing, I guess, is the only question."

"The wise thing to do would be to wait until we've had more time alone together." When she nodded in agreement, he continued. "I don't want to do anything to wreck what we have. I want—" Frank stopped and jerked his gaze away from the road long enough to look at her. "I don't want to lose you, Shelby. But sometimes it seems as if everything is working against us. I wonder how we'll ever make it." He paused for a moment, a frown showing on his face. "I have to confess that the other day I went to visit my grandmother and we prayed about it."

"Really?"

"That's how afraid I've been."

"Actually, I tried to pray the other day, too. It didn't work, though. How do you pray to a God you don't know? But don't you think, Frank, that we can work these things out on our own? Millions of other people do it. Sure, what your grandmother has and what my mother has found sounds good, but I don't care what they say. There are strings attached."

"I guess so. . . ." Frank didn't seem convinced.

He said no more, and his focus went so inward that he made no response to Shelby's next comment. It was inconsequential anyway, and she just let the silence reign. Yes, she wanted to have Frank's children, but there was still so much to be worked out between them that it could be years before they were ready for that kind of responsibility.

After returning home, Shelby checked the answering machine.

Detective Poole's now distinctive voice said, "It's Saturday, five P.M. We have a few more questions for you, Mr. Stefano. Can you come to the station this evening?"

Shelby looked at Frank. He shook his head, then shrugging as if it didn't matter, reached over and pressed the Delete button on the machine.

"So sorry, Detective Poole," he said in a sarcastic tone. "Our machine is on the fritz, and I never got your message."

"Do you think that is a good idea?" Shelby asked. Her inexperience with the police made her very intimidated by them. Frank had been skirting the law for so long it probably meant nothing to him.

"I don't get Saturdays off very often, and I am not going to spend it with the police. Not when I have a wonderful, beautiful wife to be with."

He took her in his arms, kissing her passionately. And Shelby forgot all about the police.

27

BUT THE POLICE WOULD NOT let Shelby forget. The next day she and Frank were having coffee in their kitchen on a lazy Sunday morning. She was still in her bathrobe and Frank was wearing sweat pants and a white T-shirt. They were planning on a relaxing day reading the paper, walking on the beach, perhaps a light brunch at a nearby eatery.

The ringing doorbell not only changed those plans, it destroyed them.

Frank answered it because, of course, Shelby didn't want to greet anyone in her bathrobe. She listened closely, though, in case it was company and she would have to run to the bedroom and change quickly.

"Mr. Stefano." It was Detective Poole. "We thought we'd see you yesterday."

"Why is that?" said Frank innocently.

"You didn't get the message?" That was Liscom.

"You left a message? On the answering machine? I was beginning to wonder if it was working right. I thought it was strange that I hadn't received any messages for a couple of days." Frank lied so well. "So what did you want to see me for?"

"When we called we had some more questions," Poole said.

"But a few things fell into place last night," stated Liscom. "Now it's more than that."

"Oh?"

"We're here to arrest you, Mr. Stefano, for the murder of Gloria Herrera." Liscom's tone was triumphant. "Be advised that you have the right to remain silent, the right to—"

"This is ridiculous!" Frank exclaimed.

Shelby barely heard anything after that. She was reeling. Frank arrested? That was impossible. She actually swayed on her feet and had to grip the edge of the table. They were making a horrible mistake. They had no idea what they were doing. Frank . . . murder. . . ? That was ridiculous. Impossible. Unthinkable . . .

She was shocked to glance up and find Frank next to her.

"Frank. . . ?"

"Shelby, don't worry. It's going to be all right. I have to go with them now, but I won't be long."

"No. You can't . . . ." Tears choked her voice.

He put his arms around her. "Please, my love. It will be okay."

"I'm going with you."

"You're not dressed. Just wait here. I promise you, I'll be back soon." He kissed her cheek and turned to go. When she tried to follow, he shook his head.

Shelby watched him go, feeling helpless and sick and afraid. He seemed so calm it had to be a mistake. Any evidence the police thought they had must be wrong because Frank was innocent.

Shelby dressed and spent the rest of the morning nervously pacing about the condo or trying to distract herself with the television. She thought about going to the police station but kept hoping Frank would walk through the door at any time. Two hours later the phone rang. She grabbed it like a lifeline.

"Shelby," said Frank's welcome voice.

"Are you still with the police?" It was a dumb question, but she didn't know what else to say.

"This is my one phone call."

"But if they are going to let you go . . ."

"This might take longer than I thought."

"Frank, no!"

"Shelby, you need to find me a lawyer."

"I don't want to hear this, Frank. I can't handle it."

"I need you to keep your head. I've got to have your help."

She took a breath, as if that would give her the strength she needed. "I . . . I don't know any lawyers."

"I don't, either, except for drug lawyers, and I don't think they'd help my case."

"Maybe your grandmother knows—"

"No. I don't want my family involved."

"That's pretty impossible, Frank. They'll find out, and I know your grandmother will want to do something."

"For now, I just want them left out. Maybe I'll be out soon, and they won't ever have to know." Shelby noted dismally that now Frank was saying *maybe*, and his earlier assurance had diminished.

"How bad is it, Frank?"

"Find a good lawyer, Shelby. I need to go. Come when you can. I want to see you."

"I'll be there as soon as I make a few phone calls. I love you." She hoped he heard her final words. The phone had clicked the moment they were said.

Shelby called Christie first, but her friend wasn't home. Then she called Dawn, who said she'd be right over. Dawn also knew a lawyer, someone who went to her church. She said he was a real nice man— actually, he'd asked her out a couple of times but she had turned him down. She was trying not to jump into a new relationship the minute an old one ended. Dawn didn't know what kind of lawyer he was, but if he wasn't a criminal attorney, he'd surely be able to recommend one.

Dawn met Shelby at the police station, and together they went in search of Poole and Liscom.

"This isn't a hospital," Liscom said when Shelby asked to see Frank. "We don't hold visiting hours."

"But—"

"Have you contacted a lawyer?" asked Poole.

"Yes, but I don't understand why I can't see him for just a few minutes," Shelby tried again.

"This is his wife!" put in Dawn irately. "She has a right to see him."

"Frank Stefano is being held on murder charges, do you understand that?" Poole asked, but Shelby could only nod mutely. "This is very serious and something you, Mrs. Stefano, ought to think about long and hard. He is suspected of murdering his *ex-wife*. It's true, isn't it, that you've known Stefano little over a month?"

"Which means," Liscom interrupted, "that maybe you ought to be thinking about your own health."

Shelby gaped with disbelief at these words.

Dawn put an arm around Shelby. "Don't listen to them, honey." She shot a rabid glare at Liscom before leading Shelby to a seat in a waiting room. "When Alan gets here," she said after they were settled, "he'll get you in to see Frank. By the way, my friend from church *is* a criminal lawyer. He used to be with the district attorney's office before he began private practice. He knows what he's doing. His name is Alan Rosenthal. He's a nice man about my age, very handsome, too, with curly dark hair and a few touches of distinguished gray. He's a widower and—" She stopped. "I'm sorry, you don't care about all that now."

"No, go on. Tell me all about him. Sounds like you are interested in him," Shelby welcomed the distraction.

"Who wouldn't be? What a catch. But he's not exactly my type."

"What type is your type?"

"Oh, you know, athletic, short on sensitivity, long on strong and silent. Rough and arrogant with little respect for women. Your dad was the exception, of course, though he was definitely athletic. But Alan is shorter than me and very scholarly. He's more like Socrates than Ulysses."

"Maybe that's what you need to break the cycle."

"Well, it's only been six months since I left Jim, my last guy, and after rehab and becoming a Christian, I swore I wouldn't louse up my life again. Not that Alan would be a bad thing, but I just need to find my own way for a while. I have horrible luck with men."

"Maybe that runs in the family," Shelby said dismally.

"Don't say that. I'm sure Frank is a wonderful guy."

"I wish you could meet him. Maybe you'd see something I missed."

"Shelby, you have to stop thinking like that. You have to have faith in him."

"I wouldn't be the first woman in history to be duped by a smooth-talking man."

"Is that what you really think? Do you think he is a murderer?"

Dawn's words were sobering, like being splashed in the face with ice water.

"I'm so afraid . . ." was all Shelby could say before she broke down in tears.

Dawn wrapped her arms around Shelby and cooed, "There, there . . ." over and over again.

Alan Rosenthal got Shelby in to see Frank for a few minutes. She entered a small interrogation room with dingy gray walls, furnished only with a barren metal table and matching chairs. There were no windows in the room, no light save from the single bulb in the ceiling. Frank was slumped in one chair, as gray and stark and empty as his dismal environment. Wearing only the T-shirt and sweats he'd had on earlier, he seemed small and helpless—and it had little to do with the handcuffs binding his wrists. Shelby had always been so drawn to his quiet strength—but that was gone now, replaced with something that frightened her even more than his mercurial moods: hopelessness.

Alan explained to both of them that Frank would have to stay in jail until he was arraigned and bail could be set. The lawyer then told them that the police case was built on three main elements—traces of Gloria's blood found on Frank's boat, several witnesses who not only saw Frank visit Gloria at her home the night before she was reported missing but also heard them argue, and witnesses who heard Frank threaten Gloria a few days prior to her death. When Shelby asked why it took the police so long to arrest Frank, Rosenthal said the neighbors were slow to co-operate. Apparently they were aware of Frank's involvement in drug trafficking and feared Mafia-style retribution.

"It's not a strong case," said the lawyer, "but considering your history with Gloria, Frank, they might be able to make it stick. Because you have no drug-related convictions, I'm going to ask that your drug activities not be admissible unless the prosecution can prove they specifically relate to the murder. As it stands, the only motive the prosecution can prove is that a disgruntled and perhaps jealous ex-husband was driven to murder. However, more often than not that motive can win over judge and jury."

"But Frank is innocent," said Shelby.

"And let's just hope that will carry him through."

Frank did not look very hopeful. "When's the arraignment?"

"Day after tomorrow."

"And Frank will have to stay in jail until then?" asked Shelby.

"Yes, but we will get the court to set bail."

"How much will they go for?" asked Frank.

"It won't be cheap. Neither will your defense, I'm afraid to say. Hopefully you have some assets you can draw upon."

"I have my father's house," offered Shelby.

Frank shook his head. "That won't be necessary, Shelby. I can mortgage the condo. That should bring a few hundred thousand since I own it outright."

Shelby couldn't hide her surprise at Frank's revelation, but Frank avoided her gaze. Instead, he glanced at the lawyer. "So are you going to take my case?"

"I'd be happy to." Rosenthal stood. "I'll give you two the last few minutes alone now. I'll be back tomorrow and we can get going on this."

When they were alone, Frank said, "Shelby, do you mind starting the ball rolling on the mortgage? At least get the paper work for me to fill out." Shelby nodded mutely. "I've got a file on the condo in my office at the restaurant. Could you pick that up and bring it here? It may take time to get a loan approved. I'll probably have to stay here after the arraignment until we get the money. . . ." He paused and looked, really looked, at Shelby. "If I can't get out . . . if I'm convicted—"

"Don't—"

"No, listen to me. How long have we known each other, Shelby? Not even two months. I don't want you to waste your life on someone you've only known two months."

"We knew from the beginning, Frank, that time had nothing to do with what we have. Two months, two years, two decades—it's all the same to me. You are part of me and I am part of you. That's all there is to it. Don't talk like that again. It trivializes what I know we have." Suddenly Shelby was confident in her words despite what she had expressed to her mother earlier. There seemed to be a million facets to her feelings about Frank. She only knew she couldn't lose sight of the foundation of it all— their love—or they would be doomed.

A faint smile quirked his lips. "I should have known better." He reached out to her, forgetting about the handcuffs. He stopped, frustrated and helpless. Shelby threw her arms around him instead.

Passion and desperation became one as she held him tightly. Quiet tears spilled from Shelby's eyes when the guard came and ended her visit.

Two days later bail was set at one million dollars. It took a week to come up with the ten percent necessary to get Frank out of jail. When he came home, he and Shelby tried to proceed normally with their lives. Of course, having a murder trial hanging over their heads did not make that easy. They went back and forth to their jobs, they went sailing on the weekend, they bought a new sofa for the living room, they had a romantic Valentine's Day just like millions of other couples.

But a storm was brewing, and only time would tell whether they could survive its fury.

28

ALAN ROSENTHAL MET WITH the prosecutor who was handling Frank's case. They knew each other from Alan's days in the district attorney's office and could talk candidly.

"Doug," Alan said over a cup of coffee in a place near the courthouse, "you can't win this case. You've got one piece of physical evidence, and the rest is circumstantial and hearsay. My client has no priors—"

"Come on, Alan, you and I both know he's deeply involved in drug trafficking."

"There are no convictions on record. But even if he was, the fact is that for the last year he's been a model citizen, working at a regular job, married, a regular contributor to charities. I got him bail on those grounds, and I am certain I will get him acquitted, too."

"You're dreaming, Alan. Not only is he guilty but there is tremendous pressure for a conviction in this case—preferably a murder one conviction."

"Pressure. . . ?"

"You know, of course, that the dead girl's father is Charles Herrera, not only a prominent local attorney but also a good friend and college classmate of the district attorney. He's been calling the DA's office twice a day to apply pressure. There is also the ethnic issue. Do you realize what percentage of the DA's constituency is Hispanic? There is no way our office can go soft in this case."

"I should think the fact that both the victim and the accused are Mexican-American would balance things out. Nevertheless, I would be very disappointed in you, Doug, if you bent to political pressures."

Doug Waller grimaced. "I have never prosecuted a person I did not believe to be guilty, and I won't start now—politics or not. Stefano is guilty, I'm convinced of it. Her blood was on his boat."

"Anyone could have used that boat, especially since he was out of the country."

"Which is another pretty damaging bit of evidence—his convenient trip to Mexico."

"It could be just as easily turned in his favor. I mean, he's too smart of a man to do something that appears so suspicious."

"What about the domestic violence?"

"What? That he grabbed her in a bar?"

"That incident strengthens our case. Those prior threats support motive. But I'm talking about her visit to the ER five years ago." Alan's blank look was indication enough of his ignorance in this matter. Doug continued. "So he said nothing to you? Well, it would have come out in discovery. And you'll have to admit it doesn't make the man look good—even with his 'model citizen' act."

"Do you want to tell me about it? Or should I wait to read your report?"

"I'll tell you all about it."

Shelby tried to forget the accusations, the implications, and even the tiny nagging doubt that tried to settle upon her heart. Until their meeting with Alan Rosenthal.

"I just spoke to the assistant DA," Alan said. Frank and Shelby were in his office for a scheduled meeting and were seated across from his desk. "I arranged the meeting in hopes of working out some kind of deal. I was certain I could get the charges against you reduced to manslaughter. I don't believe they have a case they can win in court. But I can't do anything for you, Frank, if you don't tell me the truth about your relationship with Gloria."

"You mean the incident in the bar?" said Frank. "I told you about that. I admitted I threatened her. I even grabbed her. I was furious."

"I don't think you ever indicated just how deeply your anger went. Tell me about it, Frank."

"Since Ray got out of prison, she'd been using him. I asked her—I pleaded with her—to lay off him. She kept him supplied with drugs. She didn't make him pay for them—not with money, anyway. I'd just seen Ray; he was wasted, and I couldn't take it anymore. I went to Lotto's. I knew she'd be there."

"You sought her out?"

"Yes, I sought her out! I wanted to—" Frank stopped, his eyes turning skittishly toward Shelby. "I don't know what I wanted to do."

"But you went to the bar and had words?" prompted Alan.

Frank chuckled dryly. "You could say that."

"Very heated words?"

"Yeah."

"What exactly did you say to her?"

Frank licked his lips, now studiously avoiding Shelby. "I don't know. 'Leave Ray alone or else.' Something like that."

"What were your exact words? Surely you can't have forgotten."

"I said, 'If you continue to destroy Ray, I'll destroy you.' She laughed at me like always and started to turn her back on me."

"That's when you grabbed her?"

"I didn't hurt her, for crying out loud! I doubt I even bruised her—but I wish I had. She needed hurting—" He broke off again, this time obviously dismayed at what he'd said.

"Is that what you felt like five years ago, Frank?" asked Alan softly, pointedly.

"What do you mean, five years. . . ?" Again Frank paused as realization and pain wracked his expression. "No, not that!"

Shelby looked back and forth between her husband and his lawyer, bewildered. Hearing about the incident in the bar for the first time was hard enough, but what new revelation was about to be rained on her?

"Do you want Shelby to leave while we finish talking about this?" asked Rosenthal.

Frank looked at Shelby, and she could see it wasn't easy for him. "She may as well stay." But the despair in his tone made Shelby's stomach knot.

"Tell me, then, what happened five years ago?" asked Alan.

Frank rubbed his face and shook his head. "Why should it matter now? It was five years ago!"

Alan picked up some photographs that had been lying inconspicuously in front of him and spread them out before Shelby and Frank. There were four snapshots of a barely recognizable Gloria Herrera. Her beautiful face was swollen and bruised; both eyes were blackened.

"These photos will be shown in court," said Alan. "No one's going to care how old they are. All a jury will think is that if you were capable of doing this five years ago, you could very well be capable of violence now."

Shelby sat woodenly in her chair, stunned. Not Frank . . . not Frank . . . not Frank . . . her mind screamed. But the photos screamed back accusingly that pictures don't lie.

"Shelby . . ." Frank said softly, but she could not look at him. "I don't care what anyone else thinks, as long as you can believe I didn't do that to Gloria."

"Didn't you, Frank?" she replied in a strangled voice, and though she hated the disbelief in her tone, she couldn't help it.

"Frank is innocent until proven guilty, Shelby," said Alan.

But she remembered Frank once saying that there were no innocents. Still, she had to let him defend himself.

"We'd been married a year," Frank said, and even though his voice sounded hopeless it was nevertheless determined. "By then I had a pretty good idea that Gloria was not exactly being faithful to me. In fact, I doubt we had a male friend she didn't sleep with. Somehow, though, she managed to maintain her sterling image—to our families, at least. That was very important to her. Actually, I think what was most important was the fact that she was able to so expertly deceive others. She reveled in how my mother practically said a novena to her. All at my expense, of course. I was the devil, she was the angel. At first I didn't mind—I sort of relished my bad boy status. But I didn't enjoy having an unfaithful wife."

"And that's what brought this about?" Alan nodded toward the photos.

"I didn't do that to her. It was . . . someone else. I don't expect to be believed. In fact, back then I *let* everyone think the worst. At the time it seemed better than having people think I couldn't control my new wife. I was very into my macho image then . . . I guess as much as Gloria was into her angelic one. We reached a compromise. She wouldn't press charges against me if I wouldn't deny it. And, to tell you the truth, it kind of lifted me in the esteem of many of my acquaintances. I never dreamed that one day my life would hang on those stupid, sick lies."

"And it does, Frank. We'll be hard-pressed to convince a jury of what you've just told me."

"I don't care about a jury." Frank turned to Shelby. "Do you believe me, Shelby?"

Shelby brought her hand to her mouth, trying to keep back the tears that had been threatening since Alan had first mentioned the abuse. She felt like she was suffocating, slowly crushed by the weight of broken promises and dreams. She thought about what he had once told her about the jealous nature of Mexican men. His father had beaten up a man for merely winking at his wife. What would a man do in the face of adultery?

She didn't know what to feel about the abject devastation on his face. She looked at his scar, and knew that it, too, was a result of violence.

Perhaps he felt her scrutiny, for his hand went to the scar and he rubbed it as if it were suddenly painful.

"I've done a lot of things," he said after a long, heavy silence. "I've never lied about that, Shelby. I told you from the beginning. There's violence in the drug world. I've given and I've . . . received." He fingered the scar again. "But I have never hurt anyone except out of self-defense. Nor have I hurt anyone who could not defend themselves, including women. Even Gloria, who was hardly a helpless, simpering woman."

Shelby finally found her voice. "Have you ever hurt anyone in order to protect your brother, Frank?"

"That's how I got this scar."

"What about Gloria?"

He covered his face with his hands, shaking his head dismally. "No . . ." was all he said.

On the drive home from Rosenthal's office, Frank and Shelby were silent. The attorney had said he was going to keep working on the DA to get the charges reduced to manslaughter. Shelby tried to convince herself that if a man like Alan Rosenthal—a lawyer carefully trained to read people—believed Frank, then why shouldn't she? It was, in fact, the noble thing to do. Stand by your man and all that. She desperately wanted to be that kind of woman. And searching in her mind, reviewing all her times with Frank, she could conjure nothing to keep her from trusting him. He had never once indicated a violent nature. He might be brooding at times, even mysterious. He might even have lied to her. But there had never been a hint that he was the kind of man who could, or would, inflict upon her or anyone else the kind of damage displayed in the photos of Gloria.

Frank had showed her nothing but tenderness, love, sensitivity.

But Shelby had only known him a few weeks. Again, she asked herself if it were possible for a person to be that great of an actor. And again her heart said no—not Frank. And she heard her father say, *"Follow your gut, Shelby."*

29

ALL THROUGH DINNER at the condo, their conversation consisted of strained and sporadic small talk. Finally, as if he could take it no more, Frank said, "I guess I should be thankful you're still here. You'd have every right to leave."

"Only if you were guilty of the things they say."

"I have no reason to believe you think otherwise."

"I'm sorry, Frank, for not reassuring you enough. I guess my mind is mush right now. I do believe you, but I have to be honest and tell you there is a small—very small—bit of doubt in me."

He touched her cheek in that gentle way of his, but all Shelby could do was wonder if that same hand could have pummeled Gloria's face.

"I hate myself for what I've done to you. I thought I could escape to an idyllic life with you, but instead I've dragged you into my nightmare."

As if on cue, the doorbell rang. It was Ramon, and Shelby didn't know whether to be relieved at the interruption or frustrated.

"Frank, I'm in trouble," he said without preamble after they invited him in. He sat on the new sofa and ran a hand through his hair, unkempt and oily, his normal hyperactivity heightened by a new agitation. "I don't know what to do."

"What's wrong now, Ray?" asked Frank, an edge to his tone.

"Frank has troubles of his own," said Shelby defensively.

"What? Gloria's murder? He doesn't have to worry about that. I'll take care of you, bro. I won't let nothing happen to you."

"I told you I didn't want your help. Besides, you're hardly in a position to help me. And coming here is hardly a great idea."

"Do you think I'd come if I wasn't desperate?"

Frank sighed. "What is it?"

"I just need a place to crash for one night. I haven't slept in three days and I can't go another. I need a safe place, just for tonight."

"Why, Ray?"

"It ain't my fault, Frank. It was set up perfect; I did everything right. Just like you said, I laid low in the dinghy on the backside of one of those little islands, and I slipped in under the cover of darkness. It was slick, man."

"What's he talking about, Frank?" asked Shelby, the wariness she'd been fighting since the session with Rosenthal inching back upon her.

"You want honesty, Shelby?" Frank asked, and when she nodded tentatively, he continued. "That trip to San Diego wasn't about racing and having fun. I did it to help Ray buy some drugs so he could pay off Barcelona. That fight I picked with you? It was to keep you from coming with us. I was backed up against a wall, Shelby. All I wanted to do was get Ray out of trouble. Lot of good it did."

"Everything we did that weekend worked out fine," Ray said defensively. "These things happen in the business, you know that. It's the risk we all take. I just can't convince Cuervo."

"Who is Cuervo?"

"The Columbian I met in prison. You see, I was able to pay off Barcelona and set up my deal with Cuervo. I was in really tight with him. He fronted me two kilos of heroin—"

"So you're into heroin now?"

"It's the new wave, man. One pellet the size of my finger is worth ten grand. It's worth ten times more than coke. Less to transport for a far higher yield. Since we did our little run to Mexico last month, I've made five successful exchanges of heroin, netting a hundred grand each. Me and Cuervo had a good thing going until things started going sour. One deal gets screwed up and he's after me. . . ."

"One deal?"

"Okay, there was another problem before that, but I was able to make it good with my own money. But you know how those Columbians don't like to get taken. I tried to tell him it wasn't like that." Ray jumped up and started pacing. "I didn't betray him, I got ripped off! The money was there—I saw it. But somehow they switched briefcases before the actual exchange. I got ripped off. Two kilos, man! Do you know what that's worth?" Without waiting for an answer, Ray went on, the words spilling from his mouth in fast, almost unintelligible succession. "Cuervo won't believe me. This was our biggest exchange yet. Almost a half a mil worth of dope. I can't make it good this time. No way do I have that kind of money."

"I thought you made five hundred thousand in your other deals."

"I had to make good the last time, and then there are . . . well, other expenses."

"How much is your own habit costing you?"

"Hey, man, you aren't gonna start browbeating me, are you? I don't need preaching. I'm not asking you for money. You said you wouldn't deal anymore the last time and I'm not gonna ask. I just want to crash. I'll die if I can't sleep. I've been on the run for a week. I gotta rest."

Shelby's mind was whirling once again over the news of what had happened in San Diego. But right now she forced herself to focus on what Frank's response would be to Ray's plea. Shelby didn't want to be cold-hearted, but she was far less concerned with Ray's needs than she was with her husband's. Frank needed to distance himself from his drug-dealing brother, not entertain him as a houseguest.

"What makes you think Cuervo won't trace you here?" asked Frank. "How do you know they haven't had someone watching my place all along? You've done some pretty stupid things, Ray, but this tops all of them. I've got a wife to think of."

"I checked the street over real good. No one is on to me. I promise I'll be outta here first thing in the morning." Ray stopped pacing and faced both Shelby and Frank. "Please, man. I'll never ask another thing of you again."

Frank shook his head, obviously not believing for a minute that final line. "All right, but you've got—"

"Frank!" exclaimed Shelby, angry not only that he was going to do it but also because he hadn't discussed it with her first.

"Shelby, he's my brother."

And that, of course, sealed it. It didn't matter that Frank had already admitted that his aid in the past had not helped Ray. The two brothers might have a completely dysfunctional relationship, but it was too strong for her, a mere wife, to fight. Besides, the last thing she and Frank needed right now was another fight. Still, she couldn't give her total blessing.

"It's late, I'm going to bed," she said. "There are some leftovers in the frig, Ray. I get up at six for work, but I doubt I'll see you because you'll be gone, so I'll say good-bye now."

She had crawled into bed when Frank came into the room. Silently he changed for bed and got in next to her.

"He'll be gone," he said finally. "I gave him an alarm clock."

"Whatever . . ."

"You can't expect me to turn my back on my own brother."

"And what about next time, Frank? And next time. When will it stop?"

"I don't know. Maybe never."

Frank turned off his bedside light and rolled over. Shelby said a quick good-night and did the same. Her last thought before finally falling asleep was to wonder whether she would have married Frank had she known what kind of baggage came with the man.

Shelby wasn't surprised to hear Ray snoring in the guest room when she woke in the morning. Passing the guest bathroom, she noticed the light on and the door open. There was a mess by the sink—a small bowl from her kitchen with a plastic drinking straw beside it. She saw a residue of a white, powdery substance in the bowl and some sprinkled on the counter.

Shelby was totally appalled. She felt invaded, as if a thief had broken into her home. It was bad enough to have Ray there high on drugs, but for him to actually be using them in her house—the idea made her shake with fury. Her first instinct was to storm into Ray's room and bodily drag him out. But her anger was overshadowed by a greater desire to avoid an ugly scene. Instead, she went to the kitchen and tried to cool off by putting on a pot of coffee. Then she went back to her bedroom but was still too shaken to wake Frank. Afraid she'd just take out her ire on him, she went into the bathroom and took a shower. After toweling off and slipping into her bathrobe, she returned to the bedroom to find Frank awake and putting on his sweat pants.

"Is he gone?" he asked.

She shook her head.

He started for the door, but she caught up to him and put a restraining hand on his arm. "Frank, please understand. I don't want to be cruel, I'm just afraid for you. He's been using drugs here, Frank, and if the police were to come here and find that . . ."

"I understand," he said gently. "I doubt that would happen, but I do understand your fear. Now, get dressed, and I promise he will be gone by the time you are done."

She took a simple ecru skirt and a floral sweater from her closet and dressed quickly, though she didn't know the reason for her hurry. Did she think Frank would be firmer with his brother if she was present? So be it. And from the sound of the voices outside her door, it appeared that might be the case. Frank's voice could be heard several times saying, "Come on, Ray, up and at 'em." Only vague grunts could be heard in response.

Shelby put on a little blush and mascara, her only makeup, and a pair of earrings, then stepped into the hall, feeling like the Bible guy she'd once heard about who had been thrown into a lion's den.

By now, a very groggy and disheveled Ray was shuffling from the guest room. Threading his hands through his hair, he was saying, "What's your problem? It's six-thirty in the morning!"

"That's first thing around here, Ray," said Frank.

"Man, I'm dying!"

"Come on, you gotta go. I promised Shelby."

At that moment Shelby's presence was noticed. Both men looked at her with entirely different expressions. Frank's was apologetic. Ray's bordered on hostile.

"I thought you were cool, Shelby," said Ray. "Man, was I wrong!"

"I'm trying to look out for Frank," she replied with as much calm as she could muster.

"He's a big boy. Let him look out for himself!"

"Maybe for once, Ray, you ought to think of someone besides yourself!" Shelby retorted, suddenly tired of seeing him constantly pampered.

"You don't know what you're talking about! You don't know anything—ah, forget it." Ramon grabbed his jacket and stormed toward the front door.

"Wait, Ray," Shelby said. "It's just that I—" But he opened the door and slammed it behind him, cutting off her attempt at an apology. She turned toward Frank. "Well, I don't think I was wrong," she murmured, still feeling the need to defend herself. "You don't need this, Frank. *We* don't need this!"

"He'll get over it," Frank said.

"What about you?"

"I've nothing to get over. I understand."

"Why do I feel so horrible, then?"

Frank said nothing.

"I could have at least given him breakfast," she said.

"You don't owe him anything."

"I guess it's more about what I owe myself, and you. If he had been a needy stranger on the street, I would have shown more compassion than I did to your own brother. I don't want to be a hard, mean person." She sighed and opened the door. "I can't have him leave with such hard feelings."

As she stepped out into the hallway she heard Ray, at least she supposed it was Ray, descending the stairs. She hurried after him while Frank followed her. When she reached the bottom of the stairs, Ray had already crossed the street and was reaching for his car door.

"Ray," she called.

He opened the door, then paused. "What?"

"I've got a fresh pot of coffee."

"Hope you enjoy it."

"Come on, Ray, join us so we can part on a better note."

"You were probably right."

"Let's talk about it at least."

He shrugged, slammed the door, and walked toward her.

Shelby turned and smiled at Frank who had come up beside her. And in that instant they were shaken off their feet by an explosion. Shelby first thought an earthquake had struck, but it was too violent, too abrupt. And the awful deafening sound was not from an earthquake. Then something struck the ground in front of her, and Frank threw himself over her to shield her from flying debris.

"You okay?" Frank asked after the initial fallout had settled.

"Yes, but what—?"

Then she saw flames leaping up around Ray's car, and in the next instant, Frank was running toward the destroyed vehicle.

"Ray!" he was yelling.

His brother had been thrown several feet from the car and lay motionless in the street. Frank bent over him, then yelled at Shelby, "Call 9–1–1."

Shelby was already running up the stairs to the condo.

30

WHOEVER HAD MEANT TO KILL Ramon with the car bomb must have been disappointed. Though his injuries were severe, the doctor was confident he'd survive. He had a concussion, a broken leg that would require surgery to set, and several broken ribs that had caused the worst of his injuries— a punctured lung and a lot of internal bleeding. No one else had been injured in the early morning blast, but a good portion of two shops across the street from the condo had been destroyed.

Shelby and Frank sat with Ray until his parents showed up, then made a quiet retreat, Frank promising Ray he'd be back in the morning. The police had come by to take statements from each of them. Ray told the police he had no idea who'd want to kill him. But the police knew Ray's record and weren't buying his story. To Frank, Ray said it had to be Cuervo. Shelby had heard stories of how Columbian drug dealers killed entire families when they wanted to execute a traitor so there would be no one left to take revenge. Frank assured Shelby that was just a movie plot.

"But, Ray," Frank had said to his brother, "this might put a new slant on Gloria's murder."

"What do you mean?"

"Was she involved with Cuervo?"

"Involved?" There was a defensiveness to Ray's tone.

"I don't mean romantically," Frank said. "Was she dealing with him?"

"You're saying the cartel might have executed her?"

"Isn't it a possibility?"

"Yeah . . . sure. That is a possibility . . . a real possibility."

"So she had dealings with them?"

"You know Gloria."

Frank nodded, and when he and Shelby left the hospital, he said he wanted to pay a visit to his lawyer. Rosenthal listened to Frank's case against the Columbian cartel.

"First we have to prove Gloria was involved," he said. "Can you do that?"

"Gloria was involved in everything, but she was an expert at *looking* clean. For instance, she was not a heavy user—a little pot or coke at parties was all I ever saw her do. She always had her head about her. The police didn't find anything related to drugs in her apartment. And she was very careful about money. She drove a modest car, lived in a modest apartment, but I'll bet she had millions stashed in the Caymans or somewhere."

"I can put an investigator on this," said Rosenthal without much enthusiasm, "but you have to understand that if you take this kind of defense, it might end up being brutal on your ex-wife's character."

Frank glanced at Shelby, a half smile slightly lifting one corner of his lips. "Go for it."

Shelby couldn't help being surprised at this response. She could not begin to fathom or explain it. Maybe she didn't want to.

Frank went every day to the hospital to visit his brother, timing his visits so as to avoid his parents. Physically, Ray improved daily, and after two days he was stabilized enough to have surgery on his leg. At first he did not experience any severe symptoms from drug withdrawal. In fact, he slept for the first twenty-four hours. He denied to the hospital staff that he was a drug user, even after his toxicology screen came back positive for cocaine and traces of heroin. The doctor ordered Vicodan for pain, but the nursing staff was careful not to overdo it, for fear of trading one addiction for another. When Ray wasn't sleeping in those first days, he was concocting ways of getting more Vicodan.

But as the dose of pain medication was gradually decreased a few days after his surgery, Ray's agitation increased. Five days after being admitted, he began to display a serious bout of withdrawal. Nausea, vomiting, cramping, and diarrhea hit him hard. But the worst of it was the terrible depression caused by the cocaine withdrawal.

"Frank, I'm jonesing, man. I need something." He was perspiring and pale.

"This is a good opportunity to kick it, Ray."

"Don't give me that garbage!"

"I can see if the nurse will give you some more pain killer."

"I already tried. They won't. They said I've had enough today. They don't know nothing. It doesn't even matter that my leg hurts."

Frank went out to the nurse's station, mostly because he could not bear feeling so helpless.

"He's to have pain medication three times a day, and he has already had two doses," the nurse replied. "I'm saving the other for him to have before he sleeps tonight."

"Well, he's in terrible pain now," Frank lied.

"Mr. Stefano, your brother can't be in that much pain. In fact, if his leg did not need to be kept immobile, we'd probably be releasing him in a couple of days. I think he is just giving you a snow job."

Returning to the room, Frank tried to infuse his tone with encouragement. "You can do this, Ray."

"Get me something, bro—please!"

"I can't do that."

"You've got to. I'll kill myself if I don't get something."

"That's *loco* talk, Ray."

"I can't stand it—" Ray stopped suddenly, clutching his stomach. In the next instant he lurched over, vomiting all over the bed and floor. "Help me, Frank," he moaned.

The next day Frank met his parents in the corridor as they were leaving Ray's room. They hadn't come at their usual time. Dolores Stefano glared at her son.

"Are you satisfied now?" she said. "He'll die for sure."

"Don't start with me," Frank replied evenly.

"The nurse says he's suicidal. They're going to put a twenty-four-hour watch on him. It's your fault."

"How can you lay this on me? How can you do that to me—?"

"All you can think of is yourself."

But before more heated words could fly, Tomas put an arm around his wife. "Come on, Dolores. We don't want a scene. Let's go."

He tugged at Dolores as she hesitated, still glaring at Frank. Reluctantly, she continued on down the hall to the elevator. Frank waited until they disappeared inside the elevator before proceeding to Ray's room. He paused at the door. His insides were in a knot over the confrontation with his mother and over what he was about to face.

In the room, Ray was rolled over in the bed, his back to the door.

"Ray, you awake?"

Ray started and jerked, and something clattered to the floor. Ray cursed.

"Ray?" Frank strode around to the other side of the bed. Ray's arm was bare, a tourniquet tied around the upper arm. A syringe lay on the floor. "What is this?" Frank asked, picking up the syringe. For a moment he was puzzled to see that the syringe was only filled with air. Then it became clear. "Ray, no!"

"Give it to me," Ray demanded. "I can't take it anymore."

"Where'd you get this?"

Ray just shrugged. "They come in here, they draw blood, I distract them for a moment—nothing to it. Now give it back to me."

Frank saw that Ray was serious. This was no fake suicide attempt. His brother had been about to shoot up an air embolism. His hand shaking, Frank removed the tourniquet. Absently, Frank rubbed Ray's arm, and as he did so, he noticed older needle marks on the vein tracks and a few "burn" marks around the muscular portion of his upper arm. He supposed he shouldn't be surprised that Ray had done more than snort drugs. But it still made him sick. And the image of that first time he introduced his brother to hard drugs haunted Frank's mind again, as it often did.

"Put the straw in your nose, man, and snort it up. You'll love it."

"I don't know, Frank. . . ."

"Hey, would your big brother lead you astray?"

"Grass is one thing, but cocaine . . ."

"Everyone does it."

"You?"

"Sure. It's no worse than alcohol. Come on, we'll do it together and have a blast."

Frank hated himself now more than he ever had in his life. He looked at the syringe in his hand. Maybe he ought to be the one getting air shot into his veins. His mother had every right to hate him. And more than ever, Frank wished he could trade places with Ray, giving back to their mother the eager boy reaching out for a shining future.

The sound of Ray retching brought Frank back to the ugly reality. Breaking the needle, he tossed the syringe into the wastebasket.

"Frank, help me!"

Tenderly, Frank took a washcloth and wiped away the perspiration beading on Ray's forehead. But it wasn't what Ray wanted. He just wept and cursed and even threatened in response. Frank wanted to run away so he didn't have to hear any more, but he stayed seated by Ray, doggedly, as if accepting his punishment. But it wasn't enough.

Finally he could take it no more. "Ray, I'm leaving for a while, but I'll be back."

"You gonna bring me something, bro?"

"Yeah . . . so wait for me. Don't do anything stupid, okay?"

"I'll wait." Ray grabbed Frank's arm as he rose to go. "Thanks, man, and hurry. Please!"

In the hospital lobby, Frank called Hector Barcelona and arranged to meet him by the rescue mission in their old neighborhood. Why Barcelona would choose such a place, Frank couldn't guess. He probably just wanted to make a point about their roots.

Walking down a street of the San Pedro barrio was almost like being on a street in Mexico. The sounds of Spanish were far more noticeable than English. All the signs on storefronts were in Spanish. Everything was run down, the sidewalk was cracked. It made him think fleetingly of Puerto Vallarta, and that made him think in turn of Shelby. But that was one vision he didn't need now. What he was about to do might well crush their relationship once and for all. Yet he tried to convince himself that she'd understand his need to help his brother. It wasn't as if he was choosing him over her. He was just doing what had to be done. Shelby was so innocent of the real world. That was why he loved her. Yet it was also a wedge between them. She could never truly understand Ray's world because she could only see things in black-and-white. The real world was gray, and it took people like Frank to wade through the muck.

He saw Barcelona's flashy red Ferrari parked at the end of the street. He was surprised that Barcelona would make the delivery himself. Frank walked up to the car.

"Que paso, amigo?" said Barcelona, poking his head slightly from the open car window.

"Barcelona" was all Frank said in response. He hoped he could conclude the deal with as little conversation as possible.

"I heard about Ramon. What a shame! How's he doing?"

"Okay."

"Do they know who did it to him?"

"No."

"You know we weren't on the best of terms, but believe me, if I hear anything I'll let you know."

"Sure you will, Hector. Now, do you have it?"

The passenger door opened, and Barcelona's man, Carlos, got out.

"Take a little walk with Carlos," said Barcelona. "Hey, be sure to tell Ramon his friends are pulling for him."

Frank could only sneer at Hector's glib facade, as if the threats and beatings did not hover between them.

Frank walked with Carlos a short distance to a side street, where they turned and then walked to an alley that led behind the mission. Here Frank took an envelope of money from his pocket and handed it to Carlos, who quickly looked inside, stuffed the envelope into his coat pocket, and removed a small packet. Frank took it and quickly pocketed it. He thought vaguely of the consequences of being caught with two ounces of cocaine. It would make Poole's and Liscom's day.

It would devastate Shelby.

But he couldn't think of Shelby.

Carlos left the alley, and after waiting a minute or two, Frank followed, walking slowly. By the time he reached the main street, the Ferrari was driving away. He walked for a few minutes until he looked up and found himself in front of St. Mark's Catholic Church. The stone cathedral-like building hadn't changed much from the way he remembered it from his childhood. He took his First Communion there, but shortly after, his parents moved into a better San Pedro neighborhood and started attending a more upscale church.

Impulsively, Frank climbed the front stairway and went inside. Much to his relief, there was no one else present. The building was dimly lit, with most of the light coming in through the stained-glass windows. A few candles were burning near the altar. He hated the smell of burning wax because it reminded him of all he despised most about his parents' church. The "Hail Marys," the meaningless confessions, the rote prayers, the droning of the priests. All form, no substance.

Then he thought of his grandmother. She went to mass several times a week; she made confession; she had most of the liturgy memorized. But when he thought of his grandmother's faith, it was all substance, no form. It was one of the great contradictions of life.

All at once he seemed to feel the weight of the cocaine in his pocket. And it made him more ashamed than ever. Abuelita would never condemn him for what he was about to do, though she would be very disappointed. But like Shelby, she just did not understand the gray areas of life. She believed God could really make everything right, that He could take away the pain and the shame and the failure. She believed faith could heal and uplift. Frank wanted to believe those things, too. But he had seen too much of the underside of life to be easily convinced. Maybe God could take away all evil. Maybe God had a very good reason for allowing people like Ramon to suffer.

That is where Frank's faith got shaky. He simply could not step back and let God have His way.

Frank paused at a back pew, genuflected briefly out of habit, then sat down. His eyes focused on the altar, he murmured softly, "God, I suppose I need you like my abuelita says—I *know* I need you. I'm no atheist. That's probably the real irony. I desire what my grandmother has . . . something real and deep and abiding to overcome the rottenness inside me. But I guess I'll never have it. I'm just not good enough.

"I know what I am about to do is wrong. I know it'll hurt Ray more than it will help him. But I'm still gonna do it. I can't refuse him. I can't turn my back on him. I've got to do this for him. Do you understand, God? I've got to. If you are really the kind of God my abuelita believes in, then maybe you can somehow forgive me. I guess I'm bound to suffer either way."

Full of despair, feeling none of the cleansing prayer was supposed to bring, Frank rose and left the church. The sudden glare of the late afternoon sunlight was like being thrust into the bright, burning fires of hell after a few teasing moments in purgatory.

31

Ray's gratitude nearly convinced Frank it was worth it.

"You saved me, man! I love you, bro."

Frank helped line out a portion of the cocaine on Ray's tray table, then he held the straw to his brother's nose as Ray inhaled the grains.

"Okay, that's enough, Ray."

"Leave it," Ramon said, reaching for the bag.

"No, they'll find it. I'll bring it back tomorrow."

"Don't forget."

That would have been an amusing statement had Frank been in the mood for levity. If only he *could* forget! If only he could go home to Shelby and forget that anything else existed besides them and their love.

He was walking to his car in the hospital parking lot when someone came up behind him and started walking at his side.

"*Buenas tardes*, Frank," the man said. He was several inches taller than Frank and a few years younger. He was well built, with a shock of sun-bleached blond hair.

"Willie Cantrell. It's been a long time."

"Too long. I heard you were out of the business."

"I am."

"I saw you with Barcelona."

"Have you been following me?"

"I wasn't sure if you were still cool. I had to know."

Cantrell was a low-level dealer. He was part of the Manhattan Beach surfer crowd and supported his surfing habit by selling drugs to teenagers on the beach. Before Frank moved up in the drug business, he used to supply Cantrell and guys like him. But that area of the business, because of the number of contacts required to make money, was far more dangerous than smuggling drugs. Frank got away from it as soon as he could make money on smuggling alone. Frank had always rather arrogantly considered Cantrell and his kind "bottom feeders"—the ones selling joints like candy outside of schools and to carefree kids on the beach. Frank saw no such distinction between Cantrell and himself now.

"I need some money, Frank."

"Well, Willie, I'm tapped out. Maybe you heard, but I just had to make bail."

"Yeah, I heard. That's a bad break, man, but I ain't asking for a handout, amigo."

"What, then?"

"I'm selling . . . information, you know."

"What information?"

"That's what's gonna cost you."

"I've got enough problems right now, Willie."

"You meet me in an hour at Lotto's with five hundred dollars. I swear, Frank, you'll want this information. It has to do with Gloria."

Frank shook his head dismally. Something told him this would cost him more dearly than they both realized.

After his rendezvous at Lotto's, Frank went home. As he pulled into the garage and parked his truck, he noticed that the hood of Shelby's

Mustang was up, then saw Shelby's petite frame bent over the engine.

"Having problems?" he asked as he strolled toward her.

"Not really. Just due for an oil change and a tune-up. You've got to pamper these classics a bit, and I'm afraid I haven't been giving the car much attention lately."

"Guess you've had a few distractions."

She lifted her head and smiled at him. Her hair was mussed, and there were grease smudges on her face. She looked so beautiful and desirable he wanted to weep.

"Could you hand me that ratchet?" she asked.

He held it out to her and their fingers brushed momentarily, sending a charge through him—of longing, regret, sadness, and unrealized joy.

"Have you had dinner?" she asked, completely oblivious of the emotional turmoil he was experiencing.

"I'm not hungry."

"Have you been to see Ray?" When he nodded, she added, "How is he?"

"Better."

During the ensuing silence she returned her attention to the spark plugs she was working on. After a couple minutes, he said, "I'll go on up to the condo. I don't want to disturb you."

"I don't mind your company."

"But this is your therapy, isn't it?"

She gave a little shrug. "I guess."

"I'm surprised you haven't done more of it lately."

"Maybe things aren't as bad as we think," she replied lightly.

He laughed dryly, then said earnestly, "They couldn't be worse, Shelby."

"What do you mean?" She straightened her back and focused her full attention on him. He wished he hadn't said anything.

"I've been arrested for murder, someone tried to blow up my brother, my mother blames me for everything. Could it get worse?"

"We can't give up hope that everything is going to turn out all right."

He reached out and touched one of the smudges on her face. "I'm sorry, Shelby, that I couldn't give you a 'happily ever after' ending."

"Do you think that's what I want?"

"Isn't it what we both wanted? A whirlwind romance and marriage while on a perfect vacation in Mexico? What else could we have been looking for? We must have been thinking and hoping that love and romance would wipe away all of life's problems."

"I don't think so. We're not that shallow."

"I wish we were."

"What's wrong, Frank?"

"I wanted to give you the happy ending. I wanted to give you it all. But at least you haven't invested a lifetime in this relationship. It's only been two months. You could walk away. . . ."

"What are you saying?" Shelby's voice betrayed her desperation and fear.

"Nothing," he said quickly. There was no way he could repair all the damage he had done or was about to do. "I'm just talking gibberish. I guess all the pressure is finally getting to me. Forget I said anything."

"Let's go upstairs and talk some more." She grabbed a cloth lying on the fender and started wiping her hands.

"No, really. I've gotta go back out anyway."

"Frank, don't do this to me."

"Please, believe me, it's nothing—just frayed nerves. I need to clear my head a bit. You've got your car. I think I just need a walk on the beach."

Frank got back into his truck and drove off. Shelby would probably think it odd that he needed his truck for a walk on the beach, especially when the beach was just across the street. But before too long, that would be the least of his problems.

It was after seven in the evening and Alan Rosenthal's office was closed, but the lawyer had given Frank his home address and told him his door was always open.

Rosenthal welcomed Frank into his Beverly Hills apartment. "What's up, Frank?"

"I've been doing a lot of thinking lately."

"Did you come up with anything else about the Columbians?"

"The Columbians . . . that was just a fake out, Alan. I can't do it anymore."

"Do what?"

"Lie to you."

They both looked closely at each other as they sat in Rosenthal's stylish apartment. The lawyer didn't look shocked or upset. Maybe a little puzzled.

"Alan, I want to change my plea. I want to plead guilty to Gloria's murder."

Now Alan's expression did register surprise, but he was still calm. "So you are saying you killed Gloria?"

"Yeah, that's what I'm saying."

"What brought about this change of heart? Or change in your story?"

"I know the truth will come out. Maybe the DA will go easier on me if I confess and save everyone a lot of trouble."

"Let me make some coffee, and you can tell me all about it."

Alan went into the small kitchen while Frank sat on a tall stool by the bar that separated the kitchen from the dining room.

"It's pretty much what the cops think," Frank said as his lawyer measured coffee into a filter and filled the pot with water. "Gloria cheated on me through our whole marriage. And she loved flaunting it in my face. She emotionally emasculated me. Do you know what that's like for a

Mexican man? I finally ended the marriage, but I never stopped hating her."

"But you were divorced well over a year. Why wait that long to kill her?"

"It ate at me all the time, but I am not a killer. I never believed myself capable of that—until I saw her doing the same thing to my brother. She chews men up and spits them out. I could take only so much, then I decided to confront her, make her leave him alone."

"That's when you confronted her in the bar?"

"Yes. She laughed then and she laughed when I went to see her later."

"But you left again only to come back yet another time?"

"I got drunk and I got angrier."

"So you returned to her apartment. Were you planning to kill her then?"

"I don't know. I was furious—and I just lost it. I hit her. And still she laughed. It drove me mad with rage. I hit her again and again until she fell and struck her head."

"And that killed her?"

"I thought so. Her head was bleeding a lot, and she was unconscious. I didn't think she was breathing. I thought she was dead. Everything crashed in on me. I wasn't thinking straight. I wrapped her up and got her outside to my truck, took her to the boat, and dumped her into the ocean."

"Then you went off on a vacation to Mexico?"

"I was hoping I could set up an alibi."

"So you fell in love and got married. Or was that just part of the alibi?"

"No . . . I mean, yeah, it was. That is, I did love Shelby, but I thought getting married might make me look less guilty."

"Why didn't you just stay in Mexico?"

"I didn't want to spend my life as a fugitive. I figured if I returned, that would be the best way to look innocent."

Alan was silent for a long minute. Then he said, "That's a very interesting story, Frank." He faced Frank, wearing an odd expression. "It raises several questions. For one thing, after your arrest your car was checked and nothing was found. How come there was no blood there, but blood was found on the boat?"

"I had her wrapped up good in the car, but . . . the . . . the cover slipped off after I got to the boat and things got messy."

"Messy, you say?"

"What? Don't you believe me?"

"The question is, will the prosecution?"

"Why not? They want to nail me—they're getting just what they want."

"Before you carry through with this confession, Frank, I want you to give it some thought. The prosecution does not have a strong case. You might get off—if you go to trial. At the very least you could get only voluntary manslaughter, carrying a maximum sentence of eleven years, of which you'd only have to serve half. Five and a half years is not a long time, Frank. If you confess, the DA will have what he needs to press for murder one. They want to put you away for life, Frank. Gloria Herrera's father is laying on the pressure. He wants the charges to include special circumstances—he wants you executed. And the man has a good deal of clout with the DA. You've got to consider all the angles, Frank."

"There's nothing to think about. I killed Gloria, and I want to confess. I'm going to the police in the morning."

32

SHELBY AWOKE AT HER USUAL TIME, then fell back on her pillow groaning when she realized it was Saturday and she didn't have to go to school. That's when she noticed Frank wasn't there. He hadn't been home all night . . . again.

She lay there for some time trying to make sense of all that had happened. But everything was so convoluted that she finally dozed off. The ringing telephone woke her again. It was now eight o'clock.

Grabbing the phone, she said thickly, "Hello."

"Hi, Shelby, this is Alan."

"Alan?"

"Rosenthal—Frank's lawyer."

"Oh, I'm sorry. I guess I'm still asleep. Frank's not here."

"I was hoping I could catch him before he did anything foolish. I want to make sure I'm there if he decides to go to the police."

"What do you mean?"

"He's planning to change his plea."

"I don't understand."

"You didn't know?"

She absently shook her head, then answered, "No . . . what other plea is there?" She couldn't have heard Rosenthal correctly.

"He wants to plead guilty—"

"What!"

"He's ready to go to the police to confess."

Shelby sat upright, now fully awake. "That's crazy. What's he thinking? He's innocent."

"Not according to the story he told me last night."

Shelby talked to Rosenthal a few more minutes, then hung up, promising to call him the minute she heard from Frank. He promised to do the same. She jumped from bed and dressed quickly. She had to find Frank and stop him. She hurried out, got in her car, and drove out of the garage. It was only as she turned on to the street and noticed the buildings the bomb had destroyed that she determined the first and best place to look for Frank.

Before Frank went to the police he wanted to see his brother. When he got to the hospital, Ray was in his bed but wide awake.

"Just the man I wanted to see," Ray said brightly.

"How are you doing?"

"Better now that you're here. You got a little something for me, bro?"

Frank took the bag of cocaine from his pocket. Ray took it by himself this time. When he was done, he examined the bag. "This'll keep me supplied for a while," he said. There was about an ounce left in the bag.

"You better go easy on it, Ray. I can't get you any more."

"Is it the money?"

"You've got to kick it, Ray."

"Forget it."

"Ray, can you still remember when you were a kid? Do you remember the dreams you used to have? You were going to be a doctor and save the world. You were a whiz in science. I couldn't believe how smart you were.

But you also had such compassion. The kids in the neighborhood used to bring their hurt pets to you because they couldn't afford a vet. Remember that dog that got hit by a car? It was an ugly stray but you nursed that mongrel day and night."

"Until it died," Ray put in bitterly.

"That dog died knowing love for the first time in its life."

"I prolonged its suffering. What kind of compassion is that?"

"Well, that's not the point," said Frank with some frustration. "You had hopes and dreams back then. And I took them away from you—"

"Come on! Don't talk like that. You sound like you're starting to believe our mother. Even I know it's not true. I made my own choices."

Frank shook his head. "You would have made different choices if it hadn't been for me. The fact is, I was the one who got you started."

"I don't want to hear this."

"Listen to me, Ray," Frank said firmly. "I took away your life, and now I want to give it back to you."

"Oh, and how are you gonna do that?" Ray asked skeptically.

"That's not important. What's important is that in order for that to happen, you have to do one thing—you've got to kick your addiction."

"What if I don't want that so-called life back? What if I'm happy just the way things are?"

"Are you, Ray?"

"It doesn't matter. I can't do it."

"Promise me this one thing, Ray. When the time comes—and you'll know when it is—would you take my gift? Would you kick drugs and at least try to take back your life?"

"You're sounding weird, Frank, like you're going to die or something."

"If I were gonna die, would you grant me my dying wish?"

"This is too weird."

"Will you?" Frank pressed.

"Yeah, sure, if that's what you want. But let me just finish off this bag. No sense wasting the stuff. Then I'll clean up my act, I promise."

"You don't need the rest of that—"

Ray was already sprinkling more cocaine from the bag.

Frank jumped when the door suddenly opened. Ray was snorting, too caught up in his pleasure to give a thought to hiding the evidence. When Frank turned, he didn't know whether to be relieved or even more distressed to see Shelby instead of a nurse standing there taking in the scene with immediate awareness.

Shelby just stood there staring, full of dismay.

"Shelby, it's not what it seems—" But Frank stopped, knowing how lame and foolish his words were.

"I don't know what anything seems like anymore," she finally said.

"Hey, don't get down on him," Ray said, removing the straw and taking a quick swipe at his nose.

"You're right, Ray, it's not all his fault," she said. "You don't care who you bring down with you. You're just a selfish, self-centered jerk. I thought maybe you were worth all the agony Frank suffers because of you, but I was so wrong."

"And I was wrong about you, too," Ray retorted. "I thought you were cool—"

"Come on," Frank tried to intercede.

But Shelby was just warming up to the anger inside her. "I ought to call in the police. Maybe you just haven't felt enough consequences for your dirty habits."

"Just get out of here and leave me alone!" Ray yelled. "Frank, make her leave. I don't need to hear her preaching."

Frank glanced from Ray to Shelby. Was he really going to have to choose between them? But wasn't that exactly what he was going to do when he went to see the police? Shelby was strong, she didn't really need him. She would make it fine without him. Ray's need, on the other hand, was so immediate, so desperate.

"I'll go," Shelby was saying. "I won't force you to make that kind of choice, Frank."

Shelby left, and Frank hesitated only a moment before he hurried out after her. She was only a few paces away when he caught up with her.

"Shelby, I wish I could make you understand. . . ."

"So do I. Why can't you, Frank?" She didn't ask, she challenged.

"I told you. Ray is a burden I can't let go of."

"I really don't want you to have to choose between us."

"But I have . . ." Frank sighed. He so needed to hold her, but he made no attempt. It was the best way.

"Frank, does Ray have anything to do with you wanting to change your plea?"

"No," he said quickly. "I . . . just can't live with the lies anymore. I've destroyed a lot of lives, many I've never even met. The worst, of course, are those close to me—Ray, my mother and father, and even Gloria. Let me at least try to spare you."

"How? By leaving me? By going to prison? How do you know that won't destroy me, also?"

"It won't. You'll feel bad at first, but then you'll get on with your life."

"I can see it won't help to argue this point with you, Frank. What I really want to know is why you changed your plea."

"Because I'm guilty."

"I don't believe it."

He shook his head and almost smiled. But the ache inside made smiling impossible. Her open simplicity was what he loved most about her. It wasn't shallow at all, but rather of such profound depth only an innocent child could truly understand it.

"And I know it won't help to argue that point with you," he said dryly.

"Then you killed Gloria?"

"Yes, I killed her."

"I married a murderer?"

He nodded, and she shook her head at the same time.

"I told you many lies," he said. "I deceived you many times. And you know there is a part of you, however small, that realizes this. That knows

I am a killer, a dope pusher, a deceiver. I hope you will hate me for the lies. I deserve nothing less. But there was one truth in all the lies—I did fall in love with you there in Puerto Vallarta. I love you still. But in this case, love is not enough. Even you must see that. I trampled your love with my dishonesty. And my own love was so paltry I couldn't trust you with the truth."

"What about now? What of this sudden outbreak of truth?" There was sarcasm, questioning, and even hope in her tone.

"It's too late," he said flatly.

"I know you are going to call me naïve and innocent, maybe even shallow, but I don't think it's ever too late. It might take work, but—"

"Shelby!" he exclaimed, frustrated. "I know you are stubborn, but I don't think you really understand what's going on here. I am a murderer. I'm going to prison, maybe for the rest of my life. *Our marriage is over!* I want you to leave the condo. I want you to take back your life." He thought about what he had said to Ray. Would it be as impossible for her as it seemed it would be for Ray?

"You are my life!"

"Stop it!" He grabbed her shoulders to give them a shake. But he shouldn't have touched her. Before he could stop himself, he had pulled her roughly to him and his arms were around her. "It's over," he murmured into her soft, pale hair. "I don't want to see you again." But the trembling passion in his arms contrasted painfully with his words.

"Please, Frank . . ."

He made himself break away, but his hands still shook and his knees felt weak. "I'm sorry," he breathed. But he didn't see fear in her eyes, as he'd expected, or anger. What was wrong with her? Why couldn't she make this easy by despising him?

"Maybe we need a little time to think," she said, incredibly. "I'll go to my old house for a while, but that's all. To think." She started to walk away, then briefly turned back. "I forgot that I brought something for you. You must have taken it from your wallet." She held out his photo of his ideal family.

He took it and shook his head. "I didn't think I'd need this again." He slipped it gently into his pocket. "Good-bye, Shelby."

"For now . . ."

And she walked away.

33

ALAN ROSENTHAL WAS FURIOUS that Frank went to the police without him and threatened to quit the case, then finally relented only because of Shelby's and especially Dawn's pleadings. He spent hours with Doug Waller, trying to get the charges reduced to manslaughter, but Frank's confession practically confirmed premeditation because of his return trip to Gloria's apartment. The situation looked bleak, and the best Rosenthal could hope for was second-degree murder with life in prison. This was appealing to Waller if it meant avoiding a trial. It should also appease Herrera and the Hispanic community. The DA's office was going to deliberate on this and give an answer in a couple of days.

Frank refused to see Shelby when she went to visit him in jail. Only after several attempts did he finally relent. Wearing an orange prison jumpsuit, he looked rather pathetic. It didn't help that there were dark circles under his eyes from lack of sleep, and a stubble of unshaven beard on his face. He did indeed look like a criminal. Shelby still would not believe in his guilt. What had truly convinced her of his innocence was, oddly enough, his confession. It simply did not ring true to her. She'd heard enough of his lies—and been taken in by them—to be certain that this was the greatest lie of all. It helped that Rosenthal believed the same.

Yet why he would claim guilt when he was innocent was a mystery.

Perhaps he was somehow protecting his brother. But Shelby could not conceive that even Ray would allow his brother to go to prison for a crime Ray committed. It would take a heartless beast to do such a thing, and while Ray was a lot of things and had a lot of problems, that wasn't one of them.

Shelby's one visit with Frank was completely demoralizing. He told her not to come back, that he really would not see her again. He told her to get on with her life. Forget him. He wasn't worth it.

Deflated, Shelby drove home—to Whittier. She was still staying in her old house, for many reasons both practical and impractical. For the most part she just felt more secure there, safer. After the bombing she had been able to handle the condo only because of Frank's presence. Now that he was gone, she felt vulnerable regardless of Frank's assurance that the Columbian drug dealers were no threat to her.

But physical safety aside, she simply welcomed the comfort provided by the surroundings of a life that had been pleasant and happy. Two months ago she had tried to escape the memories of life with her father by going to Puerto Vallarta and falling in love. Now the escape had become her prison.

Shelby spent the rest of the afternoon trying to focus on preparing lessons for school. She had been missing a lot lately, and yesterday she spoke with her principal about taking a leave of absence. They decided Shelby would work until the end of the week and a substitute could start on Monday. That would give Shelby time to prepare her students for the change in their routine and also to prepare lessons for the substitute. But Shelby's mind was far removed from dinosaurs and phonics. The doorbell was a welcome interruption, and even more so when the caller turned out to be her friend Christie.

She had a pizza in one hand and a six-pack of soda in the other. "I hope you haven't had dinner yet."

"I didn't even realize it was that late," said Shelby.

"Well, let's eat while the pizza is still hot."

Shelby gestured for her friend to come in and unload her burdens. She led Christie into the kitchen where they served up slices of pepperoni pizza and grabbed cans of cold soda, then went back into the living room to eat. Christie kept the conversation rolling—Shelby was no good at small talk. Before they had gotten their second slice of pizza, Shelby knew all the gossip at Christie's advertising firm. Then Christie turned to the subject of her love life, which got them through the second slice of pizza. By then, however, the one-sidedness of the conversation was becoming quite obvious. There appeared to be an unspoken agreement between them that this evening should be kept light. Shelby searched her own mind for topics, but it seemed there was nothing trivial happening in her life lately.

"I'm going to take a leave of absence from work," she said. "They've got a substitute to start Monday."

"That's a big step, isn't it?"

Shelby shrugged. "It's just until . . . I don't know when. I'm useless at school. I can't think, I—" She stopped and looked apologetically at Christie. "Let's talk about something else."

"I've about run through my repertoire of conversation," said Christie.

"I'm kind of a drag, aren't I?"

"Look, I'm here whether you want to talk or whether you don't. We can go out to a movie if you really want to avoid it."

"I don't know what I want."

"I wish I knew what to say."

"You always know what to say, Christie."

"Maybe the problem is that what I have to say may not be what you want to hear."

"Oh . . ." Shelby pondered whether to press her friend further. But she didn't want the kind of relationship in which they had to walk around each other on eggshells—it was enough to have that in her marriage. With a determined sigh, she continued. "Let me have it, Christie. I'm so confused now, I need some fresh insight."

"I just think you are making a mistake right now, giving up your life to be the long-suffering wife. It's a no-win deal, Shelby."

"What do you mean?"

"Frank is a murderer—"

"Don't say any more," Shelby said, almost pleading.

"You got me started now, and I'd be a rotten friend if I wasn't honest with you. He has confessed, for heaven's sake! Maybe it was an accident, maybe it was self-defense, but he deceived you. Worse than that, days after killing his ex-wife and covering up the crime, he is in Puerto Vallarta wooing you. Shelby, how can you stand by him? Even if he didn't mean to kill her, which is open to question, what kind of man can fall in love and get married with blood practically still on his hands?" She let out a sharp breath. "There, I said it. I hope you won't hate me. I just had to say it for your sake."

"And the things you just said, Christie, are the very reasons I believe him to be innocent."

"Shelby, don't be so naïve."

"I am not naïve!" Shelby retorted, sick of once again being accused of ignorance. "I did not marry a murderer!"

"He *confessed*." Then more gently, Christie added, "I know how hard it must be to face having made such a terrible mistake in your marriage. But don't make it worse by compounding it."

Sudden tears filled Shelby's eyes. Trying unsuccessfully to hold them back, she said, "I didn't make a mistake. I . . . I couldn't have." Christie reached out to her but Shelby pulled back. "Is that what I am? Some stupid, empty-headed female duped by a smooth-talking man? It was so real . . . so . . . good. Was I really so blind?"

The doorbell rang again, preventing a response from Christie, who got up to answer it thinking to send whoever it was away. But it was Dawn. She, too, was carrying a pizza in one hand and in the other a couple of videos.

"It's not a very good time," Christie said.

Shelby turned, swiping at her teary eyes with the back of her hand. "Dawn," she said in a shaky voice.

"What's wrong?" Dawn asked, stepping fully inside. Christie took the pizza and carried it to the kitchen while Dawn went to the sofa and sat down next to Shelby.

"I'm just getting a lesson in reality," Shelby said.

Christie came back into the room. "Maybe the lesson was too brutal."

"Maybe it wasn't," said Shelby, her voice much steadier. "Tell Dawn what you said."

Reluctantly Christie repeated her observations.

"How could you say such things?" said Dawn indignantly.

Christie was obviously surprised at this reaction. "I was just being honest with my feelings. That's the kind of friendship Shelby and I have. But don't tell me, Dawn, that you also think Frank is innocent."

"I don't have enough information to make that kind of judgment."

"But how do you *feel*?" pressed Christie.

"I've never been able to trust my feelings."

"Maybe Shelby inherited that—" Christie stopped suddenly, her eyes shifting from mother to daughter. "I think I better shut up before I really step in it. I think I'll take off. Shelby, we can talk again, maybe when we can both be a little more objective. I really don't want to do anything to hurt our friendship." She paused, gave Shelby's shoulder a squeeze, then headed for the door. "We'll talk soon, okay?" It was both a statement and a question.

"You've got yourself a good friend there," Dawn said sincerely after Christie was gone.

"And maybe she's . . . right." Tears filled Shelby's eyes again. "Maybe I'm just too proud and stubborn to admit I got duped."

"One thing, Shelby. I don't want you to believe that stuff about you inheriting poor judgment from me. I don't think that kind of thing is inherited—it's learned. And your dad taught you well. That's what you have to believe."

"How will I ever be certain? There are so many things with Frank that don't add up—or rather, add up to be terribly incriminating. Wouldn't I be the utter fool to give him my loyalty, only to have him turn out to be—"

"You're no fool!" Dawn exclaimed with assurance. "Do you want some advice?"

"Yes, anything."

"You've got to decide what the truth is, and then stick by it. I know the hard part is making the initial decision. But . . . well, I hope you won't be offended, Shelby, but I have been praying for you." A self-conscious smile played at Dawn's lips. "That sounds so weird and pretentious, as if my prayers are powerful or something. But my prayers, or anyone's, are only worth something because God listens to the people who love Him."

"You don't have to apologize, Dawn. In fact . . . it almost makes me feel good knowing that. As if I haven't been all alone."

"You don't have to be alone, Shelby."

"I really do appreciate the way you've been there for me—"

"You can't count on *me*. Oh, I'm here now, and I fully intend on sticking by you—and I fully intend on living out my commitment to God. But you know better than anyone that I can be kind of flaky. I can't promise what will happen in the future. But I can tell you that Jesus isn't flaky. He will never walk out on you. He will *always* be there for you."

"Kind of like Dad was."

Dawn smiled. "Yes. But your father was only human, too. He couldn't help dying. . . ."

"And leaving me."

"Jesus won't do that. He already died, and He was resurrected so that He could be with us eternally."

"Dawn, how do you know? How do you know what you have is real, that it's not just some emotional trip or something?"

"I wondered that, too, when I was first confronted with faith in Jesus. And the answer is so simple, I suppose it's almost silly. You just know.

And it is a knowledge that grows daily. I have a deeper sense of the reality of God now than when I first believed."

"And this faith will make me feel good, happy, and all that?"

"It won't take away sadness and pain. Faith just gives you the strength to face those things. It's not a 'feel good' pill. But when you know God and you are in trouble, you have something that is so much better than just being happy and feeling good. You have support, comfort."

Shelby lifted her eyes to look fully into her mother's face. For the first time in her life, she felt like a child clinging to her mother. "Will God make everything all right with Frank?"

Sadly Dawn shook her head. "That's not what it's all about, honey."

Shelby sniffed back a new flow of tears. "I know. I suppose I just had to ask."

"I'm sorry." Dawn took Shelby's hands into hers.

"Mother . . ." Shelby smiled through her tears. "Would you pray with me?"

Dawn was crying, too, as she nodded.

34

Ray was having a rough time since his brother stopped coming to the hospital. Not only was Ray furious Frank would drop him without any explanation, but he was physically regretting it, as well. He tried to enlist some friends to sneak drugs to him in the hospital, but none were willing to take the risk, especially since he had little money to offer them. Ray was in the habit of doing one or two grams of coke a day—a tremendous amount for most people, but Ray seemed to have a huge capacity for the drug. His habit easily cost him fifteen hundred dollars a week. If his fortunes didn't change soon, he wondered what he was going to do. He'd considered many times escaping the hospital—after all, he wasn't under arrest. But even if he did try to split from the hospital, he wouldn't get far with his leg all pinned up. He was stuck. And all he could think of was the pleasure a nice hit of coke could give him.

Trying to distract himself, he turned on the television. The evening news came on, and Ray would have immediately changed the channel except a phrase caught his attention.

". . . the largest drug bust of the year. Over six hundred pounds of controlled substances were confiscated last night by Drug Enforcement Agents. I have with me now Detective Brian Anderson of the L.A.P.D. Drug Task Force, who was working with the DEA on the bust. Mr. Anderson, do you have anyone in custody?"

"Yes, we were very fortunate this time. We have Hector Barcelona, whom we believe to be a major player in the Southland drug scene."

Ray smiled and turned up the volume.

"Detective Anderson, what would the street value be of the drugs confiscated?"

"We estimate it to be several million dollars."

"What drugs specifically?"

"Cocaine and heroin."

"Do you have a strong case against Barcelona?"

"I can't really discuss the details at this time, but we are confident we will be able to put Barcelona away for a long time. This is a major coup for our department, and I would like to say that this is what can be expected when various law enforcement agencies work together. . . ."

Ray switched off the television. The last thing he wanted to hear was some cop droning on about how noble and heroic they were. He'd heard enough anyway. Barcelona was nailed. That was the sweetest news he'd heard in weeks. He gave no thought to how this might affect him until the next morning, when Detective Anderson, the cop from the news, came to see him. He wanted Ray to testify against Barcelona. Ray played dumb. He didn't like the idea of cooperating with the police, even if it meant striking a blow against Hector. Besides, they had nothing to offer him in return for his cooperation.

At eleven o'clock that night he had another visitor. Barcelona slipped into the room quietly. Ray wondered if he had escaped jail, but Barcelona wasn't that stupid.

"So they turned you loose, Hector?" Ray said casually.

"I got me a good lawyer, amigo. I'm out on bail."

"Congratulations," Ray smirked.

"I hear the cops paid you a visit today."

"Yeah, they did." Ray understood now the reason for Barcelona's visit. "They got you worried, Hector?"

"Why should I worry? Old compadres stick together, eh?"

"Compadres? Seems you were ready to kill me a couple of weeks ago. I'm still not certain who blew up my car."

"I swear by the Virgin Mary herself I didn't do that! Ramon, amigo . . ." Barcelona's tone was sickeningly sweet. "Sure, we have our differences every now and then. Just like real brothers, eh? You got to know, I love you like my own brother." He paused and reached into his pocket. "See how I care about you? I don't come empty-handed." He held out a bag.

Ray reacted immediately to the white powder in the bag. His mouth watered, his heart throbbed. It was better than seeing an old friend. He reached for it, then stopped. "What do you want in return, Hector?" He almost didn't care what the answer would be; he knew he was going to take the bag.

"This is a gift, amigo. Enjoy."

Ray glanced toward the door.

"Don't worry, Ray," Barcelona assured. "The nurses are changing shifts and distracted, that's why I came now. They're also busy with a big emergency, a freeway accident. And Ricardo is outside the door. No one's gonna bother you. You must be really jonesing. How long has it been? I promise, no strings attached."

Ray grabbed the bag. After a long, satisfying hit, Ray lay back and let the effects of the drug wash over him. In about three minutes the rush came. He loved the rush. Everything became so sharp and clear, like coming out of a haze into a bright, beautiful day.

"This is pretty pure stuff," Ray said.

"You bet. As pure as it comes—never been stepped on. Nothing but the best for my friends."

Ray took another deep snort.

"You better go easy on it, man," said Barcelona.

"Don't worry about me. I can handle it. You just worry that no one comes in here."

"No one's gonna bother us, Ramon." Barcelona pulled up a chair and sat down. "Now, Ray, like I said, the coke is a gift, but I do gotta talk to you about something. I know you won't turn on me. You did time protecting me before, so I know I can count on you. But I am a little worried about Frank."

"Frank is cool. There's no way he'd rat on you."

"I wish I could be sure, but with Frank going down for Gloria's murder, he may just think he has nothing to lose."

"He's not going down for killing Gloria," Ray said with confidence. It was real confidence, too—not from the coke, because he knew he would not let anything happen to Frank.

But Barcelona replied, "After confessing, what else do you think will happen?"

"What do you mean, confessing?"

"You don't know? He changed his plea to guilty. They're gonna put him away, man."

"That can't be . . ." But Ray suddenly understood why Frank had stopped his visits to the hospital. He must be in jail.

"It's true, Ramon."

"The idiot! The stupid idiot. What's he thinking?" Ray asked the question mostly of himself. He had nearly forgotten about Barcelona. "I gotta talk to him. He can't do this." He sat up, and giving his injured leg a shove, swung his legs from the bed. Pain shot all the way through his body, and he fell back again.

"Are you supposed to be doing that?" said Barcelona.

"Help me get outta here!"

"I don't know, man. You could hurt yourself."

Struggling, Ray kept trying to get out of the bed. Finally Barcelona gave him a hand. Leaning on Barcelona and ignoring the pain in his leg, Ray stood shakily.

"Come on," Ray urged. "Let's go!"

"Don't you want to get dressed?"

Ray gave that a moment's thought, but with the cocaine rushing through his body and his heart racing, he just wanted to get moving. Still, he couldn't very well run through the streets in a hospital gown. "Get my stuff."

"Okay, but let me hold on to that coke before it gets spilled everywhere."

Ray was reluctant to do so, but he handed it over. He'd get it back later.

Dressing proved to be a useless endeavor. He couldn't get his trousers over the thick bandages on his leg, and his hands were shaking too much to properly button his shirt. Tossing the useless items aside, he started toward the door and would have landed on his face if Barcelona hadn't held him up. They made it into the corridor. Suddenly a pain like none Ray had ever experienced assailed him. It made the pain shooting through his leg pale by comparison. It struck his chest like a sledgehammer. He lost his hold on Barcelona and crumbled toward the floor.

He heard Barcelona say, as if from a great distance, "What's wrong, man?"

When Ray only gasped in response, Barcelona yelled toward the nurses' station. "Hey! Help us!"

A nurse came running. She bent over Ray, lifted his eyelids, then listened to his heart. She also yelled at the other nurse in the station. "Brenda, he's gone into arrest!" Then she began pumping his chest, but that was all Ray remembered.

Frank heard the news the next day from his lawyer.

"A heart attack? But he's not even twenty-five."

"They say he would have died if he hadn't been in the hospital already. His tox-screen was soaring. He'd very recently been taking drugs."

Frank dropped his head in his hands. So much for trying to give back a life.

But Frank had little chance to stew over his brother because Rosenthal's original purpose in coming had been to be present during a questioning session between Frank, Liscom and Poole, and the assistant district attorney. Rosenthal was still asking that the charge be reduced to manslaughter, but Doug Waller had been fairly unmovable in his determination to keep the charge at first-degree murder. However, that morning the assistant district attorney had called Alan and told him they were willing to talk.

Apparently the police had arrested an old associate of Frank's, and they wanted Frank's testimony against this man. Waller was willing—and here the assistant DA acted like he was the next thing to Santa Claus in his generosity—to make certain concessions to Frank in exchange for his testimony. In consideration of that, and in view of the fact that Frank appeared to have cleaned up his life, the state would consider reducing the charge in the Gloria Herrera case to voluntary manslaughter.

Frank did not want to be executed for murder nor go to jail for the rest of his life. All he wanted was to take the guilt for Gloria's murder. If he could do so while receiving the least number of years behind bars, so much the better. However, he refused to save himself by bringing down Barcelona. He and Barcelona had been equals in the drug business. Moreover, he and Barcelona had once been partners, compadres, even friends. Frank remembered many times when Hector had stood up for him, saved his skin, and bailed him out of trouble. True, as they had become more enmeshed in the drug world Barcelona had changed, become harder, more ruthless, even as Frank had become more disheartened and sickened by it all. In a way, Frank saw Barcelona as a victim every bit as much as Ray. Today, Frank might think of his old friend as a snake or worse, but he could not betray the past. Though they were all going to pay for their crimes in one way or another, Frank would not be the one to force the payment.

After several grueling hours of interrogation and bargaining, it was clear Frank would not budge. And Doug Waller, quite unhappy with the outcome, seemed more adamant than ever that Frank should be charged with first-degree murder. It took Alan Rosenthal two more days of hammering away at the assistant district attorney before finally convincing him that the murder of Gloria Herrera was not a premeditated crime and that because Frank had no record he ought to be given a break. The fact that several other witnesses were willing to testify against Barcelona also put the district attorney in a better mood.

The concession was a formal charge of second-degree murder, carrying a life sentence with no possibility of parole. Alan was disheartened and told Frank he was ready to go to trial to fight for the reduced charge, but the chances of winning were slim. Frank just shook his head. He would not put Shelby through the agony of a trial. He'd hurt enough people in his life. He deserved to go to prison.

35

WHEN RAY NEXT BECAME AWARE of his surroundings, he noted there were wires and tubes all over his body and he was in a different room than before. He could hear the steady *bleep* of a monitor. But at least that terrible pain in his chest was gone, though his leg was throbbing. He tried to remember what had happened, how he had ended up here.

Barcelona . . . he had been talking to him. Barcelona had been arrested but was out on bail. He was worried. . . .

Suddenly it all came back to Ray. "Frank!" he yelled and began to struggle against the tangle of wires and tubes. He pulled at a couple of wires attached to his chest and vaguely heard an alarmlike sound. All at once two nurses were at his side.

"It's okay, Ramon," one was saying in a calm tone.

"I have to get out of here!" Ray cried.

"You've got to stay here so we can get you better." Her voice sounded so sweet that Ray almost wanted to stay.

But then he remembered his brother. "I need to save Frank. I gotta see him."

"You have to stay in the hospital, Ray. You are a very sick man."

"Frank's in trouble. . . ." He fought again, but the nurse's hands held him. He writhed and struggled. He had to go to his brother.

"I think he's having a psychotic episode," one of the nurses said. "I better call the doctor."

Ray continued to struggle, knocking over the I.V. bottle, sending it crashing to the floor, which in turn ripped the needle from the vein in his hand. "Get the police! I have to talk to the police!" he yelled over and over.

When the doctor arrived he ordered Valium for Ray, then tried to talk to him. "Ray, you're going to give yourself another arrest if you don't calm down."

"Get me the police."

"When you are better you can talk—"

Ray grabbed the doctor's lab coat. "Now! I have to talk to them now!"

"Will you promise to calm down if I let you do that?"

"Yeah. Just get them here."

Liscom and Poole arrived about an hour later.

"You've got to let my brother go," Ray told them. He was still very agitated. "He didn't kill anyone. I did, do you hear? I killed Gloria. Let Frank go."

"You're confessing to Gloria Herrera's murder?" said Poole.

"Yes! I didn't mean to do it. Things just got out of hand. I was pretty stoked up, you know, doing speedballs and I don't know what else. But she just kept playing with my head. She was cheating on me and she loved seeing me suffer. I went crazy. I hit her a couple of times. She fell and hit her head."

"Sounds pretty much like Frank's story—"

"But I'm telling the truth!" Ray yelled.

"Maybe you're just confessing to protect your brother," said Liscom.

"You don't get it! *He's* trying to protect *me*!"

"You got any hard proof?"

"I put her in my car to take her to the boat. There was blood in my car. I tried to clean it up, but you guys can always find traces—like you did on the boat."

"Only problem with that, Ray, is that your car blew up into a million pieces."

Groaning in despair, Ray fell back against his pillow. Ever since Frank had been arrested for Gloria's murder, Ray had been confident that his brother would get off. In the first place, he didn't believe the police had a strong enough case to convict Frank, especially since Ray *knew* his brother was innocent. Ray was indeed the killer—it had happened just as he had told the police. But in the off chance Frank was convicted, Ray planned all along to then turn himself in. Frank had ruined everything by confessing.

"Look," said Poole, "we'll take what you have said into consideration. We'll investigate it and see what we come up with. Now, you better relax because you're not gonna help your brother if you're dead."

Poole and Liscom left Ray's bedside in the Cardiac Care Unit. As they walked to the elevator, Liscom chuckled.

"What a piece of work," he said. "But you gotta give it to those Mexicans, they stick together."

"You think he's blowing out air?"

"Of course."

"Maybe he's not."

"Wait a minute, Ed," said Liscom, stopping to face his partner. "We have the man we want in custody. We don't have to look anywhere else."

"We have the man we *want*, but do we have the murderer?"

"We've got a drug-dealing scum ball, and we have a chance to put him out of commission for a long time. We are also in a perfect position to nail another piece of scum. Frank Stefano will give us Barcelona if he thinks he can plea-bargain the murder charge. Now, that's a good day's work."

"I heard that Stefano refuses to testify against Barcelona."

"Just give him time. A few weeks in lockup might make him crack."

"And what if the real killer goes free in the meantime?"

"Ray Stefano is nothing, a nobody. The way he's hitting the dope, he'll be dead in a year anyway. We've been wanting Barcelona and Frank Stefano for a long time. We got them both. I can let Ramon go because he is too stupid to be any threat in the drug world. Besides, Ramon probably only confessed because he thinks he's gonna die anyway, so why not rescue his brother before he goes."

"On the other hand, maybe he wants to clear his conscience before he dies."

"Like I said, we have the right man in custody."

They started walking again, reached the elevator, and Liscom punched the button.

"I heard Frank Stefano cleaned up his act, that he isn't in the business anymore," said Poole.

"It's a big front. Once you're in you never get out. And even so, he still ought to pay for the past."

"That's not my job, Marv. My job right now is to find Gloria Herrera's killer."

"We *have* found her killer."

"I'm not so sure," said Poole.

The elevator arrived and they stepped inside.

36

SHELBY HAD HEARD THROUGH ALAN that Ray had had a heart attack and was not doing well. He had also confessed to Gloria's murder, but the police had given little credence to it, writing it off as an attempt to protect his big brother. This, however, reinforced Shelby's faith in Frank's innocence. She knew Frank well enough to be able to perceive him as the rescuer of Ray rather than the other way around.

At Frank's formal sentencing Dawn sat with Shelby and offered tremendous support just with her presence. Shelby had begun attending Dawn's church and was feeling more and more certain that she had made the right choice in giving her life to God. She believed she could not have sat there and heard Frank's fate or watched Frank's strained countenance without the support of her growing faith.

She wanted desperately to talk to him, but he was still refusing to see her in prison. The instant they were dismissed by the judge, she hurried to the front, not debating her actions or worrying about causing a scene in court.

"Frank . . ." she said from behind the wooden barrier separating the spectators from the front of the court.

When he didn't respond, Alan nudged him firmly. "Talk to her, Frank," he said.

And much to Shelby's surprise, Frank turned. "Hello, Shelby," he said formally.

"How are you?" was all she could think to say, though the answer to that question was obvious.

"Fine."

After waiting so long to talk to him, Shelby was suddenly dumb-struck. She didn't want to waste this precious time with trivial words, yet this was hardly the place for deep soul-searching.

"I love you, Frank." The words managed to squeeze past the lump in her throat.

"Shelby, I can't keep you from trying to see me, but I can ask you not to." He did not look directly at her as he spoke. "It serves no purpose. Alan is in the process of drawing up divorce papers. You could even make it easy on both of us by applying for an annulment. Alan says you have valid grounds for one. It will be like the marriage never happened."

"That can't be what you want."

"It is what I want."

At that moment the guards came, and Frank let them lead him away, not turning when she called his name.

"Alan," she said to the lawyer, "tell me this isn't so."

"He's quite determined about it."

"Can it happen without my cooperation?"

"Possibly. But fighting it won't help, Shelby, especially with him in prison. You will have to think about getting on with your life."

After that, Shelby rattled around her empty house for about a week before going back to work. She "got on with her life" like everyone kept telling her to do, but she did so only because there was no other choice. Ray also seemed to be getting on with his life, but not in the way Frank would have wanted. After a week in the Intensive Care Unit and another week back on the regular medical-surgical floor, he was released from the hospital. Mrs. Querida told Shelby that she and his parents had tried to make him get into a rehab, but since he was an adult, they could not force the issue. He assured them, however, that he was dried out and was going to stay away from drugs. No one believed him.

A month passed and spring came in full force to Southern California. The Santa Anna winds blew away some of the smog, and the temperatures warmed up to the eighties. Shelby tried to get excited about spring projects with her class. They were going to make Easter baskets with real grass they would grow themselves inside the baskets. There were also bunny projects and units about butterflies and new life. Shelby's own new life, her life in Christ, was continuing in spite of her growing listlessness. She was determined, however, not to give up on God simply because things were not working out to her satisfaction.

That determination was bolstered considerably from reading the Bible given to her by her mother. On Dawn's advice she began in the New Testament. Shelby had never read the Bible before, and even the most common Scriptures were obscure to her. But as she began the Gospel of Matthew in a modern English version, she discovered it was like reading a regular story. Suddenly the text was exciting and came alive for her in a way she'd never expected.

Eventually Shelby reached the book of Romans. It was not as riveting as the previous books because it was less of a story and more of, in her mind, a sermon. But she read it doggedly—until she reached chapter eight. It was there that a verse reached out and grabbed her. This was an entirely different sensation than even the excitement she had experienced in her previous reading. The verse may as well have been written in neon.

"And we know that God causes everything to work together for the good of those who love God and are called according to His purpose for them."

It practically shouted at her. In fact, as she read it, she was nearly sure she had really *heard* her name. *"Shelby, all things will work together for good because you love me and I have called you according to my purpose."* She'd heard some people say how God spoke to them, and she wondered if this was what they had meant. Could God actually be speaking to her? The very idea made her heart pound and her head spin.

When Shelby told Dawn about it, her mother only said with a smile, "Isn't that just like God."

Shelby's only response was "Wow!"

She clung to that verse, allowing it to give her hope and lift her spirit. She didn't know why Frank had gone to prison when she had prayed so hard for a miracle to keep him out. But Shelby knew—she really knew!—that somehow good would come out of it. Maybe there would yet be a miracle.

Ed Poole did not consider himself to be the sentimental type, even though his partner, Marv, often called him a "bleeding heart." He wanted to put away low-life drug dealers as much as anyone. But from the very beginning, from that first time he had questioned Frank Stefano about the Herrera murder, he'd had mixed feelings about the man. For years he had known that Stefano and Barcelona were smuggling major amounts of drugs into the country. But they had been practically untouchable. They were smart and careful, so that any sting attempts by the police inevitably failed.

The closest they had come to getting the two was when they arrested Ramon Stefano on that "possession with intent to sell" charge. But the younger Stefano had gone to jail rather than implicate his brother. Poole learned from the vice cops who had been keeping an eye on Stefano and Barcelona that Stefano had appeared to taper back his dealings considerably after Ray's arrest—either that or he was putting on the best front ever. Except for occasional contact with his brother, Frank seemed to have cut off almost all contact with the drug world.

Liscom refused to believe Frank had changed, but Poole, who considered himself to be a pretty good judge of human nature, sensed a real sincerity in Stefano. If Frank did murder Gloria, he did so truly believing it was the only way to protect his brother. But Frank Stefano simply did not appear to be the kind of man who would brutally attack a woman, even in a fit of passion, then drag her body to a boat in order to dump her at sea. This seemed more the behavior of a poor, lost kid whose head was messed up by dope.

Unfortunately, Poole was having a hard time proving this. Several months ago the vice department had given up on Frank Stefano—they were too busy to keep after a man who was leading them nowhere. Thus, they had not a clue about Stefano's visit to Gloria Herrera, nor were they even apprised of Stefano's subsequent trip to Mexico. As far as the evidence implicating Stefano in the Herrera murder, Poole doubted it would have been enough to convict Frank if he had not confessed. And there was nowhere else to look for solid evidence. Gloria Herrera's apartment had been rented to someone else. Ray's car was demolished. The witnesses who placed Frank at the scene were all that was left of any substantial use. But the brothers looked enough alike to be mistaken for each other. Frank had said he had made two trips to Gloria's place. The first time he had argued with his ex-wife, and he had left only to return later and end up killing her. So the neighbors might have indeed seen him once and just assumed it was him the second time. Had they been questioned at a trial, this discrepancy might have been discovered.

No trial meant no chance to either prove or disprove Frank's guilt. That was too bad, because Ed Poole really hated to send innocent men to jail.

The phone blared on Ed's desk, and he shoved aside the report he was working on to grab the receiver.

"Yeah, Poole here," he said. After pausing to listen, he responded, "Uh-huh, Mr. Lazar. I can see how that would disturb you. Uh-huh . . ." The conversation continued for a few moments with Poole nodding and interjecting "uh-huhs" at appropriate points. Finally, "I'll talk to him, sir. I can see where he might make you nervous, but I am sure he is harmless enough. Sure . . . I'll talk to him."

Poole hung up the receiver, a bemused look on his face. This Stefano case was getting stranger and stranger. Ramon Stefano seemed to be conducting his own investigation—at least he had approached one of the witnesses a couple of times. The man, Mr. Lazar, said Ray was practically badgering him to change his story. Ramon had even asked Lazar if it could have been he, Ramon, whom Lazar had seen return to Gloria's apartment that night. By itself that was odd behavior, but coupled with the fact that Ramon Stefano made regular appearances at Poole's desk to inquire about any new findings in the Herrera case, it added up to peculiar indeed. For a once-convicted drug addict to come within a mile of the police on his own volition made one rethink things.

Ramon's persistence had to be more than a noble attempt to rescue his brother. He'd have to realize by now that it was lame—unless he was certain Frank was not the killer. But Poole simply did not know how to get at the truth. He'd been over all the reports from the case a dozen times. So much of it was circumstantial. Fingerprints, for example, showed that both Frank and Ramon had been in Gloria's apartment, but they both knew her and had been there many times. The blood on the boat was their best solid evidence, but it only showed that Gloria Herrera had been on the boat and left some blood. The logical, and most likely correct, assumption was that she had been there on the night of her murder, but she had been on the boat on previous occasions and could easily have cut a finger then and left her blood. Of course, the most prohibitive element in attempting to prove anything was the time factor. It had been hard enough to gather evidence when Herrera's body had been found three weeks after her death. It was only getting more difficult. And Poole had a dozen other cases demanding his attention; he didn't have the time to devote to a closed case, one that was supposedly solved.

What he needed was a break in the case—a big break.

37

Ray's fortunes were improving by the minute. Barcelona's arrest, along with his henchmen, Carlos and Ricardo, had left his entire operation up for grabs. And Ray was in the perfect position to step in and take over. It had only been a couple of months since he'd fallen out of grace with Barcelona, so he was still well-known to Barcelona's contacts—in fact, many preferred dealing with Ray over the ruthless Barcelona. Within a couple of weeks after his release from the hospital, Ray was back in business. And his own personal consumption of cocaine was also back to normal. He needed the energy and the sense of confidence the drug provided in order to handle the responsibilities of a big-time operation.

Two problems, however, still weighed on him. He couldn't do anything about Cuervo. He'd just have to live with that threat hanging over him, although it was seeming less and less of a real threat. Barcelona's Columbian contacts did not share Cuervo's vendetta against Ray, proving that Cuervo didn't have as much influence in the cartel as he had tried to make Ray believe. In fact, the drug lords were on the verge of completely disassociating from Cuervo. Rumor even had it that there was a contract out on Cuervo.

But by far the most weighty problem was Ray's brother. Ray was going to do all he could to get Frank out of jail, even if it meant helping him escape. That's why it was so important to start bringing in cash. It was going to take money to save Frank, one way or another. And he was tireless toward both ends. Pumped up on coke, he could go days without sleep, and he did so often. The world was in slow motion, while he was constantly in fast forward. Even if Cuervo did still want to kill him, he'd have a hard time nailing Ray down to do so. The only thing that slowed him down at all was having to hobble around on crutches. In two weeks, Ray made two trips to Miami in order to set up a meeting with the Columbians and then a trip to Columbia. He was there for three days enjoying an incredibly high life, compliments of a major drug lord—living in a fortress, drinking Dom Pérignon, socializing with beautiful women, and especially, indulging in the purest drugs the world had to offer.

In this situation it was very hard to remember what it was all about— that his brother was serving time for a crime he, Ramon, had committed. Under the influence, Ray had complete confidence that he'd save Frank. In fact, he was certain that he could save Frank and himself, as well. No sense either of them going down for Gloria's murder. Anyway, Gloria hadn't really been murdered, not technically speaking. It had happened just like he told Poole. Only he had left out a few details. Like walking in on Gloria while she was with another man. Ramon had indeed been very high that night, and her betrayal only intensified his rage. He had let himself believe that he was the one man Gloria was true to . . . she had led him to believe that, as well. To realize what a fool he had been was more than he could handle. That's probably one reason why he hadn't mentioned Willie Cantrell to the police. Ray was too humiliated—not only that Gloria was cheating on him, but that she was doing it with a loser like Cantrell. Ray understood what Frank had always said about Gloria, that she reveled in making men feel small. It was her sick way of maintaining control.

But Ray was glad he had kept Cantrell's part in all this to himself for another reason. No sense mentioning an eyewitness, or at least someone who could prove Ray had motive, if there was still a chance for both Ray and Frank to be spared. And he was glad Willie had had enough sense to keep quiet about it, also. Ray was just not as sentimental as Frank and saw no point in going to prison, like a lamb to slaughter, to save his little brother. Ray was far more pragmatic. Anyway, he'd gone that route once, hadn't he? He'd already served time for Frank—well, not exactly *for* Frank, but he could have gotten a far lighter sentence if he had turned in Frank.

As Ray sat in his apartment, he determined to be neither sentimental nor stupid. He'd prove to his brother once and for all that he could take care of himself and Frank, as well. He began thinking more and more of a prison escape. He could easily get Frank a passport, and Frank could hide out in Columbia. No one would be able to get to Frank if he was holed up in that drug lord's fortress.

Tomorrow Ray would work on making all the proper contacts, both in prison and out. He'd make this happen. For now, though, he needed a little pick-me-up. He took out his supply of coke, sprinkled some on his kitchen table and, with a butter knife, lined it out carefully. Soon after inhaling it with a straw, he grabbed his crutches and jumped up, deciding he didn't have to wait for tomorrow. It was only ten in the evening— prime time for most of his contacts. After stashing his supply of cocaine, he grabbed his coat and headed for the door. Suddenly he stopped and gasped as pain like a blow hit his chest. He staggered back against the door. It wasn't quite as bad as last time, but it was bad enough to bring tears to his eyes. Gasping for breath, he frantically tried to think about what to do.

He made it to the phone and punched in 9–1–1. As he waited for an ambulance, he wondered if he'd make it. They said he had almost died the last time, that he would have had he not already been in a hospital. All his previous confidence and bravado was suddenly overshadowed with fear. He started shaking. What if he died now? There would be no one to save Frank.

"What have I done?" he groaned.

Hearing a siren approach in the street outside his apartment gave him

no hope. He could still die. The pain responded a little to the nitroglyc-
erin tablets the doctor had given him but not enough to revive his confidence. He grabbed at the phone once again and keyed in a number he
had by now memorized.

"Poole . . . I gotta talk to Detective Poole . . . Ramon Stefano . . ."

But the pain started again in full force, squeezing his chest like a vice,
and Ray dropped the receiver. Then there was pounding on his door, and
in a moment paramedics charged in.

Ramon Stefano was in bad shape and might not make it through the
night, but at least he had done the right thing before he lost the chance.
He had given Poole the break he needed. An eyewitness.

From Ramon's bedside in Intensive Care, he had told Poole of a Willie
Cantrell who had seen Ramon with Gloria on the night of her death—
after Frank's visit. Not only that but Cantrell's reason for being at Gloria's
apartment also provided a perfect motive for Ray. It all fit so much better
than Frank Stefano's lame little scenario.

Poole found Cantrell at the beach house he rented with six other surf-
ers and beach bums. For once, Liscom's strong-arm tactics paid off. He'd
had the foresight to get a search warrant before picking up Cantrell, so
when they got to the house they were able to throw their weight around
a bit. They walked in on a mad scramble for the bathroom, but the old
toilet there couldn't flush fast enough and it overflowed, belching up
doobies and plastic Baggies and other suspicious paraphernalia. Poole and
Liscom hauled in everyone at the house, including Cantrell.

At the police station, with prison hanging over his head, the hapless
surfer was more than willing to spill out his guts. Ray had gone berserk
when he caught Willie and Gloria together. He had attacked them both,
but Willie had managed to escape. He insisted that he believed he was in

more danger than Gloria and that if he left, Ray would calm down. But when Cantrell returned about thirty minutes later to make sure Gloria was okay, he watched covertly as Ray put something in the backseat of his car—obviously a body. Of course, calling the police had been the furthermost thing from the drug dealer's mind.

After several hours of interrogation, the police had enough to properly solve the Herrera murder. But Poole did not feel victorious. Ray Stefano was as much a victim as Gloria Herrera.

Poole called Doug Waller, the attorney who had handled the Stefano case, and told him all he'd discovered. They met a couple of hours later, and the man looked over all the new evidence and was convinced. And he was pretty upset that he'd locked up the wrong man. Poole understood because he felt the same way. Of course, Frank Stefano hadn't helped with his false confession.

"Is Ramon Stefano still alive?" asked Waller.

"He's hanging on, but barely. How long before Frank can get out of jail?"

"These things take time, Poole. You know that."

"It'd be rotten if Frank couldn't see his brother before he died. Couldn't you pull a few strings?"

"I'll see if I can expedite a kick-out order."

Quite miraculously, the assistant DA was able to get Frank out in two days. Even more amazing was the fact that Ramon was still alive.

When Poole drove out to the Chino Prison Facility to personally see to Frank's release, he did not receive a grateful reception. Frank had known all along of his brother's guilt and had been ready and willing to take Ray's punishment. Learning of his brother's hospitalization and the serious nature of his illness did not improve his disposition.

Poole hoped that one day Frank would come to realize that his act of sacrifice would most likely not have spared his brother. Ray's self-destructive nature would have doomed him one way or another.

When Frank arrived at the hospital the morning of his release from prison, his grandmother greeted him with a loving embrace. Her joy at seeing Frank vied with her worry over Ramon. But she kissed Frank's cheek and held tightly to his hand.

"They let you out of jail, Frank. Just to see Ramon?" She looked around, perhaps to find Frank's guards.

"They let me free, Abuelita." He didn't have the heart to tell her why just then. She and the family would find out soon enough about Ramon's guilt. For now, there was enough pain.

"Your brother has been asking for you."

"How bad is he?"

Mrs. Querida shook her head. "Let's go see him."

She led Frank into the room. His parents were standing at Ray's bedside. Dolores looked up at his entry, and immediately all the tenderness she had been directing at Ray left her expression as she glared at Frank. He looked away, unable to meet her gaze. Then she left the bed and strode quickly up to him as if to bodily restrain his approach.

"Haven't you done enough?" she spat.

Frank stared at her. There was absolutely no response to make. Mrs. Querida spoke instead. "Dolores, you know Ramon has been asking for him. Don't do this to either of your sons."

Dolores hesitated, then stepped aside. "Only because it will stress Ramon otherwise. He never did know what was good for him."

"Mama . . ." Frank attempted.

But Dolores turned her back on Frank, though she did not leave the room. Frank walked past her and stepped up to Ray's bed.

"Hey, Ray, it's me, Frank," he said softly.

Ray's eyes fluttered open. "Hey, bro . . . they gave me last rites . . . guess the party's over, man. . . ."

"They don't know anything, Ray."

"At least they knew enough to let you out of jail." Ramon smiled weakly. "I wouldn't have let you go down, bro."

"I know."

There was a brief silence as Ramon seemed to gather his strength to speak again. "I can't die, Frank, knowing you're gonna blame yourself."

Frank bowed his head, tears filling his eyes. "Okay . . . I won't . . ."

"Don't blow me off, man!" Ray's voice, which had been a strained whisper, now rose considerably. "You ain't your brother's keeper, you never were. Don't you realize how demeaning that is to me?" He paused and closed his eyes. A minute later he opened them and spoke, his voice much weaker. "I'm so afraid, bro. . . . Don't leave, okay?"

"I won't."

"Guess I need you after all. . . ."

Frank stood by Ray's bed for the next hour. Mrs. Querida sat by him quietly praying, while Dolores and Tomas stood on the other side. Again, Frank avoided his mother's eyes, especially when Ray cried out as a new attack seized him.

The family was shoved aside as the doctor and nurses rushed in and tried to revive Ray. Frank listened from outside the curtain as the doctor shouted orders. They worked on Ray for half an hour, defibrillating him twice. But it was no use. The line on the monitor stayed flat, lifeless.

Ray was gone.

When the doctor came out shaking his head, Frank fled the room and found his way to the one place he hoped no one would think to find him—the hospital chapel.

There were only six small pews and a stained-glass window of an empty cross above the altar. Frank sat in the front pew, and only then did he let his emotion overwhelm him. He wept as he had never wept before. No matter how Ray had tried to absolve him, nothing could change the fact that he was responsible for his brother's death. He wished he had remained in prison. He deserved no less. Maybe he was innocent of Gloria's murder, but he was in no way *truly* innocent.

"Francisco . . ."

He had been so caught up in his grief that he had not heard his grandmother approach.

"Abuelita . . ." he wept, and as she sat beside him he wrapped his arms around her, laying his head on her shoulder as she murmured comforting words in his ear. "No, Abuelita, don't try to comfort me."

"You will carry this around on your shoulders for the rest of your life, then?"

"There's nothing else to do. It is my fault. Everything my mother says is true. I know you want to believe the best of me, but don't fool yourself, Abuelita. I brought Ramon to this. I cannot escape it."

"You can't live like this, Francisco—"

"You're right. Before, I hung on because there was hope that I could make Ray change. But now . . . there's no reason anymore."

"You would kill yourself, then? Is that what you are saying? Oh, Francisco . . ." Pausing, she took his face into her ancient, withered hands and lifted it to meet her eyes. "Nieto, you must have learned by now that you do not have to carry this alone."

"Nothing has changed from before, Abuelita. I don't deserve God's forgiveness any more than I deserved Ray's."

"Of course you don't. What you did to your brother was a terrible thing. Even I must admit that. But one life destroyed is enough. What good does it do to continue to punish yourself? Accept God's forgiveness and experience the life you have always dreamed of living. In this way you can honor Ramon. You can allow his death to have some meaning."

"I do want those dreams, but how can I have them when the weight of guilt is so heavy?"

"You know the answer to that, don't you, nieto?"

Frank nodded. She had told him many times about how God would carry his burdens, even his guilt. But it still seemed too easy.

"I don't know," he said. "I don't know . . ."

"Think of Shelby," said Mrs. Querida. "Would you destroy her life, as well?"

"She'll get over it." But even as he said the words, he knew they were empty. He wanted desperately to have a life with her.

"Pray with me, Francisco," Mrs. Querida said quietly but with compelling force.

Frank realized then that his grandmother would not let him go. And he sensed that God was that way, also. Gripping him with strong hands, not allowing him to slip over the edge. It had always been true, though he still had no idea why his grandmother or God thought him worth it. The only way to stop them was indeed to take his own life. But he wasn't going to do that. He didn't want to die. There was only one other thing to do—he had to find a way to live with his shame. And his grandmother was offering the way.

"Okay, Abuelita."

They bowed their heads. She crossed herself, then prayed, "My heavenly Father, please surround my dear nieto with your love and lift the weight of shame and guilt from him. Show him the path to true joy and happiness not so much by erasing his pain but by learning how to daily surrender it to you. In the name of the Father and the Son and the Holy Spirit, Amen."

In the brief silence that followed, Frank wondered what he would say to the God he had been running from for so long. It was bad enough to reject God, but it was so much worse to do so *knowing* that only He has the answers that would give him hope. But it hadn't really been God he had rejected, rather the forgiveness, the absolution that had so frightened Frank. He was still frightened of all the good things God had to offer, but he was even more fearful of the alternative—an empty, miserable existence without God, eternally confronting his shame with no hope to sustain his wretched existence.

"God," Frank prayed at length, "I give up. I surrender to you. If you can make something of my miserable life, then I beg you to do so. I can't bear any of this alone. I beg you also, then, to help me. No, I need more than mere help. I cannot do *any* of it by myself. I am completely helpless. Every time I close my eyes I see my brother's broken life. You are my only hope. If you can't rescue me, I am truly lost."

38

SHELBY MIGHT NOT BE ABLE to see Frank, but that did not keep her from thinking about him and about the life they could have had together. She had not been in communication with Frank or his family since that last day in court. She had thought about calling Mrs. Querida but decided that speaking with the woman who so loved her grandson would simply be too painful.

By all appearances that short but deeply important chapter of her life was over—if only she could accept that in her heart.

In the meantime she proceeded with her life—school, church, getting to know her mother, seeing her old friends—hoping to build a world that would cocoon her.

It had rained yesterday, but now the sun was struggling to come out, and the clouds in the sky were the big, white, promising kind. Shelby had been wanting to wash and wax her car, so she got right to the job when she came home from school. Dressed in a gray sweat shirt and blue jeans, she attacked the task with the enthusiasm of one who fears the quiet of inactivity.

Soap splattered her and water dripped from loose strands of her hap-hazardly tied-back hair as she took a chamois cloth and began drying water from the car. She thought about her dad and remembered that the last time she had waxed the car, they had done it together. It seemed so long ago, but it had been less than six months since his death. Would he have been disappointed in what she had done with her life in his absence? He'd always been so careful to protect her from her impulsive nature. He never said it outright, but she had known, nevertheless, that his greatest fear had been that she would turn out like her mother.

And now it looked as if she had done just that. Well, Daddy, maybe it's not such a bad thing after all, she thought. Dawn had been such a support for her these last few weeks, and Shelby still marveled at their new relationship.

Removing the last bit of water and squeezing out the chamois, Shelby turned to get the can of Turtle Wax. Suddenly she stopped and gasped. It was like seeing a mirage in the desert. It couldn't be real. Then he spoke.

"Hi, Shelby. I couldn't help watching you a minute." He smiled tentatively, as if it was too much to hope that he'd be welcomed.

"Frank . . ." In her shock she was unable to move, though her heart was pounding. Then she suddenly came to life and her pesky impulsiveness served her well this time. She dropped the can of wax and ran to him, throwing her arms around him, holding him so tightly that if he was a mirage, he still could not slip away from her.

"My dear Shelby," he breathed into her damp hair, "I don't know what I would have done if you would have responded any other way."

"You're really here . . . I can't believe it—" Stopping abruptly, an awful thought came to her. "Frank, you're not. . . ?"

He chuckled. "No, I'm not a fugitive. I'm a free man—in more ways than one."

"What do you mean?"

Reluctantly, he let go of her, and taking her hand, he led her to the porch steps where they sat. "I've so much to say to you." He clasped her hand between both of his and brought it to his lips. "Can you forgive me for what I did in the courtroom?"

"Of course. I know how difficult it was for you. But how did you get out, Frank? What happened?"

"I've been out for a couple of weeks. I would have come sooner—in fact, it took all my strength not to—but there were things I wanted to do before I saw you." He sighed, and for the first time, his eyes flickered away from her. "Ray is dead."

"Oh, Frank! No! How. . . ?"

"He had another heart attack. But before he died he revealed evidence that conclusively proved that he . . . that he was responsible for Gloria's death. He kept it back all along, thinking he could get us both off. That's what the coke did—gave him such false confidence. But when he had the second heart attack, he realized he could die, and I'd be lost forever."

"He didn't mean to kill her, did he?"

"No. It was the drugs. Ray was a good boy, he really was."

"I know. Frank. . . ?" Her entreaty made him turn his gaze toward her once again. "How are you with it all?"

"I'm okay. I'm relying on God to get me through."

"God?"

"I finally stopped running from Him. I hope that won't be a problem—"

Her smile made him stop. "I never had a chance to tell you, Frank, but I've been relying on God a lot, too."

"Really?"

"Kind of incredible, isn't it? That we both should end up in the same place when we were so far apart."

"Maybe it's not as incredible as you think. I mean, it seems to me exactly like something God would do. I won't even venture to guess if our marriage was His will in the first place or not, but I'm certain that once it happened, the survival of our marriage became vitally important to Him. And as things were, it would never have survived without His intervention in our lives as individuals. Prison wasn't the worst thing keeping us apart. My freedom, without Christ in my life, would have meant little to us. I could never have truly received your love and the happiness our marriage promised with all the shame and guilt from Ray hanging over me."

"And now it no longer haunts you, Frank?"

"I'm getting more free of it every day. I'll always have to live with what I did to Ray and to others like him. Some scars, I know, heal but don't completely disappear. But now I hope I can use those times of pain and remembrance to bring me closer to God."

"We will do it together, Frank. You, me, *and* God."

He took her once more into his arms, and she marveled at how complete she felt—so much more so than she'd ever felt before.

"I've made a few other changes in my life, Shelby, that perhaps you should know about. That's part of the reason why I took so long to return to you. I know God requires nothing of me but my sincere heart. Yet for my own benefit I knew I had to make a complete break from the past. Before when I tried that, I couldn't let it all go. There was a part of me that was afraid of being stripped naked and not having anything to put in its place. Now I have no fear at all of that. In fact, I have a sense of anticipation for what lies ahead. I put the condo up for sale and already there are several interested buyers. I'm going to donate the money to a couple of D.A.R.E. programs and to a rehab clinic. I sold the truck and the boat. . . ."

"Oh, Frank, not the boat!" That more than anything made her realize his complete transformation.

"There will be other boats—maybe a *Shelby Dawn*. Even if there isn't another boat, it doesn't matter. Right at this moment, I have all I could ever need or want. I don't have a single possession except for those of a restaurant manager. But I am a richer, more complete man than I ever was." He paused and reached into his jacket pocket and took out his photograph of the "ideal" family. "And this, I know now, is but a vague shadow of what lies ahead for me . . . for us." He started to tear it up, but Shelby stopped him.

"Don't, Frank. Let's keep it as a reminder of what God has done and will do in our lives. Just imagine, Frank! Imagine what is in store for us!"

"I still find it almost too awesome to fathom that God would give so much to a man who has done such evil. It's easy to see with you—"

"But we are all the same to God. My mother said that she felt the same as you until she realized that God's love has no degrees. It is simply impossible for Him to love one of his children more than another. He died for us all."

They were silent for a few moments, as if basking in the wonder of what they had found in their new faith. Shelby thought about how a few minutes ago, before Frank had appeared, she'd had so many questions about the direction of her life. Now suddenly her doubts, her fears, her questions were quelled. Certainly she hadn't seen the last of such emotions—they were part of life. But this experience surely was building her faith for next time. She was growing! And it felt great.

"Shelby," Frank said after a while, "I have something for you. Wait here." He jumped up and strode toward his car—actually, his grandmother's Buick, not his Ranger. He took a package from the front seat and returned to the steps, holding it out to her. "I wanted to give you something, but I had nothing that was special enough. Abuelita suggested this."

Shelby took the gift wrapped in a floral paper with a blue ribbon. As carefully as possible, she removed the ribbon and paper and lifted the lid of the box. Moving aside the tissue paper, she stared with awe at the contents, tears quickly welling up in her eyes. It was Mrs. Querida's lace mantilla. "Oh. . . !" she said in a choked voice, then touched the fine lace no longer in its protective plastic.

"I would be honored if you'd wear it for our wedding," he said.

"Our wedding?"

"I feel very strongly, Shelby, that our marriage has never ceased being valid. And I don't wish another wedding because I somehow feel the first one didn't count. Still, after all that has happened, after my rejecting you as I did, I feel that we are due for a new beginning."

He smiled, and for the first time ever, Shelby saw Frank as he was meant to be—clear, unclouded, and full of joy.

39

How odd for a wedding day to begin in a cemetery. But for Shelby there was deep significance to such a journey.

She hadn't been to her father's grave since the day of his funeral. She carried his memory in her heart so the place where his body lay was not of huge importance to her. However, today she needed a more tangible connection to him. Perhaps his chair at home would have been just as good, and indeed, she had sat in that chair today, as well. But it seemed more fitting to leave her special gift at the cemetery.

She laid the bouquet of flowers on the grave. It was identical to the one she would carry in the wedding ceremony.

"Daddy," Shelby murmured, "Frank and I have planned a wedding so our loved ones could witness our commitment. But I want you to be there, too. I want you to be part of this day as you were part of every important event of my life. That's why, Daddy, I am going to walk down the aisle alone, so that you will be at my side in spirit.

"Dawn thinks that in the moment before your death, God might have revealed himself to you so that you are with Him now. She's certain that once you really saw God, you would accept Him with all your heart. I believe that, too, Daddy. It's because of the kind of father you were to me that I am able to truly know God now. You showed me what a father's love ought to be, pointing me toward my heavenly Father. I thank you for that, Daddy."

Shelby sighed and wiped a tear from her eye.

"Well, I guess it's time to get married. Just so you don't worry, Dad, I love Frank, and he loves me. I mean *really* loves me. What we had in Puerto Vallarta was just a glimpse of what our love has become. I'm going to be okay, Daddy."

Frank walked to the front of the church from a vestibule door. He was followed by his best man, Carla's husband. Choosing a best man had been difficult because it reaffirmed to Frank that he had very few friends after abandoning his criminal associations—not that most of them were true friends. And Frank was reminded that the one person who should have filled the position of best man—his brother—was gone forever. But Frank determinedly pushed such thoughts from his mind. He thought instead of a Scripture his grandmother had quoted to him last night. *"Weeping may endure for a night, but joy comes in the morning."* He clung to this promise and marveled at how faithful God was to fulfill it in him this wonderful day.

The organ quietly played a medley of romantic tunes. The soft glow of candles filled the church. Only four pews were occupied in the large sanctuary. Shelby's friend, Christie, was there with a date, along with Shelby's aunt Lynn and her family. And, of course, Dawn was there in the front pew with Alan Rosenthal. There were also a handful of friends from Shelby's school.

Surprisingly, Frank's side of the church was well balanced with Shelby's. His sisters and all their families took up an entire pew. Frank had heard that his father had issued a rare command to his children: "Be at Frank's wedding, or else!" Mrs. Querida sat in the front pew with Tomas

Stefano. Frank was shocked to see his father there, for he'd assumed he'd stay away with Dolores, who continued to hold a deep grudge against Frank. The sight of his father lifted Frank's spirit immensely, almost making up for the absence of his mother.

This was the happiest moment of his life—even better than Puerto Vallarta. After coming so close to losing Shelby, he now prized her love more than ever.

As the organ began the first notes of "The Wedding March" and Shelby began walking down the aisle toward him, Frank's usually reserved expression opened into an unabashed grin. Her creamy satin gown was elegant in its simplicity, but Frank would have gazed with just as much awe had she been wearing her customary jeans and T-shirt. He was, however, very impressed with how she so perfectly graced the old lace mantilla fastened to her head with Abuelita's pearl-encrusted comb. With Shelby's pale hair and skin, she was no Spanish rose, but the mantilla still suited her ideally as its lace folds fell about her beautiful face.

Everyone stood and Shelby grinned, though there was a glistening in her eyes that indicated her joy, too, was tempered by sadness. No doubt she was thinking of her father and of how proudly he would have walked beside her and given her to her waiting groom. At least Frank hoped Mike Martin would be pleased with his daughter's choice of a husband.

Shelby reached the front of the church, and the minister asked, "Who gives this woman to be married?"

Dawn, also through smiles and tears, said proudly, "Her father and mother."

But before stepping up to Frank, Shelby paused to embrace her mother, kissing her tenderly on the cheek. Dawn's tears multiplied, as did Shelby's.

"I love you, Mom!" Shelby murmured just loud enough for Frank to hear.

Then Shelby moved beside Frank, and he wanted to hold her in his arms, but using great restraint, he just took her hand. They smiled at each other, then turned to face the minister. They had been married six months already, but the expression of their vows to one another that day was fresh and new. Six months ago they'd had no concept at all of what they were doing. Now they deeply understood the kind of commitment—truly for better or worse—that marriage involved. And they welcomed it together.

Books by Judith Pella

Beloved Stranger
Blind Faith

LONE STAR LEGACY
Frontier Lady
Stoner's Crossing
Warrior's Song

RIBBONS OF STEEL†
Distant Dreams
A Hope Beyond
A Promise for Tomorrow

THE RUSSIANS
*The Crown and the Crucible**
*A House Divided**
*Travail and Triumph**
Heirs of the Motherland
Dawning of Deliverance
White Nights, Red Morning
Passage Into Light

THE STONEWYCKE TRILOGY*
The Heather Hills of Stonewycke
Flight from Stonewycke
Lady of Stonewycke

THE STONEWYCKE LEGACY*
Stranger at Stonewycke
Shadows over Stonewycke
Treasure of Stonewycke

THE HIGHLAND COLLECTION*
Jamie MacLeod: Highland Lass
Robbie Taggart: Highland Sailor

THE JOURNALS OF CORRIE BELLE HOLLISTER
*My Father's World**
*Daughter of Grace**

*with Michael Phillips   †with Tracie Peterson